THE STORM

ALSO BY R.J. PRESCOTT

The Hurricane

The Aftermath

The Storm

withdrawn

THE
STORM

R. J. PRESCOTT

The Storm
By R.J. Prescott

ISBN 978-0-9931838-5-0

Interior Formatting by Leigh Stone of Irish Ink Formatting
and Graphics

Editing by Hot Tree Editing

Cover Design by Louisa Maggio of L.M. Cover Creations

Maireann lágo ruaig ach maireann an grágo huaigh.

A day lasts until it is chased away, but love lasts until

the grave.

PROLOGUE

KIERAN DOHERTY-
THIRTEEN YEARS EARLIER

"It's time, Kieran," Father Pat said gently from Da's bedroom door. He'd asked me to stay outside for a few minutes, but I wasn't feckin' stupid. He was there to read Da his last rites. I knew I should hurry. There wasn't long left now, but I couldn't get my stupid legs to move. Because this was it. The minute that I got up and walked through the door, I was saying goodbye. And I wasn't ready. I was nowhere near ready. Father Pat sighed deeply and came to sit next to me.

"You know it's not forever, son. You'll see your dad again someday in Heaven," he said, as though that would be of any comfort.

"Yeah, well, it feels like forever," I replied, kicking the toe of my shoe against the floor.

"As long as you remember him, he's not really gone."

"Sorry, Father, but that's just shite. He's a good man and he never did anything wrong, so how come God punishes us by picking him. It's not feckin' fair." I sniffed to stop the tears from falling. Rage consumed me. I wanted to scream at the world and everyone in it.

"It's not fair, Kieran. All you feel now is hurt and pain, and that's not going to go away any time soon. But I have a theory, that God handpicks his angels. Some of them are women and children, and some of them are loudmouthed, surly Irish men. But all of the angels are picked because they are the very best of us. Your dad is strong, brave, and kind, and he loves you and your ma something fierce. God isn't taking him from this earth so he can snuff out that light. He's putting it in Heaven so it will shine eternal. The way you're feeling right now will last a long time, but it won't last forever. One day something, or someone, will make the sun come out, and you'll smile again. I promise."

I didn't believe him; I didn't think I'd ever laugh again. I felt like I was in a deep dark hole I'd never be able to climb out of. Me mates would still be able to see me, but I wasn't the same. Nothing was the same, and without Da, nothing would be again.

"Come now. Come and say your goodbyes. He's waiting for you." I stood up slowly, my steps sluggish. I swallowed back the tears as I walked in to see my old man laid out in bed. The gentle giant who was always hoisting me up on his shoulders looked so small and fragile now. He smiled as he saw me, the twinkle in his eye showing me the man I knew so well. As frail as he was, his chest didn't sound as wheezy as it did of late. It was a kind of cruel false hope that he seemed better just before the end.

"Hello, son," he said, smiling.

"Hey, Da," I replied with a sniff.

"Cheer up, Kier. It's not the end of the world," he said. He was joking. I knew he was joking, but it was the end of the world for me. He could see the minute that I lost it, and he held out his arms just as I dove into them.

"I'm so sorry," I said through my sobs. "For everything I ever did bad. For the times I didn't make you proud. I don't want you to leave."

"There's nothing to say sorry for. I've always been proud of you, little man. You are so much like your ma. You just listen to her and do what she says, and you'll be fine," he said.

"I promise, Da" I answered, my sobs subsiding. He coughed and his whole body was racked with it. As he caught his breath, we just stayed still. I didn't want to make him talk because I knew it hurt him, and right then I was content to lay there and get a hug from my old man.

My last hug.

"Ah, there's my girl," he said to Ma, who was leaning against the doorframe watching us. "Now a woman as beautiful as you, darlin', should never look so sad. Come over here and give me some lovin', and I'll put a smile back on your face." I kissed Da on the cheek, then climbed off the bed to make room for her.

"Con is downstairs waiting for you, love," she told me as she lay down. I nodded, not trusting myself not to cry again, and wiped my now runny nose along my sleeve.

"I love you, Kieran," he said gently.

"Love you too, Da." Then I left to give Ma some time with him.

"You know, Kathleen, you are just as beautiful now as you were the day I met you. And not a minute has passed since that I haven't counted my blessings for finding you," I heard him say gently to Ma. The strength in his voice was gone, and he sounded almost wistful.

"And you are just as charming now as you were then, James Doherty," she replied.

"I'm so tired, love," Da said and coughed slightly before settling. "How 'bout singing me something?"

Her voice was so beautiful as she softly sang his favourite U2 song. When she got to the end, she broke down and sobbed harder than I'd ever heard her cry before. I knew then that he'd passed. I slid down the wall to the floor and, burying my head in my knees, I let my own tears run free. Eventually, Father Pat came in with Mary, my friend Tommy's Ma. She wrapped me in her big arms and hugged me so hard I was havin' trouble breathing. I didn't tell her though, 'cause I needed that hug so bad. But long after my tears had dried, I could still hear Ma's.

Da told me once what fallin' in love was like. "Son," he said, "true love ain't the passenger train that pulls up at the station so that you can board when it's time. It's the freight train that ploughs into you when you least expect it. That's how it was for me at any rate. There's just no getting over something like that, and if you find someone who makes you feel that way, you hold onto her forever."

I didn't think anything of it at the time. Da was always saying soppy shite about Ma. Now watching Ma's suffering, I knew what he meant. She would bounce back and take care of me, because she was the strongest person I knew, but she'd never be the same again.

Finding your soul mate might be great, but losing them was like watching a person get torn in half. If Father Pat was right and this shite feeling ever got better, I was avoiding trains at all costs. 'Cause there was no fucking way I was ever going through this again.

CHAPTER ONE

KIERAN

The Royal Oak pub in Camden Town, London was always busy, but that Friday night it was absolutely packed. St Paddy's Day was tomorrow, and the local Irish band Attree's Ashes was playing over the weekend. Taking a long, hard drink of me pint, I joined the rest of the pub in singing "Wild Rover" at the top of my lungs. I was relaxed, happy, and ready for a good weekend of celebrating.

Me and the boys would take it easy tonight. We were all off to church tomorrow at ten o'clock, and it wasn't somewhere you wanted to be hungover. I'd say we were going to ask for forgiveness for all the sins we'd likely commit when we were too drunk to remember our own names, but Father Pat, our local priest, would be joining us in the pub later in the day. He and my trainer, Danny, were partial to a good single malt whiskey, so it was doubtful that he'd remember any of my sins any better than I would. Besides, St Paddy's Day was a holy day, and I was pretty sure God forgave all manner of sins on a holy day.

After the last strains of the song had rung out, I made my way back to our table where my best mate, Con, had a round of drinks waiting.

"Ah see, that's why you're me best mate. You know what I need, even before I do," I said, rubbing my hands together in anticipation of my icy-cold pint of Guinness. He snorted in amusement.

"Looks like I got them just in time too," he said, nodding towards the bar. The queue to get a drink was probably five people deep now the band was taking a break.

"Where's Em?" I asked, referring to Con's wife. We were a pretty tight-knit group, Em included, so I was surprised not to see her there.

"She and Nikki have gone to the movies. I've warned her what tomorrow's going to be like, and she doesn't want to be hungover."

"Probably best. I could open a bottle of beer next to her and she'd probably get drunk just from the fumes," I said, grinning. Em drunk was a sight to behold. She was the only person I knew who could projectile vomit after five drinks. It was one of the reasons I highly doubted that my buddy would be wasted tomorrow. To call Con protective when it came to his wife was a major understatement. He was getting better, but Em had her own reasons for not feeling comfortable drinking in public, so Con always made sure he was fairly sober. Nothing would ever happen to her with all of us around. Hell, she was like a little sister to all of us. But to Con, that girl was his whole world, and it wasn't something he took for granted. I'd always said that I didn't want that kind of love for myself, but I'd be lying if I didn't feel a kind of longing while watching them both together.

"She's bringing Nikki tomorrow, so she's staying over at our place tonight. That way I won't have to worry about Em coming home alone," he explained.

"We still meeting at St Paul's?"

"That's the plan," he replied. "Seamus O'Donnell's is doing fried breakfast and a Guinness for five quid, so we're heading there after." Mass followed by a full day of drinking might seem odd to some people, but that was St Paddy's Day for you.

"Hey, ladies, thanks for keeping my seat," Tommy said, as he slid onto the stool next to me and stole a sip of my drink.

"I spat in that," I told him.

"Fuck you did," he replied, putting my glass down and eying it suspiciously. "Why would you say that anyway?" The little fucker had the gall to look hurt, like I was being mean.

"Because you can get your own drink, ya tight arse," I said with a chuckle. "I don't know why you're so fussy about getting a bit of my saliva anyway. You've been sticking your tongue down anything with a vagina since we walked in here."

"Can you blame me?" he asked, his eyes following the women filling the pub. He looked like a kid in a sweet shop. "It's wall to wall women, and they all love a bit of bad boy Irish charm. There just ain't enough of me to go around."

I rolled my eyes at Con, but he just laughed. Tommy was a fucking force of nature when it came to woman. The kid was constantly in heat, and there was no shortage of girls lining up to clench his thirst. I didn't like to make it easy for him though. Fucking with his head was pretty much my favourite hobby.

"All those women, yet you still come back to me," I said.

"What the fuck are you talking about now?" he asked.

"Well, first you try to make me jealous with all those girls. Then you pull your stool up next to mine, which is pretty intimate, and now we're sharing drinks. I mean, I'm flattered and all, but I've told you before that I just don't feel the same," I said, and rested my hand on his leg, which made him jump a mile.

"For the last fucking time, *I'm not fucking gay!*" he shouted at me. Con, by this stage, was doubled over in his seat with laughter.

"You know, I'd believe you, but I think you're protesting too much. All the signs are there, Tom. It's time you came out of the closet. We're all friends here," I replied.

"We're not friends, and I'm not fucking gay," he said, in case I hadn't heard the first time. Standing up, he moved to the stool next to Con on the other side of the table.

"Don't try it on with me. I ain't gay either," Con said, joining in.

"Fuck the pair of you," Tommy said, swiping one of the pints Con had bought and taking a drink.

"Who's gay now?" Liam said, putting his drink down before taking off his jacket and sitting down next to us.

I'd known Tommy and Liam near enough my whole life, but the two of them couldn't have been more different. Tommy was maybe a few inches shorter than me, with shaggy brown hair that always looked like it needed cutting. He wasn't stocky, but like most of the guys at the gym, he was ripped. Liam, on the other hand, was a tank. At six foot six inches, he probably only had about an inch on Con, but he had shoulders like an ox. The guy was huge. But unfortunately for Danny, he was a gentle giant. He liked to train and keep in shape, and he'd spar with either me or Con when we needed it, but he lacked the killer instinct that made Con unbeatable. When the rest of us were shouting our mouths off, Liam was the one thinking and taking it all in. Of us all, he was the voice of reason.

"Kier thinks that Tommy's gay," Con said, letting Liam know we were fucking with Tommy again.

"Yeah?" he replied, looking at Tommy. "I am too."

I shit you not that you could hear a pin drop while we all tried to work out whether we'd heard him right.

"Well, looks like you're not alone in the club, Tom," I said, figuring that Liam was yanking our chain. I looked at Con, expecting to see a grin, but he just shook his head sternly at me, telling me that Liam was being serious.

"Actually, he's not my type," Liam said, taking a sip of his pint. He looked nervous and embarrassed, and then it hit me that he was telling the truth. I was absolutely floored.

"I knew it. I fucking knew it. It was bound to happen someday. There's no way having this on display, half naked and sweaty, all these years didn't turn someone. I'm just surprised it ain't happened sooner," Tommy said. Just to illustrate his point, he stood up, lifted his top and started rolling his arse and abs in some kind of weird mating dance. Fuck knows why it worked on chicks, 'cause it was making me feel kind of nauseous. It didn't look like it was doing much more for Liam either.

"Put it away, Tommy," Con finally told him.

"Are you serious?" I asked Liam. "Because if you're messing

with us, this is low. I don't know whether to hug you or kick your arse."

"I'd really appreciate it if you did neither," he replied.

"Shit, man, you've seen all of our dicks," Tommy said. It was apparently the wittiest response he could come up with.

"Yeah, so?" Liam said.

"Well, how do I know now that you ain't thinking of my dick when you rub one out?" Tommy asked.

"If you've ever seen your dick, you'll know why," Liam answered.

"Are you implying I've got a small cock? Because there's nothing wrong with this beast." Tommy gestured towards his junk.

"It's because you've got little baby hands," I explained. "Makes it look bigger when you're holding it than it really is." He lifted his hands to check out their size, then gave me the finger when he realised I was playing him again.

"So, do we have to wear them rainbow hot pants and walk in parades and stuff with you now?" Tommy asked, 'cause apparently stupidity knew no bounds.

"Absolutely, and I think wearing 'em to the Paddy's Day parade tomorrow would be a great way to start showing Liam our support," Con answered, his face serious. A brief look of panic washed over Tommy's face before his usual cocky smirk was back.

"Fuck it," he said, finally. "As long as you promise you ain't thinking about my beast when you're beating the meat, I could fucking rock sparkly rainbow hot pants."

"Since when did they become sparkly?" I asked, half choking

on my beer.

"If we're gonna do it, might as well go all the way," he said with a shrug.

"You'd do that for me?" Liam asked, quietly.

"Fuck no," I said, then paused to look at Tommy. "Well, Tom might, but hot pants would make my arse look big. But I will march shoulder to shoulder with you and kick the arse of anyone who has a problem with you being gay."

"I'd do the hot pants too, but that's because I'm a better mate than dickface," Tommy added, pointing a thumb at me. "Women fucking love gay guys anyway."

"I'm pretty sure that marching in sparkly rainbow hot pants is something you'll never see me doing, but I appreciate the support. This shit's been weighing heavy on me for a long time. Frankly, I expected you guys to give me a harder time about this," Liam said.

"Why? More women for me," Tommy replied. Liam finally cracked a nervous smile, and I loved that Tommy could do that for him.

"I can't say I'm not shocked. If Tommy came out, I wouldn't be at all surprised. It's just a matter of time really, but you? Well, you kept that secret pretty good," I said.

"It's not like it's something I've always known. You grow up taking it for granted that you're straight, until you meet someone that makes you feel different. I fought it for a long time, but it ain't something that goes away," he explained.

"But how can you be sure? What if you just like the idea, but then you get with a guy and realise you don't actually like riding the meat train?" Tommy asked.

We all looked at Liam, waiting for the answer. I mean, he was the youngest son in a strict Irish Catholic family. Coming out was a big fucking deal in our world, especially if he'd never been with a guy before and wasn't absolutely certain. He didn't say anything, but his cheeks reddened and the corner of his mouth tilted slightly in a wry smile that had us all grinning.

"You dirty bastard. You've already done the deed, haven't you?" Tommy said. "How is it possible that we haven't seen you on the pull?"

Liam's answering grin was almost smug. "I've met someone," he said.

"Fair play, you don't hang around, I'll give you that," I said. Inside, I was kind of relieved. What Liam was facing ahead would be a lot easier with someone by his side who knew what he was going through.

"So, when do we get to meet him?" Con asked. It occurred to me then that Con knew all about this and hadn't told me. I'd be having words with my so-called best friend later.

"I don't know," he admitted. "He's just come out to his family, but he hasn't told his mates yet. You guys *are* my family, so I'm telling you first. But when people see us together, it's only a matter of time before me ma finds out. I was just hoping we could have more time together before we have to deal with all the shite me family's gonna throw our way."

"So don't tell them yet," Con suggested. "Besides Em, and probably Earnshaw, there's no one outside this circle who needs to know yet. As long as you ain't all over each other when we're out as a group, there shouldn't be any reason for people to put two and two together. Bring him tomorrow. You can introduce him to everyone and spend the day with him without raising suspicion."

"And if they guess he's gay, then we'll just say he's with Tommy," I suggested. "That's totally believable."

"How many times do I have to tell you? *I am not gay!*" Tommy said, getting riled up before he looked at Liam and remembered. "But don't worry, mate, if I ever thought I was, you'd be my first port of call."

"Charmed, I'm sure," Liam replied sarcastically.

"Speaking of gay boys, where's Earnshaw?" I asked.

"I'm here, but it's nice to know you guys are missing me," Earnshaw replied, putting his bottle of Bud on the table and joining us. Heath Earnshaw looked like your typical all-American golden boy. He'd left a high-flying US sports agency when Danny hired him to be Con's Manager. He'd also left all of his family behind in the States, except for his younger sister who had a job in London. I couldn't pretend that we'd given him the warmest reception, but he'd more than proved his loyalty and was pretty much one of us now.

"What did I miss?" he asked.

"Liam told us he's gay and in a relationship, but his family don't know he's got a boyfriend or that he bats for the other team," I explained.

"Shit, that's a surprise. It can't have been easy telling everyone, but your family loves you. That's not going to change just because you're gay," he replied.

We all stopped and turned to look at him, Liam included.

"What?" he asked.

"Not to burst your happy bubble, but he's the youngest son in a strict Catholic family. We might as well be back in 1950's Ireland for how this news is going to go down," Tommy explained.

"I think I'm gonna puke," Liam admitted, and ran his hands down his face in despair.

"Could you give him up and keep pretending to be straight?" Con asked. "If all of us and your family told you to, could you break it off with him today and never see him again?"

"No. Never," Liam replied firmly.

"Then you know what to do," Con said, smiling sympathetically. "Your ma and da might tear you a new one, but they have lives of their own, and if they want to be part of yours, they need to learn how to accept things. And if they don't, that's their choice, not yours. All you can do is the best you can to live a happy life and do right by the one you love."

Liam nodded as he accepted the truth of what Con had said.

"It changes you, doesn't it? Meeting that one person that knocks you for six," Liam said.

"Shit yeah," Con replied. "But I wouldn't change it for the fucking world."

The band, back from their break, plucked at their instruments as they warmed up for their next set.

"Well, girls, as fun as this sharing your feelings and shit has been, I'm off to find myself a warm body for the night," Tommy said, knocking back the last of his drink and wandering off into the crowd.

It wasn't too long ago that I'd have been following, but things were different now. Whilst I wasn't ready to talk to the boys about it, I'd met my game changer too. The only difference between me and them was that I had absolutely no fucking clue what to do about it.

CHAPTER TWO

MARIE

I stood in front of the mirror and, for the umpteenth time today, held up both tops as I tried to decide what to wear. I'd never celebrated St Patrick's Day before, and Em had told me to dress casual. I wasn't exactly a converse and hoodie sort of girl, so casual with me usually meant skinny jeans, heels or boots, and a form-fitting top with a scarf and jewellery. It was probably the dressmaker in me that couldn't abide baggy, misshapen clothes. My clothes were me. Even on my worst days, they gave me confidence—and that was the most important thing a girl could wear. Finally deciding to go festive, I settled on the emerald green one. After dressing quickly, I curled my hair with the irons and added a little light makeup. If I took a bit more care than usual, it was because it was going to be a fairly big day out. It had absolutely nothing to do with a certain sweet-talking, brown-eyed Irish charmer.

Absolutely nothing at all.

The taxi beeped from outside, making me jump. Deciding against carrying a bag around, I stuffed my card, money, and ID into my pocket and locked the door behind me. It didn't take me long to get to the pub where I'd arranged to meet Em. A few months ago, I'd moved apartments to be closer to my mum. My new apartment was a little smaller than the old one, but living closer to my friends was a bonus. When the cab pulled up outside the bar, I started to have second thoughts. It was only midday, but an Irish band was pumping out tunes and the place was so packed that patrons had poured out onto the pavement. Knowing it would be rude to back out on the girls, I took a deep breath and braved it.

The music was loud, but the sound of the crowd belting out songs along with the band was almost overwhelming. Typically, I wasn't great with crowds, but the atmosphere in here was absolutely electric. I was accosted by a girl who insisted on stencilling a shamrock onto my cheek and successfully fended off two proposals of marriage before eventually finding the girls. Liam, Heath, Nikki, Max, Albie, and a load of other guys from the gym sat around two tables that had been pulled together. Em was sitting across Con's lap. He smiled smugly as she leant back to whisper something in his ear. Sometimes, it was as though they were both in an untouchable bubble, where everyone else in the world ceased to exist. It often made me yearn for something I would never have.

"Marie!" Tommy shouted at me. "I've been waiting for you to get here for ages!" He seemed a little hyperactive and very excited, like a little kid at Christmas. Given the number of hot girls in here wearing tight jeans and low-cut tops, it probably was a little like

Christmas for Tommy.

"Don't listen to him," Liam said. "He's already kissed two girls, and we haven't been here for more than a couple of hours."

"Is that right?" I asked, one eyebrow raised in mock disapproval.

"It's not my fault! Amy just lost her job and needed cheering up. Then Amelia got jealous," he said, like that totally explained his locking lips with both women.

"Sisters?" Liam asked.

"Twins," Tommy confirmed, winking knowingly at him.

I smiled, because total manwhore that he was, you just couldn't help loving Tommy. He exuded life and fun, and I adored that about him.

"Hey, you made it!" Em said, climbing off Con's lap to give me a hug.

"Thanks for inviting me," I said. "I can't believe I've never celebrated St Patrick's Day before!"

"Well, the Irish don't do anything by halves," she replied.

"Hey, Marie," Con said, leaning over to kiss my cheek. "First things first, let's get you a drink. I've a feeling you've some catching up to do," he said, nodding towards Em.

"How many have you had?" I asked.

"Two leprechauns and a shamrock shake up," she replied, reaching for some green concoction on the table.

"Fucking criminal to be drinking anything other than Guinness today," Tommy said, shaking his head as he looked at Em's drink.

"The pub's doing two for one on all cocktails today, but I have a feeling that Jerry got a bit carried away with the rum when he knew it was for Em," Con said, keeping his hand on the small of Em's back. It took a long time for Em to feel comfortable in a crowd after going through some difficult stuff with her dad, and I knew that Con's touch made her feel grounded.

"So, do you fancy one, or would ya like something else to drink?" Con asked me. The guys were so generous and chivalrous. Whenever I went out with them, they rarely let the girls pay for anything, despite our protests.

"You should try one. They're delicious!" Em said, her rosy cheeks a testament to how much liquor was in them.

"Maybe later, I think I'll just stick with a beer for now." I didn't drink much, and I didn't want to be throwing up in the bathroom in a couple of hours.

"I've got this, Con," said a voice from behind me. I turned around to see Kieran holding a pint and a bottle my favourite beer. It was pretty weak and one of the few drinks I could handle. I had no idea how he knew what I'd order. Maybe it was just coincidence, but a small part of me hoped not.

"Thanks," I said, trembling slightly as I took the bottle from him. Whether it was adrenaline or excitement, he was the only man to ever make me feel that way. I feared and craved it at the same time. He was so tall that I had to tilt my head to look into his eyes.

And damn those eyes.

He had eyes that made love to a woman before he even took her clothes off. Big, brown orbs that made you feel like you were swimming in chocolate. And boy did he know how to use them. That slight head tilt and half smile was so obviously a ploy, and I mentally kicked myself for falling for it. Kieran was a player. He'd probably always be a player. If only my stupid, treacherous body would listen to my brain, I'd be fine.

"I haven't seen you around for a while. How've you been, darlin'?" he said with that deep Irish lilt that just about melted my knickers off every time I heard it.

"I'm good, thanks," I replied. "Wedding season's coming up in a few months, so I've been pretty busy getting my orders ready."

"Em said that you're making a lot more of your own designs now," he said.

"I started off doing one or two and putting the dresses in with the others in the shop, but now my designs are outselling the other stock," I told him proudly. A few years ago, I'd scraped just about enough money for a deposit on my own business, and with a loan from the bank and a *lot* of help from my family, I started my own wedding dress boutique. I loved my shop, and I was proud of what I'd achieved.

"I don't know how you do it. How do you even know where to start?" he asked.

I paused, not wanting to start waxing lyrical if he was only making conversation. But he seemed genuinely interested, which made me relax a little.

"I haven't really had any formal training, but my mum and her mum were both dressmakers. They made their own patterns too. That's the real talent behind it. You can learn to follow a pattern, but designing the dresses and creating patterns takes a lot of skill," I said.

Anyone listening would probably say I sounded smug and conceited, but I didn't mean to. I loved what I did for a living, and I couldn't help but let my passion and enthusiasm for it bubble over.

"So they taught you how, but where do you get inspiration from? I mean, sorry to sound like a guy, but all wedding dresses look alike to me," he said.

I smiled, knowing that lots of people thought the same thing. Honestly, I felt a little flattered that he was taking so much of an interest.

"I get inspiration from everywhere. It could be seeing flowers while walking through a park, or reading a magazine on the bus. I have a notebook that I keep all of them in, and whenever I see something that inspires me, I whip it out and sketch it before I forget it."

"Why wedding dresses?" he asked. "Why not just dresses in general?"

"Hopeless romantic, I guess. There's nothing more magical than helping a girl become a princess for a day. I love that I get to be a part of it."

"So, have you designed one for yourself?" he asked. It may have been my imagination, but I thought his voice dropped slightly when he asked, like the answer was important to him.

"Of course not," I replied. "That would just be weird."

Of course I did! The most perfect design, and the one dress I'd never make.

Two women, who were clearly drunk, came barrelling into us. The place was packed, but most people dancing to the band had congregated on the dance floor. These girls were dancing right next to us, meaning that I was taking the brunt of their revelry. As soon as Kieran saw what was happening, he put down his beer and moved behind me. With his hands on my waist, he steered me to swap our positions.

My calm demeanour disintegrated with his touch, and I shivered from the heat of his palm so close to my skin. I couldn't rationalise my reaction to him and the nervous butterflies that took flight as I caught the faint scent of soap and aftershave. I wanted to move deeper into his arms as I imagined how it would feel to have those huge biceps around me.

His left arm was tattooed in a full coloured sleeve that ended at his chrome watch. The other arm was completely bare, but I'd bet he had more tattoos somewhere. These boys loved their ink. He moved away from me, just in time to take an elbow in the back.

"I'm so sorry," the drunken girl who staggered next to him said. "We were just having fun. I totally didn't see you there."

"No problem," he replied with a grin. "It might be safer if you hit the dance floor though. This place is filling up pretty quick."

"Oh my God, I love your accent. Say something else!" she screeched, pulling at her friend to witness the spectacle that was an Irish accent in an Irish bar on St Patrick's Day.

"Tommy!" Kieran called out. "This lady over here wants you to show her the pot of gold at the end of your rainbow." Apparently this was code for something because Tommy rounded the table with lightning speed to throw his arms around the girl's shoulders. The one who'd ploughed into Kieran looked disappointed at the brush off, and I couldn't help feeling a little smug. He leaned in towards my ear to talk when the band struck up a lively tune and the place erupted.

"Come on," Kieran shouted, a mischievous smile on his face. "Let's dance!"

"What? No!" I said in a blind panic. Unlike most women my age, I was a rubbish dancer. I could belt out a good tune, but shaking it in public was not my forte. Someone once told me that seeing me dance was like watching a zombie on speed get a cramp. The horrified look on his face told me that he wasn't joking. Up until that point, I'd been convinced I was totally killing it on the dance floor. Now, when absolutely forced, I did the two-foot shuffle until I could politely make my escape. Of course, in my bedroom with a hair brush, I was still freakin' Beyoncé.

Apparently my objections didn't carry with the rest of the noise, and I was in the middle of the crowd before I knew it. I needn't have worried though. Alcohol had evened the playing field as far as coordination was concerned, and I was far from the most tragic case there. In any event, Kieran led most of the time and, eventually, the dance floor became too packed to do anything other than jump around and sing. By the time we made it back to the table, I was hoarse.

"Another drink?" he asked me.

I could tell how fit he was. Apart from a light sheen of sweat, he looked fresh as a daisy. I was so exhausted from dancing, I felt like I was about to cough up a lung. I managed a nod and a "yes please," and he disappeared to the bar.

Em was back sitting on Con's lap, but looking at me starry eyed.

"What?" I asked, fanning myself with a beer mat to try and cool down.

"You guys make the cutest couple ever!" she replied.

"Slow down, Em. We're not a couple. I've told you before that I'm not looking for a serious relationship," I said.

"Come on, Marie, you two can't keep your eyes or your hands off each other. It's only a matter of time until something happens with you, if it hasn't happened already."

"Look, I'm not saying that I don't like him. I'm just not in a place where I want or need a relationship. I'm happy with things the way they are," I replied. That wasn't exactly true, but there was no need to tell Em that.

"Why does it have to be serious? Just get to know him a little and see where it goes. He really is a great guy. What's the worst that could happen?" she asked.

I'd fall in love with him. Or even more tragic, he'd fall in love with me. I couldn't allow that to happen.

"Do me a favour, Em. Don't push this. Nothing's going to happen with Kieran. We're friends, and that's exactly how I want to keep things."

"Okay," she said, with a longsuffering sigh. "But you're giving up on something that could be pretty spectacular."

"Since you got married, you want to marry everyone else off. It's quite cute really," Nikki said, pulling up a stool next to me.

"I just want you guys to be happy, that's all," Em explained, looking a little put out.

"Now don't get your knickers in a knot. What you and Con have is special, and that's pretty hard to find, but you've got to let people find it in their own way," she said, and Em nodded in reluctant agreement. "Besides, life is a chocolate box of men, and I want to try every flavour. Unless I find that one mythical chocolate that makes me forget that all others exist, I'm going to keep eating. Maybe Marie feels the same."

"What she said," I added, giggling at Em's glum expression. She really did want to see us all settled down.

"Cheer up, Em, it really is for the best. Just imagine how awkward it would be if we dated and things didn't work out? I'd never be able to come out with you guys anymore, and it would split up our group," I said.

"But imagine if you fell in love and had beautiful babies and we spent every weekend taking the kids away camping!" she whined.

"Dear God, marriage really has turned her into a monster!" Nikki said to me, and I laughed as Em poked her tongue out at her.

"Honestly, Em, we really are better off as friends," I said.

"Who's better off as friends?" Kieran asked, as he set a bottle of beer down on the table in front of me and dragged over a stool to put down next to mine.

"Marie was just shattering my dream of planning your wedding by telling me that you're just friends," Em told him glumly.

"Is that so, Irish?" Kieran said. Chuckling, he took a sip of his pint.

"Irish?" Nikki asked, before I had a chance to.

"She looks more Irish that English," Kieran explained, flicking a lock of my hair to demonstrate, and making me shiver.

"I was explaining to Em that I'm not looking for a relationship now, so she needs to bring the crazy down a notch," I said. The words were bitter in my mouth. The rational side of me knew that I was doing and saying the right thing. The irrational side of me was sitting as close as possible to the edge of my stool just to touch him.

"I get that. So how do you feel about casual, sweaty, monkey sex?" he asked. I choked on my beer, and he slapped my back until the coughing and spluttering stopped.

"You did that on purpose!" I said, wiping tears from my eyes.

"I did not," he said, innocently, "and stop avoiding the question." I looked up to see Em and Nikki perched eagerly as they waited on my answer.

"I don't think I'm built for casual sex," I replied. "I know myself, and it wouldn't be long before I was all in and casual went out the window. Friendship is pretty much all I'm capable of at the moment."

"That's a shame," Kieran said finally. "Friendship is so much better when orgasms are involved."

"Amen," Liam replied.

CHAPTER THREE

KIERAN

I hopped from one foot to another, shuffling backwards and forwards as Con moved the bag.

"Now! Right, right, left! Right, right, left!" he said, calling out combinations as I hit the bag. With everything I had I hit that fucking bag, smacking the shit out of it as hard as I could. On the rare occasion that I was in a pissy mood, just the smell of Driscoll's Gym calmed me. If it came down to calling whether I'd spent more time here or home over the years, it'd be a close one. This morning though, nothing was cutting it. I was wound up and pissed off. I just hoped I could burn off enough energy that I got rid of my bad mood as well.

"Okay, I'm calling it. What the fuck's up with you?" Con asked, holding the bag still.

"Don't know what you're talking about. I'm fine," I replied. I should have known better than to lie to him. Cormac O'Connell had been my best friend since we were kids. I didn't think he could have known me any better if we were brothers. The fecker didn't say anything, just stood there, arms crossed, with one eyebrow raised.

"That's really fucking creepy you know," I said, punching the bag. Because he'd been leaning on it, he took the brunt of the blow. Shoving it back at me, he came around and started sparring. His hands were only in wraps whereas I wore gloves, but it didn't matter. We'd been doing this forever. He might well be heavy weight champion of the world, but I could read Con like a book. There wasn't a single combination he could throw at me that I hadn't blocked at some point in our lives. We went at it for a good ten minutes, but it was still stalemate until Tommy walked in.

"You two going at it already?" he asked. Distracted, I turned to glance at Tommy, but that was all the opening Con needed. The fucker was fast and had me in a headlock before I ever saw it coming.

"Spill," he said, giving me a noogie.

"I swear, if you don't let me go, I'm gonna punch you right in the fucking balls. Let's see you explain why you can't give Em kids because you were being a dick and now your balls are somewhere between your arse and your mouth."

Con threw his head back and laughed, but released me. He didn't ask again, but I knew he wouldn't let this go until he knew what was going on.

"I like someone," I said, finally.

"Marie. We know," he said.

"What do you mean you know? How can you know? Did she say something to Em?" I asked.

"Jesus, you're so fucking needy. When she put your balls in her purse, it looks like she gave you a shot of oestrogen as well."

I went to give him the finger before remembering that I was wearing gloves, so I punched him instead.

"How did you know then?" I asked.

"It's not hard to figure it out, mate. Your eyes follow her like a love-sick puppy when she's in the room. That and you lose all game when you're with her. You could charm the birds from the trees as far as most women are concerned. When it comes to Marie, it's not pretty."

"Fuck off," I said grumpily. "Everything was going great yesterday. I was taking it slow but letting her know I was interested. Then she tells Em that she doesn't want to get involved with anyone and that we should just be friends."

He threw his head back and laughed.

"Well, I'm glad I fucking amuse you. All fucking smug now you've got Em ain'tcha. Imagine if I'd given you the same shit when you two first met," I reminded him.

"She's your Em?" he asked.

"Yes. No. I don't know. Maybe," I replied, making him roll his eyes.

"Well, I don't know what you're moping and bitching about. The answer seems pretty clear from where I'm standing," he said.

"Well?" I asked.

"If she doesn't like you, walk away, 'cause nobody likes a stalker. But if you think she might feel the same, pull up your big boy pants and fucking fight for her," he replied.

"Fight how?" I asked.

"Look, Em was exactly the same when I met her. She only wanted friendship because she was afraid. Even getting her to speak to me was a big fucking deal. So give Marie what she thinks she wants, until she realises that you aren't going anywhere and you aren't going to hurt her," he replied.

"Irish," I said.

"Huh?" he replied.

"It's what I call her. Not Marie," I explained, making him grin.

"You're in so much fucking trouble. Get ready for a ride on heartbreak train, my friend. This girl's gonna make you work for it," he said.

"Is it worth it?" I asked.

He nodded in reply. "All the best ones are."

I felt a little better after that. Con, however, made me pay for the cheap shot with the bag by putting me through five more rounds where he gave me his very best. I needed every ounce of concentration when we sparred these days. He was good when we were kids, but since he'd been training full-time he'd become unbeatable.

"You ladies finished dancin'?" Danny barked at us, making us both chuckle.

"I could go a few more rounds," I hollered back.

"Get'cha arse over here, boyo. You too, lads," Danny said, beckoning us to come out of the ring and gather round with the other lads.

"What's going on, Danny?" I asked.

"Kid, the boys and I have been talking about your future.

Princess over here has been in the spotlight for a while," he said, nodding towards Con. "But we've been watching you close too. You've been doing great since you gave up construction to work Con's corner full-time, but now I want you to consider taking a shot yourself."

"You want me to fight?" I asked, absolutely stunned. I'd honestly never considered having a career as a professional fighter. Con was the one with all the drive and determination. I didn't know if I had it in me to do what he did.

"I do. If you can find the right fuel for your fire, you could be a bloody great fighter. At the end of the day, you don't know until you try. Give it your absolute best shot. Give me absolutely everything you've got in the tank, and when you step out of the ring after your first fight, you'll know for sure whether this is what you want."

I looked up at the faces of my mates, and there wasn't a hint of surprise on any of their faces.

"You fuckers all talked about this?"

Con, Liam, Earnshaw, and Tommy all nodded in agreement.

"What about Con?" I asked. After all, my job was to act as his corner man and prepare and train him for his next professional fight.

"He doesn't have another title fight for a while, and he'll keep in shape training you," Danny replied.

"Time for you to feel the pain, my friend. I've got a tractor tyre out back with your name on it," Con said, rubbing his hands together.

"Bit excited there about putting me through the ringer, aren'tcha? You've more faith in this working than I do," I replied.

"Please, you've been training with me toe to toe my whole life.

In months, you could be ready for a title fight. You just need the right motivation, that's all. Maybe all this angst and shit over your bird will be it," he said.

"Jesus Christ, not another one of you getting all loved up. I've only just gotten over the last feckin' wedding," Danny replied.

"Thanks, Con," I said sarcastically. "I'm not loved up, Danny. Con is talking bollocks."

"Well, nothing new there," Danny said.

Con flipped me the bird, making us all chuckle. "Stop thinking about how it would feel to lose, and think for a minute about how it would feel to win," Con said.

With the boys all in agreement, I started to wonder if I could really do this. Everyone knew me as the lover, not the fighter. Being who other people wanted you to be was easy, finding out what you were made of was hard. Em came out of the office and headed over to us. As well as being Con's wife, she did the books for the gym, and I had no doubt that Con and Danny would have talked to her about this.

"What do you think?" I asked her. She wasn't exactly a lover of boxing, not with how worried she got that we'd get hurt. It was how I knew I'd have an unbiased opinion, a voice of reason.

"I'd prefer it if you didn't get knocked around," she replied.

"Don't worry, Sunshine, I'll teach him to duck," Con said, wrapping his arm around her shoulders and kissing her affectionately on the head.

"But, a very wise man once said, 'a ship in harbour is safe, but that's not what ships are for.' You're a fighter, whether you know it or not. Maybe you have one fight in you, maybe you have hundreds. There's only one way to be sure."

"That Albert Einstein sure knows his shit," Tommy said.

"How could you possibly know that was Einstein?" Liam asked.

"Beer mats at Seamus O'Donnell's. They have loads of 'em with deep shit written on the back," he replied.

Em nodded enthusiastically. "It's where I read it."

Pretty much all of us rolled our eyes at their goofiness.

"Are we doing this shit then, or what?" Con asked.

Fuck it. At worst I'd be humiliated and get my arse beat. I'd get over it. But I was pretty sure that sitting in my rocking chair as an old man and wondering about the chance I didn't take would haunt me. Con was kind of right anyway. This shit with Irish had me feeling stuff I'd never felt before. Being able to vent that in training didn't seem like such a bad idea.

"Me ma's gonna feckin' kill me," I said finally.

"She'll smack you upside the head for agreeing to do it, and she'll smack me for talking you into it, but she'll be in the front row cheering you on when you hold up that belt," Con said.

"So what now?" I asked.

"We try for the same belt Con did when he went for his first title. We've three months to train, and we're already set up for it, thanks to Con's training. Your ranking is ridiculously low, but you'll get a shot on the back of his name," Earnshaw said. Although he was officially brought in as Con's manager, he was employed by Danny and promoted fights for all the club guys.

"Great," I said sarcastically. Trading on the back of Con's name was not something I ever wanted to do.

"This is a gift horse, Kieran. Don't look it in the mouth," Danny said.

"How do you mean?" I asked.

"You're getting a shot because you're in Connell's camp and because his trainer also trains you. But your ranking is low because you don't have many fights outside this place behind you. It works in our favour. It makes you a wild card, someone they can't predict," Earnshaw explained.

"It means they can't study your form, Kier. You get to fight any way you want and they won't be expecting it," Con said. I could see how that would make sense, and Con didn't seem to give a shit how I got the fight.

"When do we start?" I asked, almost afraid that Danny would say now. I knew what was involved in training a professional fighter, and I needed to stockpile on all the foods I wouldn't be allowed for the next three months.

"Tomorrow morning, 6.00 a.m. And, Kieran, you know my rule. As long as you're in training, no sex. So whatever flirtation you've got going on, better go on the back burner until you're holding that title. And I ain't feckin' about with this rule, boyo. You even think of fornicating or goin' to town on yourself, and you can find another feckin' gym to train at. I ain't wasting my time over someone who ain't taking this seriously," Danny told me.

How the fuck I could forget that rule I didn't know. As far as Danny was concerned, it was ironclad. No fighter, married or not, was allowed to come until after the fight. It was the old way that he'd been taught. The theory was that it built the testosterone steadily until the fight where you could release it in one blast. It was a shit rule, and I wasn't entirely sure my dick could go three days without at least a hand job, let alone three months. The 'no sex' thing wasn't so bad though. I hadn't been with a woman since I first met Irish anyway.

"Fine," I agreed, with a long-suffering sigh. "But if my balls literally explode before then, it'll be your fault," I reminded him.

Danny took his cigarette out of his mouth. "I'm sure I'll live with the guilt," he deadpanned.

"Well, unless you need me for anything else, Danny, I'm going to sack off the rest of the day and enjoy my last few hours of freedom," I said.

"Of course," Danny replied.

"Really?" I said, kinda surprised that he wasn't giving me shit.

"Of course feckin' not. Didn'tcha listen to a single word I said? We might start your professional training tomorrow, but you're still a fighter today, ain'tcha? Now get your arse over there and give me fifty one-handed press-ups, then change sides," Danny said. He wandered back to the office, muttering something about wasting talent and fucking ungrateful kids. As soon as he slammed the door, the lads fell about laughing.

"Laugh it up, fuckers," I said grumpily as I started on my push ups. When I finished those, I started on the sit ups, knowing I was best going through Con's basic routines. If Danny caught me sloping off early, he'd go fuckin' nuts. I only hoped I had enough energy afterwards to down at least one Daisy burger with fries before I kissed my usual diet goodbye.

Half an hour later, Albie strolled in and started warming up on the bags. He and Em went to school together, which was how we'd all met, but he'd been training at Driscoll's for a while now and wasn't far short of being one of us. Seeing him reminded me of something.

"Liam, what the fuck happened St Paddy's Day? I thought you were bringing your fella there to meet us. Didn't think you'd bottle it," I said. The guys in earshot went quiet, waiting for his answer. As far as I knew, none of the lads were bothered at all about him being gay, but we were sure as fuck interested in who his boyfriend was. He darted a quick look across the gym, then back to me.

"I did bring him. We spent the day together and it was fucking great."

I stopped what I was doing and looked around to share confused looks with the other guys. The day might have been a little fuzzy, since I'd knocked back the pints after Marie's rejection, but I was pretty sure I hadn't been introduced to anyone.

"I wasn't drinking much that night, and I know full well that you spent the whole day with all of us, so what gives?"

"Bunch of nosy little bitches, aren't you?" Liam said. "You know I'm gay now. Can't you just leave it at that?"

"Um, no," Tommy said. "If you're giving some fucker the hot beef injection, we wanna know who it is."

Liam was one of the most placid, even-tempered people I'd ever met, but on the feckin' rare occasion that he lost his shit, you needed to stand well back. He'd been doing sit ups and chucking a medicine ball back and forth with Tommy. When Tommy opened his big, fat trap, Liam gave a low growl and chucked the ball so hard that Tommy grunted and stumbled as he caught it.

"I don't give a shit how many meaningless one-night stands you have. Some of us ain't cut from the same cloth. You're talking about someone that I care about, so how about showing some fuckin' respect," Liam said.

Sensing danger, Con jumped into the fray and stood between them both. "He didn't mean anything by it, mate. You know he runs his mouth without thinking. He gives me shit all the time, but you know how he feels about Em."

"Don't be so fuckin' sensitive, mate. If I was only dippin' my wick in one girl, you'd want to know who it was too," Tommy replied. Con sighed, knowing that Tommy wasn't helping the situation.

"I don't see it's any of your fuckin' business who I'm seeing. We'll tell people in our own time, so why you gotta push?" Liam said, still looking like he was ready to throw down with someone.

"Jesus, mate, at this rate, we're all gonna be retired before you come all the way out that closest. Stop being a whiny little bitch and tell us already," Tommy said.

At that, I jumped into the fray with Con, 'cause Tommy really didn't have any sense of self-preservation. He was a stone's throw away from getting his arse beat, and at this point, I was on the fence about whether to protect him or point and laugh.

"It's me. Liam and I are together," said a voice from behind us, quietly but firmly. We all turned to see who had spoken.

"Holy. Fucking. Shit," Tommy said, finally.

CHAPTER FOUR

MARIE

I woke suddenly and sat bolt upright in bed, still breathing hard. Sleep was a cruel kind of torture. The beautiful blond-haired child of my dream with eyes of chocolate brown was the spitting image of Kieran. His cheeky grin, the exact replica of his father's, broke my heart.

"Bye, Ma," he'd said, waving as he ran to catch up with his dad.

When I woke, my eyes were wet with the knowledge that the adorable boy would never be mine.

CHAPTER FIVE

KIERAN

There was nothing to say after that. We all just kind of stood there, slack jawed, and stared.

"Well, I didn't see that one coming," I said.

"You didn't need to say anything. I would have kept you secret," Liam said, his eyes wet with unshed tears.

"Yes, I did," Albie said. "I'm not ashamed of who I am, or who you are. We do this, we do this together."

If I had a million guesses as to who Liam's new boyfriend could be, Albie, the six-foot-three-inch, rugby playing genius would not be one of them.

"Fair play, my friend. You've shocked the shit out of all of us, but coming out like that takes some big, brass balls. I can't begin to imagine the shitstorm that you're both gonna have to endure, and I can't speak for all the lads, but, mate, I've got your fuckin' back," I said to Albie, offering him my hand. He swallowed hard before shaking it firmly.

"Thanks, Kieran. I can't tell you how much I appreciate that," he replied. He looked so relieved, I pulled him in for a hug and a back slap. All the lads followed my lead, crowding around Albie to shoot the shit and offer their support. A few of them teased him, but you couldn't come out to a bunch of rowdy Irish boxers without expecting some ribbing. There was no doubt at all though that, here at least, Albie and Liam would be accepted without judgement. While Albie was holding court, Liam slipped off to the changing room, so I followed. He stood, head leant back against his locker and eyes closed.

"You okay, my friend?" I asked him.

"You know, Kier, I'm really fucking not," he replied. "For months I've been worrying over this shit, scared that you lot wouldn't want me training here, or that you'd start getting weird around me, or that you'd find out about Albie and scare him off. I was fucking prepared for everything, except what just happened. I didn't dare to imagine that we'd be accepted or that he'd stand up for me like that. And now that I've gone through it, I'm twice as scared to tell my family, because I know for certain they won't react the same way. They'll be fucking devastated. Not one of 'em will see what a great guy I'm with." Walking dejectedly, he sat down on the bench and picked at his wraps.

Sitting down next to him, I gave the best advice I could. "That burden ain't yours to carry, my friend. The best I figure it, you get one life. Worrying and wondering about 'what if' just wastes what precious little time we have on this rock. Live every day like it's your last. Love the people you can't help but love, and don't apologise for it. Stop thinking about everything you could lose, and start thinking of everything you could gain. Let yourself be happy, and what happens, happens. You can't control how your family will react, any more than you can help how you feel, mate."

"When did you get so fuckin' wise?" he said with a chuckle.

"Who the fuck knows," I replied. "But do me a favour and don't go tellin' people. Next thing you know, they'll be thinking I'm all mature and shit, and I can't handle that sort of responsibility."

He discreetly wiped his eye with his palm while still chuckling. "Thank, Kier," he said, and I could tell he meant it.

"Anytime. Now, let's go and rescue your man before Tommy scares him away."

We walked back into the gym to see a slightly red-cheeked Albie chatting with Con and Earnshaw. Tommy stood with them, frowning as though he was confused.

"What you thinking so hard about, Tom?" I asked.

"I'm tryin' to figure out how it works?" he replied.

"How what works?" I said, confused.

"You know," he answered, gesturing with his hands. Knowing that he wasn't the sharpest tool in the box, I interpreted that to be stupid sign language for sex.

"You want me to explain the mechanics of gay sex," I said, choking back a laugh.

"Nah," he replied. "I figured out that they're dancing the chocolate cha-cha. It's just that... fuck, look at the size of 'em both. When their cocks clash, it must be like a fight scene from

Highlander." Liam, along with the rest of us, exploded with laughter. The man who barely cracked a smile caught Albie's eye and looked happier than I'd ever seen him.

"What are you fecker's laughin' at?" Danny asked, his customary cigarette hanging from his lips.

"Liam is gay and Albie's his boyfriend," Tommy blurted out, pointing at Liam. Liam sobered up pretty quick at that. Danny was the nearest thing that most of us had for a father. Unlike my own, Liam's Da was still alive, but the fecker was a waste of space. For him, Danny filled that role, and his approval meant a lot to him. To his credit, Danny's expression didn't change. He looked like he was thinking on something for a minute, before shaking a bony finger between Liam and Albie.

"No shenanigans in my gym. And that goes for the lot of you feckers. Liam, your subs are late. Make sure you square up before you leave," he said. Turning on his heel, he headed back to his office.

"As long as I live, I will never get the measure of the way that man's mind works," Con said.

"That's for damn sure," Liam replied.

* * *

"Hey, Kier, what you up to tonight?" Con asked.

"Drownin' in a pool of my own self-pity I imagine," I replied. Groaning, I eased my aching arse down on the bench and peeled off my sweaty black wraps. Stuffing one into my gym bag, I started on the other. Some of the boys stuck theirs in the gym laundry, but Con and

I were superstitious. No one else got to wear our wraps, so we took them home to wash. I ached something fierce. Danny hadn't been fucking about with the training. If I thought I was prepared for what he and Con were going to throw at me, I was wrong. It'd only been a week, but if felt liked I'd been doing this for a year. Usually Friday nights would be all about bars and babes. Tonight, I wondered if I'd have enough energy to ride my sorry arse home. How Con ran home from the gym after a full day of training, I'd never know.

"Fancy going to a movie? I'm off to see that new blockbuster with Em," he said.

"No offence, mate, but I don't fancy playing third wheel while you cuddle up and indulge Sunshine's inner geek," I replied.

"Mock all you like, but sci-fi makes her horny. If I have to sit through three hours of that shite to make her happy, so be it," he said.

"Yeah, you're really selling me on this night out. Thanks for the offer though," I replied sarcastically.

"No worries. I'll see what Tommy's doing. Em asked Marie if she wanted to come, and I don't want her feeling like the odd one out," he said. He slung his gym bag over his

shoulder and walked away.

"Hold up there, boyo," I called out as I leaned back to catch him before he left. "Give me half an hour to go home and change, and I'll be ready."

"Thought so," he said with a smirk. "See you outside the cinema at 8.30."

"Fucker," I mumbled to myself. Despite being slightly pissed that I'd been played by Con, I was reenergised. No matter how bad I hurt, I'd be spending at least three hours next to Irish tonight, and I couldn't wait.

* * *

I was so fucking eager to see her, I arrived ten minutes early. Being a Friday night, the car park was rammed. Luckily, there were still bays for bikes at the front, and I rode my Suzuki GSX-R600 into a space. Pulling off my helmet, I ran a hand through my buzz cut as I caught sight of her. Auburn hair, which shone in the lights above her, fell halfway down her back and curled at the ends. I couldn't see her eyes from here, but I knew they were the brightest blue. Everything about her was pure and wholesome and too good for the likes of me. Man, she was fucking beautiful, and my heart beat harder for everything I couldn't have.

She shivered as I strolled towards her. Instinctively, I shrugged off my jacket to offer her.

"Cold?" I asked.

"No, I'm fine thank you," she replied.

"Probably would have swamped you anyway," I said, pulling back the heavy leather coat.

"I didn't know you were coming tonight," she said.

"Would you have bailed if you'd known?" I asked.

"Of course not," she replied. "I like you, Kieran. I really do. I just... I'm just not in a place where I can offer anyone more than friendship at the moment." The sad look on her face and the note of regret in her voice gave me hope.

"I can do friendship," I replied, giving her my best cocky grin.

She sighed, but smiled. "You really have no intention of settling for friendship, do you?"

"Absolutely none," I replied. "But I'll take what I can get, until you fall for me."

"You're wasting your time with me, Kieran. There are a million girls out there who'd kill to go out with you," she said.

"Darlin', a million girls just ain't you," I answered, making her blush. "Okay, I don't want you over-dosing on all this charm too quickly. Let's head in and get the tickets and snacks."

"Shouldn't we wait for Em and Cormac?" she asked.

"I'd be surprised if they make it before the film starts," I replied.

"Are they running late?" she said.

"Con's hasn't seen Em all day. It'll take her ages to peel him off long enough to drive here," I replied.

She laughed, cutting the tension between us.

"Come on then. I've been dying to see this movie for ages, and I'm not missing the start. I'll text Em and let her know where we are."

* * *

Sure enough, Em and Con rocked up with only minutes to spare. When they finally squeezed past a pissed-off row of people to reach us, I turned to Irish and shared a secret smile. As if Con's ear-to-ear grin wasn't a dead giveaway that that they'd been getting busy, Em's bedhead sure was.

"Sorry we're late, guys. The car wouldn't start," Em said.

"You having trouble with that brand new car of yours?" I asked, making her bury her face in Con's shoulder with embarrassment.

"She's a terrible liar," he said, helping himself to a handful of my popcorn.

"Hungry, are you?" I asked him, eying his hot dogs and nachos with jealousy. Danny would pitch a bitch fit if I touched any of that stuff, and Con knew it. The popcorn was for Irish, though the greedy bastard next to me would hoover that too if I didn't protect it for her. The lights dimmed, halting any more conversation. Con wrapped his arm around Em's shoulders and threw me a wink, knowing I couldn't do the same. I gave him the finger as subtly as I could and shifted my body towards my girl. She was looking straight ahead at the screen, hands folded demurely in her lap. Even above the sickly-sweet popcorn, I could still smell the clean apple scent of her shampoo. I adjusted my jeans slightly as my cock began to thicken. I must be in a bad way if the smell of fruit was getting me hard.

An hour later and we'd both relaxed. I'd only given the movie half my attention, but it was pretty good. Irish was hooked though. Inch by inch, she'd eased back against me. She kept reaching over for the popcorn and looked surprised when she realised that she'd emptied it.

Fuck it.

I reached down to put the empty box on the floor. As I sat back, I used the opportunity to wrap my arm around the back of her chair. She looked at me with a smirk on her face.

"Smooth, huh?" I said, wiggling my eyebrows comically. Rolling her eyes, she smiled as she went back to watching the film. As she did, she twisted slightly and leaned back to cuddle into the crook of my arm.

"Don't take it personally," she said softly. "You're just a warm body."

"Whatever you say, baby," I answered. My voice was a whisper against her ear, making her shiver.

I'd done countless things with countless women, but in that moment, I couldn't think of a single one of them. None of those experiences could hold a candle to what I was feeling with Irish pressed up against me. All of a sudden I was like a fuckin' teenager again. It didn't matter that, when the lights came on, we'd go back to being friends. The darkness let us steal enough magic to pretend that we were more.

She excused herself a while later to go to the bathroom. I used the opportunity to lift the armrest between us. Con snorted with laughter as he caught me. This time I didn't try and hide the double fingers I stuck up at him, making him and Em laugh. When Irish shuffled along the row to get back to me, she didn't notice what I'd done. Or if she did, she didn't comment. As soon as she sat, I reached for her hand. I willed the movie not to end as her slender fingers wove gently through mine, her soft skin mapping the terrain of my own hard and calloused hand. All too soon the lights came back on, and our free pass was over.

As she moved away from me, I felt the loss of her warmth. I didn't understand the reason for the sad look on her face. I knew from Em that she was single, and it wasn't like she lived a million miles away. If she liked me and I liked with her, I couldn't see any reason why we shouldn't be together. In hindsight, I probably should have waited until I'd taken her home, or at least left the movie theatre, but *I'm Kieran fuckin' Doherty*, I told myself as I stood up, held Irish's face gently in my hands, and kissed the ever-loving shit out of her.

The theatre could have exploded and I wouldn't have known. That kiss had *everything*. Magic, fireworks, all that shite girls talk about, it had the lot, and I wanted more. It wasn't a taste; it was a brand. She was mine now, and I wasn't letting her go. Fuck playing it cool, Irish showed me what I never knew I wanted, and I wasn't stopping until I had it for good. She pulled her lips reluctantly from mine, but I didn't let her go.

"The guys over there are cheering and whistling at us," she said.

"Jealousy's a bitch," I replied, giving her lips a quick peck before reaching for her hand to lead her to the exit. Em and Con stopped to applaud before following us out.

"Quite the show you put on there, Kier," Con said. "So, are you two going steady then?" Con was taking the piss, but Em was looking at us like we were the cutest thing she'd ever seen.

"I'll talk her into it as soon as I can get her alone for five minutes," I said.

"Um, I'm right here, guys," Irish said. Her flushed cheeks were the prettiest shade of pink, and damn if I didn't want another taste.

"We'd better get home if you guys have to be up at five for training," Em said, always the voice of reason.

"How'd you get here, darlin'?" I asked.

"Um, the bus," she murmured. Em opened her mouth, I guessed to offer Irish a lift home, when I silenced her with a pleading look.

"I'll make sure she gets home safe," I told her and Con.

"Don't I get a say?" Irish asked me, her laugh telling me that she was more amused than annoyed at my high-handedness.

"Nope," I replied. "I'm not giving you the opportunity to run off. You freak out too easily. Besides, you'll love the bike." She rolled her eyes at me, but squeezed my hand in response.

"Take it easy, fella," Con said, giving me a back slap while the girls said goodbye. When Con leant in to kiss Irish's cheek, Em hugged me hard.

"Don't fuck this up. I really like this girl," she whispered in my ear.

"Don't worry, Mrs O, I'll be on my best behaviour," I said. "I'm keeping this one," I added.

"Just be patient with her. I have a feeling she's worth waiting for," she replied.

We waved them goodbye, and I led Irish towards the bike. I could sense her nervousness, but her tight grip on my hand gave me hope. The temperature had dropped and she shivered as we walked.

"Here, you'll need this," I said, wrapping the heavy leather jacket around her shoulders and zipping it up. It swamped her, but it would do its job. I handed her the helmet to put on, but brushed her hands away as she fiddled with the strap.

"Tell me why," I asked suddenly.

"Why what?" she said, looking confused.

"Why you aren't ready for me. Why you don't want to date," I answered.

She sighed, and I regretted that the glow from our kiss was gone under the weight of her thoughts. "You won't like it," she answered sadly.

"Maybe not," I said, straddling the bike, then helping her to climb on behind me. "But you're going to tell me why you don't think we can work. Then I'm going to show you exactly how we can."

CHAPTER SIX

MARIE

"Focus, Kieran," I said.

"If you wanted me to focus, you probably shouldn't have opened your shirt, darlin'," he replied.

He lifted his hand slowly, as though to cup my breast, before I rolled my eyes and slapped it away.

"Okay, hot stuff, eyes up," I told him.

"Um... if you want me to look at your face, can you close your shirt? I think your tits have me hypnotised," he said. Despite the gravity of what I was trying to tell him, I couldn't help but giggle. He really was loveably charming.

"Kier, I'm wearing a tank. It's not like I'm topless," I said.

"I'm sorry. Still mesmerised by your boobs," he replied.

"Okay, look about an inch above my breasts," I said.

"Holy shit, that must have been some knife fight, Irish," he said, as he saw the faint two-inch scar on the left side of my chest.

The whole evening with Kieran was magical. I'd floated through it in a bubble, imagining for one night that I was normal, that it was a real date where he and I could go home together and wake up tomorrow and do it all again. But I wasn't normal. There could be no happy ever after for the both of us. So I took a deep, steadying breath before bursting the bubble for good.

"It is from a knife, but not how you're thinking. It's a surgical scar," I explained.

His jaw dropped open as he stared back and forth between my face and the scar.

"How? Why?" he said. I could see the confusion and a glimpse of horror on his face.

"I was born with a congenital heart defect, Kier. I've been in and out of hospitals nearly my whole life. When I was fifteen, my heart finally gave out. I had several valve repair surgeries, but at some point I'll either need a replacement valve or a transplant," I explained.

He ran his finger gently along the scar, making me shiver.

"But you're okay now though, right?" he asked.

"I have a ton of medication to take every morning to keep things on an even keel, and I can't do anything other than light exercise so that I don't overexert myself, but at the moment, I'm healthier than I've been for a long time," I explained.

"So we'll go slow, and I'll be extra careful not to make your heart pound too hard," he said jokingly.

"It won't work, Kier. I can't have a fling. Not with you. I like you too much already. It would be too easy to fall for you," I said.

"Who says it has to be a fling? I don't have a lot of experience with relationships, but it's what I want with you," he said.

Tears swam in my eyes as the tiny fissures in my heart began to crack. I wanted Kieran to be mine so badly, I could taste it. Never had I felt so alive as I had on the back of his bike, my arms wrapped around his rock-hard abs, my face nestled against the warmth of his body. Just once, I wanted this fragile heart to beat for someone else. I wanted it to beat for him.

"I want that too, so very badly, but I can't do that to you. I won't. There are so many things that I'd be robbing you of. There'd be endless hospital appointments. We'd never be able to have children, because the strain would almost certainly be too much for my body. And even if you could handle all that and I didn't get sick again, this heart has a shelf life. Whenever I get sick and admitted to hospital, I never know whether I'm going to make it back out again."

He swallowed hard, looking absolutely devastated. He opened and closed his mouth. The Irish charmer with the gift of the gab was rendered speechless. Knowing what had to be done, I closed my shirt and wrapped my arms protectively around myself.

"It's all right, Kieran. You don't need to say anything. Em told me what happened to your dad, and it's not something I would put you through again. It's why I've been so standoffish. I was hoping to avoid this conversation. But I need you to know that it isn't you. If I had a chance of something real with anyone, I'd want it to be with you."

Leaning forward, I kissed him gently on the cheek, inhaling the delicious scent of his aftershave one last time.

"Bye, Kier. I'll see you around," I said.

That was probably the hardest part of this conversation. I was friends with his best friend's wife, so seeing him around was inevitable. But he'd never be mine, and there was always the possibility of seeing him one day with a girl that he'd call his for good. It would be a pain there was no medication for.

Leaving him straddling his bike, I turned around and walked stealthily towards the door of my building I didn't turn around, not once. The tears were streaming down my face, and I didn't want him to see that. When I was safely inside my apartment, I locked the door and collapsed on to the bed, pulling the fluffy comforter over the top of me.

It's for the best, I told myself. But it didn't help. Instead, I broke down and sobbed myself to sleep.

* * *

I woke up feeling tired and sluggish. My puffy eyes were still red from crying, but the sun was shining and things didn't seem as bad as they did last night. Everything always looked better in the morning. No matter how hard the previous day had been, I always tried to look for the positives when I woke. I was alive. My heart was still going strong. Today, I'd be a part of someone's dream coming true. I never felt sorry that I was helping people chose a dress that I would never get to wear. Being a part of someone's big day was a privilege that I would never take for granted.

Waiting for the water to boil for my tea, I looked out the window at the morning and allowed myself a brief minute to wonder how

Kieran was. I had no doubt that the truth had hurt him, but it was for the best. Kieran had said goodbye to his Dad after a terminal illness. I wouldn't let him fall in love with me, only to have to do the same thing again. The whistle of the kettle shook me out of my own head. One quick cup of tea and a shower later, and I was out the door, ready to start another day.

* * *

"Oh, my dear, you look sooo beautiful. This gorgeous dress suits you so well!" the crazy Maltese lady said.

Stella Kelly was a bubbly, fiery, powerhouse of a woman, who swept into my shop a few times a week and filled the place with her personality. She drove me nuts constantly, but I absolutely couldn't do without her. She was always butting into my business and second-guessing every decision I made. But when I was sick, she kept my shop going for me. When I was well, she made every bride feel like a princess and sold more dresses in a day than I could ever hope to. Luckily for me, she was my mother.

"You're absolutely right. I think this is the one," the bride said, smoothing her hands down one of my early designs.

"It's a fabulous choice. Feel free to keep it on for as long as you like. But when you're ready, make your way out front and we'll sit down and put the order through. In the meantime, can I get you a glass of anything to celebrate the occasion?" I asked.

"Oh, a glass of wine would be wonderful if you have it," she replied, clapping her hands together excitedly. I left her cooing over the dress with her mother and sisters and made my way out to the front of the shop. Pulling a bottle of white out of the fridge, I was lining up glasses for the wedding party when my mum slapped her hands down on the counter in front of me.

"What's up with you today? You look like someone ran over your horse," she said.

"Mum, I don't have a horse," I replied.

"I know you don't have a horse. It's an expression. It means you look miserable. You also look tired and too skinny, but I couldn't think of any expressions for that."

A little over thirty-five years ago, Michael Kelly ate one mouthful of Stella Bellizzi's pasta, fell madly in love, and swept her off her feet. At least that's the way Mum told the story. He left for Malta on a temporary posting with his engineering company and returned home with a wife. In the early years of their marriage, Dad kept her busy with baby after baby. I was the eldest. A quiet, shy kid, always hiding behind Mum's skirts. A year later, she gave birth to a son, and practically five minutes after that, twin boys. All three healthy, strapping, good-looking Maltese lads. Although Dad was English, he was dark haired and olive skinned like his mother. Thanks to a genetic throwback from three generations before, I inherited the pale skin and red hair of Dublin-born Niall Kelly. Someone made the mistake once of asking Mum if I was adopted. She answered in Maltese. Very loudly. I did inherit one thing from my Dad though, his weak heart. He died suddenly of cardiac arrest when I was five, leaving Mum in a strange country to raise four children alone. But she did it, and since I was already receiving medical treatment, she decided to stick it out in London.

"I'm pretty sure the expression is something like 'you look like someone ran over your dog,' and I don't have one of those either."

"That's ridiculous. Mine is much better. You'd form much more of an attachment to a horse than a dog," she said.

"How would it even be possible to run over a horse?" I asked.

"Of course it's possible. You don't think a car would hurt a horse?" she answered.

"You do realise how ridiculous this whole conversation is, don't you? I can't even remember what we were talking about," I said, smiling at her as I poured the wine.

"That's better. I don't like it when you're sad. Now eat something and sleep more, and I will be really happy," she said, squeezing my cheeks like I was a kid. Even after all the years she'd spent in England, Mum's accent still carried a distinct Maltese lilt.

As it turned out, a day in the shop was just what I needed. Everything, from the beautiful fairy tale décor in creams and oaks to the subtle scent of apples from discreetly hidden Yankee candles, relaxed me. Coming here didn't seem like work. It was more a haven. Maybe that's why it pissed me off when I looked up to see Alastair Baxter-Hall striding confidently across the road towards the boutique.

"Hello, Alastair," I said politely, barely resisting the temptation to grit my teeth. "This is a nice surprise."

"I hoped you'd think so. You look a little pale today. Should you really be working?" he asked.

I sighed, knowing that I didn't have the energy for another confrontation with him today. "I'm perfectly well, thank you. If I'm pale, it's probably because I haven't eaten yet," I replied. I could have kicked myself as I said it, knowing what was coming next.

"Well, let's rectify that now. Shut up this place and I'll take you to dinner," he said. The way he'd waved his hand dismissively around my shop as he'd said "this place," had my hackles rising. Soon after our first meeting, he made it clear that he wanted to date. I told him that I just wanted to be friends in order to let him down gently, but I quickly realised my mistake. Alastair wasn't looking for a friend; he wanted a trophy wife, someone to attend charity lunches and hang on his arm and every word. The fact that I clearly wasn't that woman did nothing to deter him. To him, my livelihood was a hobby, a means of passing the time until I married. Not even my attempts to end our association had fazed him. He'd simply announced that he'd wait until I saw sense and was ready to settle down and suggested that I didn't wait too long. That was six months ago, and not a week went by without him dropping by the boutique or other places I hung out. What started out as annoying was now becoming wearisome, and more than a little creepy.

"I can't just 'shut up' shop, Alastair. This is my busy season. I have two more fittings before I'm done for the day," I explained.

"You see! This is what I've been talking about. How can you expect to run a business in your condition? You can't even afford to take a break when you get tired. How is this kind of strain good for your heart?" he asked.

A month ago, I ran into Alastair on the way to my mum's for dinner and had tripped while attempting to make a hasty escape.. When my handbag spilled out all over the pavement, my pills had rolled to his feet. He'd read the label and stormed into the shop the next day, obviously having investigated what the drugs were for, and demanded an explanation. I didn't owe him one, but I gave it anyway, hoping it would end his infatuation. Unfortunately for me, it did the opposite. My weak heart only gave him more ammunition to wear me down.

"I'm completely healthy at the moment, but even if I were sick, I'm perfectly capable about making decisions about my own health. I've been doing it for a long time," I said.

He looked wounded, and instantly I felt guilty. I hated confrontation of any kind, and after saying goodbye to Kieran last night, I really didn't need this.

"It's only your welfare I'm thinking of, darling," he said. "We're still friends, aren't we? I'd like to think you'd look out for me if I were sick."

"But I'm not sick. Working here gives me purpose," I said, trying to explain.

"All right, I see I'm not going to get my way today. But just remember, being my wife would give you purpose too. And it's a job that won't leave you with calloused fingers," he said with a wink. I clenched my fist to hide the callouses he spoke of, then unclenched them. I was proud of those marks, not ashamed. They came from hours of hand sewing, of creating something beautiful by my own hand.

"What happens if you get married one day and your wife wants to work?" I asked him. I had no intention of ever being that woman, but until he abandoned his archaic notion that a woman *had* to give up her career when she heard wedding bells, the chances of him turning anyone else's head were slim.

"With the life I could provide for her, what woman would want to work?" he asked.

"It isn't just about making a living. This place is my world," I said, trying to explain. I needn't have bothered.

"I would be your whole world if you'd let me. Now, if I can't talk you into dinner, I might as well catch up with Geoffrey for drinks at the club. I'll see you soon, Marie. Goodbye, Mrs Kelly, you're looking as lovely as ever I see," he said.

Mum giggled as she walked up to the counter with the tiara that my bride had chosen.

"I have no idea why you fall for Alastair's charm," I said to her, feeling flat after his visit.

"He's not such a bad catch, little one. He's besotted with you and he's rich too. He could take care of you," she reasoned.

"Mum, I don't care about money. You know that."

"But if you get sick again when I am old, who will take care of you?" she asked. I knew this worried her, and my heart broke as I looked into her watery eyes. In all likelihood, I would die before her, and no parent should have to outlive their child.

"I won't marry a man I don't love, Mum, not just to have someone to take care of me."

"Yes, but, dear girl, you won't marry a man you do love either, will you?" She squeezed my cold hand.

"I can't do that to someone, Mum. I saw how much pain you were in when Dad died. It wouldn't be fair of me to knowingly do that."

She patted my hand sympathetically and shook her head. "For someone so smart, you know so little. To lose the other half of you is a pain like nothing else. But it's not his loss I remember. It's his love. It was a gift I would not trade in a million years. If you are lucky enough to find a gift like that, you'd be a fool not to take it."

With one last pat, she left the tiara on the counter and walked back to the bridal party. I heard her happy voice cooing with the bride's mother about her daughter's fabulous choice. On top of Alastair's untimely appearance, Mum now had me dwelling on Kieran and the chance of something with him that I'd thrown into the wind. In a show that would be completely unprofessional if anyone were watching, I leaned forward and rested my weary head against the cool counter. There were some days that were just made to be written off with a pint of Ben and Jerry's in bed and a Nicholas Sparks movie.

CHAPTER SEVEN

KIERAN

Stunned.

More specifically, absolutely shaken to the fucking core.

That's how I'd felt when Irish had shared her little revelation. Of all the reasons I'd thought up for the way she avoided having a relationship with me, her being sick was never one of them. Over the years, I could've had my pick of thousands of women. Wasn't it just a cosmic fucking joke that the one girl I wanted was the prime example of why I avoided commitment in the first place. Thinking back to my last memories of Da, and the months after his death where Ma struggled to go on, had my stomach tied up in knots.

I flicked on the gym lights and headed to the changing rooms to get ready. At 5.00 a.m., the gym was completely empty. I hadn't slept all night, but as bone weary as I was, I needed some outlet for my frustration. After a quick change, I rolled on my wraps and started on the bags. It wasn't my normal routine, but there was no one here to knock me back on track, and I needed the sweet burning pain of feeling my knuckles cracking against the tough leather to distract me from my thoughts. The slamming doors had me looking over my shoulder, but I needn't have bothered. There was only ever one person who'd be there at this hour.

"In early, aren'tcha?" Con asked me. I shrugged and carried on smacking the shit out of the bag.

"Did you know?" I asked, not bothering to look up.

"Know what?" he replied, sounding genuinely confused.

"Irish has a congenital heart defect. She's been sick for years, and it's only going to get worse until her heart finally packs up."

"Fuck," he replied.

"Pretty much."

He dropped his holdall and held the bag still for me. It was man code for a hug. "That's why she's been dodging you?" he asked.

I nodded, wiping the sweat away from my eyes with my forearm. "Em told her about Da, and she doesn't want to get into a relationship knowing she could be going down the same path he did."

I let rip with my punches, pouring out my anger and frustration with every hook and jab. By the time I was done, the sun was high in the sky and the gym was half full. I grabbed some water while Con went to change, before easing back into my usual routine.

"What's going down, ladies?" Tommy asked, as he threw a medicine ball at me. Danny liked to mix things up by swapping round my training partners in the afternoons. Usually Con would carry on training alongside me, but as he had no upcoming fights scheduled, he'd taken to hanging around the edge of the gym with the guys who all heckled and commentated on my performance. The lazy fucker was as quiet today as I was, and it was making everyone nervous.

"Not much," I replied. "Is that a hickey on your neck?"

"Yeah, Hoover Hayley gave me a going over last night. Man, that girl can suck," he said.

"Slut."

"Hey!" he said, indignantly. "She's a nice girl who enjoys a good time, that's all."

"I was talking about you."

"Oh. Fair enough," he replied. "Enough with changing the subject though. Why do you and Con look so miserable?"

With a deep sigh, I relayed everything I'd told Con.

"Fuck," he said, echoing Con's sentiments.

"What did you say to her?" he asked.

"Nothing. My vocal chords pretty much seized up."

He stopped, medicine ball poised midair and stared at me. "You mean to tell me that she bared her soul and you let her walk away without saying a word? You fucking pussy."

"Ease off, Tommy," Con said.

"No," Tommy replied. "There was a time I wanted to make a play for Marie, but I backed down for you."

"She deserves more than to be one of your fuck-and-dump girls, Tommy," I replied angrily. A barely caught the ball that he threw hard at my chest.

"I only ever sleep with girls who want the same thing I do, but that don't mean I couldn't have something more with Marie given half the chance."

"You are fuckin' dreamin' if you think she'd have picked you over me," I said.

"Maybe she would have if she'd known what a spineless little shit you were," he replied.

Throwing the ball to one side, I launched myself up and straight for him. Tommy lived to wind us all up, and had become a master at dodging our long jabs. But then, possibly for the first time since I'd known him, he went for me as well.

Neither of us were playing.

"Enough!" Con bellowed, grabbing me in an armlock before I could lay a hand on him. Liam did the same for Tommy, practically lifting him off the floor as he moved him away from me.

"We are not doing this shit," Con said. "Tom, you know why Kier didn't say anything, so why are you up in his face about this shit?"

"Because I like this girl, and he let her walk away, probably feeling like absolute shite, just because some bits of her don't work so good. Look, Kier, I know you lost your da, but that was a long time ago. Who's to say how long any of us have. But that girl looks at you like you walk on fuckin' water. If you don't have the stones to take a chance at what could be something amazing, that's up to you. But to just stand there like a pussy and offer her nothing, not even friendship, that's fucking low."

None of the boys said a thing, and I guess they were torn. They all knew firsthand what I'd been through with Da, but they liked Marie a lot. As I looked at each of them in the face, the reality of what I was throwing away hit me in the chest.

"You're right," I said to him. "I owed her more than that. It gutted her to tell me, and she didn't have to. She could have waited until we gave a relationship a try before saying anything."

"Don't be so hard on yourself, mate," Con said. "I wouldn't have known what to say either." It was typical of my best mate to jump to my defence.

"Yes you would," I replied. "If Em told you she was ill or had a health problem, you'd wrapped her up even tighter in cotton wool, but you'd have gone after her anyway, wouldn't you?"

He nodded in reply. "Yeah, I would've. But that doesn't mean you were wrong. You barely know this girl, and you've lived through this before. It's a lot to take on."

"I know her a lot better than you knew Em when you went after her. I know she's good and kind and that we share the same sense of humour. I know that she snorts when she finds something funny but she's trying not to laugh. I know that she's a good friend who's generous, patient, and loyal. I know that she's the first woman who's ever left me lost for words. I know that she's special. So what the fuck's wrong with me that I couldn't tell her that?"

"You want a list, arse nugget? 'Cause it's a long one," Tommy asked.

"Leave him alone, Freud," said Liam. "You've said your piece. Now that's enough."

Tommy rolled his eyes at him and looked at me pointedly.

"So now we've established what a fuckin' stupid mistake you've made, what are you going to do about it?" he asked.

I ran my hand haphazardly through my buzz cut. The idea of being with anyone else made my blood run cold. The idea of her being with another guy made it boil.

I liked this girl.

A lot.

Getting to be a part of her life was worth the chance of someday losing her. Tommy was right, for probably the first and last time in his life. There was no such thing as a sure thing in this world. Anyone of us could die in a car accident tomorrow. Diamonds were treasured because they were rare. If my time with her was finite, each moment would be more precious because of it. Da was right about that freight train, because that's exactly what this felt like.

"She'll never give me a shot now, not after I let her go without a fight. Mentally, she'd have closed the book on us by now," I said.

"Go big," Liam suggested. The big guy didn't say much. When he did, I listened. "You and Tommy are the kings of showboating. So do something big and show her that you've thought this through, that you're certain you want to make a go of it," he said.

"It's not a bad idea," Con added. "Marie is kind of shy in a group. Maybe if you put her on the spot, she'll give you a chance so you'll stop."

"Great. I always wanted a girl to date me out of embarrassment and pity," I said.

"Like you could get a girl to date you any other way," Tommy said, chuckling.

"Con," I said with a nod.

Answering with a knowing smirk, he gave Tommy a slap for me.

"Ow, fucker, that hurt," he said, rubbing the back of his head.

"Look, why don't you go and see her and talk it through

privately. If she doesn't buy it, then go big and get her attention," Liam said. It was pretty sound advice, though I was confident that Irish had made up her mind about us, regardless of what I said.

"Any bright ideas on how I'm going to get her attention?" I asked.

"I have one," Tommy said.

"Does it involve making an arse of meself?" I asked.

"Fuck yeah," he replied with a grin. "Might as well be some entertainment for us in it.

* * *

I trained hard for the rest of the afternoon while Tommy laid out the bones of his idea. By the end of the day, I felt exhausted but optimistic. I was heading for the showers when Danny called me over.

"Get in here a sec, kid," he said, going back into his office. I closed the door and sat across from him, wondering what I could have done wrong. The chair was deliberately lower than his to make us feel intimidated. It worked, because I always felt like I was in the head master's office in here.

"What's up, Danny?" I asked.

"Look, kid, I ain't being nosy, but I overheard you lot talking about why you and that girl ain't together."

"Okay," I replied, not really sure where he was going with this.

"Have you really thought through what it is you're about to do? If you fall in love with her, that's it for you. You and Con are cut from the same cloth that way. For years it could be sunshine and roses. But one day, when you least expect it, she'll get sick. And it's gonna hit you like a punch in the nuts."

"You have such a way with words, Danny."

"Laugh it up, ya' little shite, but listen to what I'm sayin'."

I perched on the edge of my seat and leaned forward, looking him square in the eyes.

"What d'you want me to say? Do I know what I'm letting myself in for? Probably not. Am I ready for it? No, I'm not. But life don't wait till you're ready before giving you that sucker punch that'll land you on your arse. If I have a chance with her, fuck everything else. I'm taking it," I replied.

He sighed, rubbing his hand wearily down his face. The cantankerous old bugger was starting to look old. I probably had a thing or two to do with that.

"And what about when things get really tough?" he asked. "You're laid back and don't take life too serious, which ain't a bad thing, but when she's battling those demons, she's gonna need someone mature, someone who's in it with her for the long haul."

"Wow. I had no idea you thought so little of me, Danny," I replied, shocked.

"For fecks sake!" Danny exclaimed. "I love you like you're my own feckin' kid. And I ain't meaning to insult you. I'm trying to save you from a world of hurt 'cause you have no feckin' idea what it does to a man to lose the woman he knows he was supposed to spend the rest of his life with."

"What if you're wrong?" I asked.

"What d'you mean?"

"Marie's spent most of her life knowing that most of her friends and family will outlive her. What if my immaturity is the exact thing that makes her happy? If you numbered the days you had left, wouldn't you want to spend them with someone who lives every day like it's their last?"

"And you? What happens to you when she's gone?"

I sighed deeply and sat back in the chair, allowing myself a moment to reflect on what it would be like to live in a world without her. Where her laugh was just an echo on the wind, and she only smiled up at me from a torn and faded picture in my wallet. The clouds would always be that little bit greyer, and the sun would never shine as bright.

"I hear ya, Danny. I do. But the thing is, this girl had me by the balls from the very first time that I met her. I'm fallin' for her. And I'm not really sure I ever had a choice."

"Maybe you didn't, kid. Maybe you didn't," he replied. "Well, they say God has a plan for us all. I guess it's time for us to find out what yours is. I ain't saying I ain't worried about ya, but it's your life. Your decision. You wanna go after this girl, then go after her. What will be, will be."

It was as close to a blessing as I was ever gonna get, but from Danny it was priceless.

"Thanks, Danny. Now, any ideas on how I can get the girl?"

He took a moment to think hard before replying. "What the fuck do I know about wooing women?" he said with a wry chuckle. "You ain't never had a problem before, kid. Just be yourself and you'll do just fine."

* * *

Using my motorcycle without a helmet was reckless and illegal, but there was nothing better in the world for clearing your head than the freedom of riding with the wind in your hair. I knew what I was doing was impetuous, but after my talk with Danny, I needed to see my girl. Of course she didn't know she was my girl yet, but that was just semantics. Pulling up to the curb, I let the bike rest on its stand while I waited astride it. The ugly grey monstrosity at the top of the wide steps ahead of me screamed government building, and I had more than one strange look from passers-by as I sat there staring at it. Finally, a steady stream of people began to trickle out. The minute the light of the street lamp bounced off that red hair, my lips turned upwards in a gentle smile.

"What are you doing here? And how did you know where I'd be," she asked, stopping stock-still in surprise as her eyes met mine.

"Em told me, and I've come to give you a lift home," I replied.

She looked left and right as though this was some sort of trick. Her confusion was kind of cute.

"Um, why? I thought we'd said everything that needed to be said the other night."

"*We* didn't say anything. You said your piece then ran out on me before I even had a chance to process it all," I said, handing her the helmet that had been secured behind me. She stared down at it and bit her lip.

"Stop thinking so hard, Irish, and climb on."

Doing as I'd asked, she put on the helmet and climbed on behind me. As her body slid closer to mine, I took a deep breath, because for the first time that day, everything felt right. Her tiny hands sliding around my waist had me instantly tensing, my cock hardening painfully in my jeans.

"Shouldn't you have a helmet too?" she asked.

I loved that she worried about my safety.

"I'm good. Now hold on tight and I'll have you home before you know it."

Dark clouds drifted across the evening sky, and I doubted we'd make it back before the rain came. It pissed me off. Now that I had her with me, I wanted to open up the throttle and just fly. I'd keep going all night, just to feel her warmth at my back and her body pressed against mine. My breath caught when she rested her head against my back and squeezed a little tighter.

All too quickly, we pulled up outside her apartment. The drizzle was getting heavier, and we dashed towards the awning above the main door for cover. She'd taken off her helmet as she ran, and droplets of rain fell down her cheeks to land on the soft curls of her hair. Man, it hurt to be so close and not kiss her. Now that I'd had a taste, I wanted those soft lips pressed against mine, to hear that breathy moan a second before I teased my tongue against her plump bottom lip. I knew she felt it too. We were moving infinitesimally closer until the air trapped between us became so hot it practically steamed. The rain beat down hard, forming a curtain that hid us from the world. There was just me and her in perfect solitude.

"Kiss me," I whispered to her. I'd meant to will her to do it, but my mouth was blurting out my thoughts without filter.

"You're crazy," she whispered back.

"Admit it. You like my brand of crazy."

"It doesn't matter whether I like it or not. It doesn't matter whether I like you or not. You know why things won't work out between us."

"Thing is," I said, teasing a lock of hair away from her face and stroking the soft skin of her cheek with my thumb, "I figured something out today. I admit, I don't use my brain often, so when I do it takes a while to warm up."

"What did you figure out?" she asked breathlessly.

"You worrying about why we won't work don't matter. Life's just one long road that takes us where we're meant to be. I was meant to be yours. It's why life keeps throwing us together."

"And if my fate is to die?" she asked.

"Ah, love, but that's everyone's fate. It don't matter how long the road is. It's the moments that make the journey matter. You can run and hide all you like, but I ain't letting you walk this road alone."

Threading my fingers through her damp curls, I pulled her gently towards me until her trembling lips were pressed against mine. It was the purest, gentlest kiss I'd ever given a girl, and it blew all the others out of the water.

CHAPTER EIGHT

MARIE

Ever wonder how one kiss can change the world? That was pretty much all I'd thought about for the last week. I hadn't seen Kieran for seven whole days, and every minute of that had been absolute torture. I was sure he would be the one to break this battered heart. It didn't occur to me that he could be the one to fix it. Most people hated the rain, but one kiss had made me addicted to it.

And it hadn't rained.

Not once in seven days.

"Why the long face, little sis?" my brother, Luca, asked.

"No reason. Just feeling a little down in the dumps today. I guess I miss the rain," I replied.

"It's a beautiful sunny day and you miss the rain? God, you're weird," he said, making me smile.

"Well, I know that's true. Anyway, what are you doing here? I thought you were going out tonight?"

"I am, but I called Mum earlier and she said you looked blue, so I thought I'd stop by on the way home and check in," he said.

"Where are the twins?" I asked, knowing that wherever one was, the other two weren't far behind.

"Tweedle Stupid and Tweedle Stupider are with Mum," I giggled at his pet name for our younger twin brothers Tristan and Matteo. All three of them followed after Dad and became engineers. Much to Mum's dismay though, they all practised engineering as roughnecks on a North Sea oil rig. It was tough, dangerous work, but the boys craved the adventure. And when they didn't have it, they drove me nuts. They were boisterous, overprotective, and overbearing, but I adored them. Technically, they might have been younger, but I'd spent so many years in a hospital bed with them looking over me, that they'd long since out grown me.

"Doing what?"

"Mum's pissed that they've cleaned out the fridge again, she's on strike until they've filled it back up," he replied with a chuckle.

"They've gone food shopping?" I said in disbelief.

"With Mum," he added. "She didn't trust them to go alone. I called and spoke to her half an hour ago, and she was screaming at them for leaving her with the trolley to chat up the checkout girls."

"I don't know what she's thinking. It probably took her longer to get them in the car than it would have to do the entire food shop on her own."

"Well, her bridge club is coming over tonight, so she's kicking us all out. Fancy coming with us?"

"Em beat you to it. She's going into town for a girls' night, and I said I'd join her."

My brothers hadn't met Em, but they knew all about her from me. Between the hospital stints growing up, I never really made many friends from school who stuck, and since then I'd been working hard to make my own business a success, not leaving much time for anything else. Em was shy, and I'd never met anyone as innocent and kind as she was. From the first day we met, when I'd fitted her for her wedding dress, we became firm friends. It was a gift I'd needed so much more than she could ever realise.

"Glad to hear it. You could do with letting your hair down a bit," he said. Of all the boys, Luca always seemed to worry about me the most. As much as he drove me crazy sometimes, it was nice having him back for a bit.

"Look, why don't you get ready at Mum's, and we can share a cab," he suggested.

"It'll be late," I warned. "I have fittings until seven, so I'm not meeting Em until nine."

"No worries, the women will wait for me I'm sure," he said, making my roll my eyes. "You need a hand with anything before I go?"

"You're a diamond. Thanks, Luca. Could you carry this tray of prosecco to the bridal party in the fitting room? They're just oohing and aahing over the dress, so they'll all be decent," I said.

"More's the pity," he replied, taking the tray with a wink and walking into the back room. I could hear the moment that he arrived by the chorus of excited shrieks. I wasn't surprised by their reaction. Luca was one good-looking guy. But I couldn't help but giggle as I wondered whether they'd still fancy him as much if they'd heard him and the twins flatulating their way through a Brittney Spears song last Christmas.

* * *

It felt so good to be cutting loose on the dance floor. It was true that I was a horrible dancer, but with the club as packed as it was, it wasn't as though anyone could really see me in the crowd. Besides, the cocktail Em had ordered for me had loosened my inhibitions enough that I didn't really care. I could still drink with my medication, but in moderation, so two drinks were my limit.

"Having fun?" Nikki shouted over the music.

"Definitely," I shouted back, smiling widely at her.

"Looks like you've got an admirer," she said, nodding her head and looking behind me. I turned to follow her gaze to where a group of guys were dancing. I used the word dancing loosely because most of them were doing the two-feet shuffle that I favoured. The guy I'm guessing she was talking about caught my eye and smiled. He was the tallest of the group, and his fitted shirt stretched tightly across a muscled chest. His sandy blond hair was stylishly messy, and he had that cute boy-next-door vibe that would have piqued my interest a few months ago. That was before Kieran and *that kiss* of course. Now, it seemed, he had ruined me for all men. I appreciated the interest from this guy, but honestly, it just made me wish it were Kieran standing there throwing some charm my way.

"He's been looking over at you for ages. You should go talk to him," she shouted.

"I'm good, thanks." I carried on dancing, distracted by thoughts of a blond-haired, brown-eyed giant whose kisses were more addictive than crack.

Ten minutes later, I was contemplating getting some water when someone bumped into my back.

"I'm so sorry. Are you okay?" someone shouted from behind me. I turned around to see that it was the cute guy, holding his hands up in apology.

"No problem." I smiled to show him I wasn't mad.

"Can I buy you a drink to make up for it?"

"She's fine," Tristan said, thrusting a bottle of water into my hands.

"Sorry. I didn't realise you were here with your boyfriend," the guy said.

"This is my brother, Tristan," I replied. The guys smirked, as though he was back in the game. He had a better chance of scoring a date in a nunnery than he did with me when my brothers were around.

"Nice to meet you. I'm Mark," the guy said. He literally moved in front of Tris, giving him his back as he leaned in closer to talk to me, acting as though he couldn't hear over the music. Matt and Luca joined Tris in giving Mark the evil eye.

"Nice to meet you, Mark. Thanks for the offer of a drink, but my brothers have me sorted," I replied politely.

"Brothers?" he said, realising I'd referred to more than one. Following my gaze, he met the stares of my three pissed-off brothers.

"I'd better get back to my friends," he said hastily, not taking his eyes off them.

"How is it you always attract stupid people?" Tris asked me.

"How do you know he was stupid? He could have been a smart, successful guy for all you know," I replied.

"You meet a girl you like, you don't turn your back on her family. It's not rocket science to figure out the guy's a douche canoe."

I rolled my eyes, but said nothing. There seemed little point in explaining that I hadn't been interested regardless.

"What are you lot still doing here anyway? I thought you were meeting your mates in Blades five minutes ago," I said, referring to the sports bar up the road.

"Trying to get rid of us, little sis?" Tom asked, slinging his arm around my shoulder. "I thought we'd hang around for a bit and meet your friends. Seems a shame to waste an opportunity." He looked around to see who I was with.

"Hell no," I replied. "I love you guys, but there is no way you're hooking up with my friends. Besides, Em's married and most of the other girls are in relationships," I lied. Well, it was true Em was married, but most of the other girls we were with were single. Still, my brothers didn't like complicated, and I had no desire to spend my evening watching them stick their tongues down my friends' throats. A few of my friends had hooked up with my brothers in the past, and it never ended well.

"You are no fun, short stuff," Tris said, smiling.

"If we go, do you promise not to hook up with numb nuts?" Luca said, referring to the guy they'd scared away.

"I promise," I said, this time refraining from rolling my eyes.

"Trust me, boys, she's in good hands," Nikki said, linking her arm through mine. The boys looked amused at her attempts to steady herself as she leaned on me. She'd been knocking back the cocktails since we'd arrived, and it looked like they were kicking in.

"Okay, sis, have a great night and call us if you need us," Luca said.

"I will," I reassured him.

They knocked back their drinks and waved goodbye as I searched the dance floor for the rest of the girls. Spotting them at a table in the corner, I dragged Nikki over. Seeing us coming, Em scooted up on the bench, making room for us.

"Was that your brothers I saw you talking to?" Em said.

"How did you know?" I asked her.

"You told me they were giving you a lift, and the family resemblance is uncanny," she said. I wasn't sure whether to be insulted or not, but she laughed at the face I pulled.

"What's O'Connell up to tonight?" I asked her. Em never drank when she was on her own, but she seemed pretty happy and relaxed as she sipped on her glass of wine.

"He's giving Kieran a hand with something," she said. I didn't reply, but she looked like she was searching my expression for something.

"What?" I asked her, finally.

"There's not a tiny part of you wondering what Kieran's doing tonight?" she asked. I shrugged, not sure what to say to her.

"Doing the right thing is tough," I admitted. "I was doing okay until he kissed me."

"He's that good, huh?" she asked. My body melted against the seat and I sighed deeply, remembering just how good it was. She smiled at my reaction. Then, after taking a sip of her drink, smiled even wider as she looked past me at something.

Suddenly, the song ended and the lights dimmed further. At the front of the dance floor was a small stage, usually filled with girls dancing. Tonight it had been cleared and a small spotlight shone down in the centre of it.

"Hold tight for me, boys and girls. We have a little surprise for you. I want you to give a warm welcome to some very special friends of mine. Ladies, put one hand in the air and use the other to stop your knickers taking themselves off. Take it away, boys...," the DJ announced cryptically from his booth. I loved hearing live bands, so I was quite excited to see who they had playing. All of a sudden, girls started shrieking and flooding the dance floor, but from my seat, I couldn't see what they were looking at. Nikki, having no inhibitions at all, stood up on the bench to see what everyone was fussing over.

"Oh no, they didn't," she shouted, laughing. She looked down at Em knowingly, who shared her smile.

"Yeah you!" the crowd sang as a band played the first bars of The Vamps' "Somebody to You."

I still couldn't see, but a guy with a voice that could melt butter began to sing. A tingle ran up my spine, and I couldn't help feeling like I was witnessing something special; I just didn't know what. The crowd joined in every time with the lyrics "yeah you," throwing their arms up and pointing at the band. The atmosphere was electric.

All I wanna be, yeah all I ever wanna be, yeah, yeah

Is somebody to you

All I wanna be, yeah all I ever wanna

As the crowd on the dance floor began to part, Em spoke into my ear.

"Be brave," she said, clapping her hands to the rhythm of the music.

Out of the throng of people, Tommy danced his way over to us, shaking his arse like a professional. As soon as he reached for my hand, I knew this was Kieran's doing. Dying with embarrassment, but secretly elated, I followed him sheepishly as he walked me to the front of the stage.

Looking up, I felt like I'd been struck by lightning. Standing at the microphone like some rock god was Kieran. It was his amazing voice that belted out the lyrics to the song. He strummed a guitar as he sang like he owned the stage. As I stood at his feet, he looked down at me with the biggest smile, and I knew then he didn't just own the crowd, he owned me too. Tommy, Liam, Albie, Heath, and even Con were dancing beside him, buoying up the crowd and making all the girls crazy.

Kieran looked into my eyes as he sang, and it was like the crowd disappeared. This was so much more amazing than a text message or a phone call. He wanted us to be together, and now the whole world knew it. As the song built to a crescendo, Em and the girls joined me, and we jumped and clapped with everyone else. I couldn't ever remember having had so much fun.

My heart was bursting when they finished, and I waited for Kieran to put his guitar down. Con reached Em first, jumping off the stage and lifting her to wrap her legs around him as he kissed her like a man possessed. Tommy dove straight into a group of screaming girls, but it was Liam who surprised me the most. Wrapping his hand around Albie's neck and into his hair, he brought their lips together in a kiss so hot that everyone around them cheered. Kieran thanked the band then jumped off the stage in front of me.

"So, have I convinced you then?" he asked, looking a little nervous.

"Convinced me of what?"

"To be my girl."

Grabbing the front of his shirt, I pulled him close. "I was always your girl," I replied.

He rested his forehead against mine and breathed a sigh of relief. "I'm not letting you go this time. No matter how hard you try to push me away."

"Promise?" I whispered, not daring to believe that we were actually doing this.

"Promise." Shutting his eyes, he closed the gap between us and kissed me gently. I sighed in satisfaction, and he swallowed the noise as his mouth moved more urgently against mine. Raising my arms around his neck, he wrapped an arm around my waist and lifted me off the floor so that he didn't have to bend down. Both of us were breathless when he parted his lips to touch his tongue against mine.

"About time, fuckers," Tommy cheered, as people whooped and hollered at us. We broke apart and discovered our friends all stood watching us and clapping. Kieran wrapped his arms around me from behind and buried his face in my neck.

"So, you can get up and sing in front of hundreds of strangers, but you're embarrassed when the boys see us kiss," I said to him jovially.

"I'm not embarrassed about the kiss, love. I just didn't think you'd want the girls seeing me hard-on," he replied, and I burst out laughing.

* * *

The rest of the night passed in a wonderful blur. We kissed, we danced, and we kissed some more. Kieran had to stay stone-cold sober as he was in training, but both of us were drunk with happiness. I was starting to get tired, but I so desperately didn't want the evening to end.

"One more bottle of water for the road?" he asked me. I nodded my yes then kissed him briefly, just because I could.

"I'm so excited for you guys!" Em said, practically vibrating with happiness.

"I can't believe you kept all this a secret!" I said. "And I can't believe Kieran actually got Con up dancing."

"Yeah, I don't think that'll be happening again anytime soon, but Kier wanted to do something big for you so you'd take him seriously," she replied.

"He's absolutely crazy, but it was so perfect." I sighed, still feeling like I was floating on air.

We laughed and chatted some more until a warm hand snaked its way around my waist. The overpowering smell of alcohol registered at the same time that I felt a hand squeezing my arse. Jerking away, I found Mark, who was now completely plastered. Then my attention jumped to a furious Kieran standing in front of me as he handed me a bottle of ice cold water.

"Another brother?" Mark asked, slurring his words drunkenly. Paying no attention to the fact that I'd already pushed him off once, he put his hand right back where it was and pressed his erection into my hip.

Moving so quickly I nearly missed it, Kieran smacked him square in the face, knocking him on his arse.

"Boyfriend actually, arsehole," he replied. "Touch my girlfriend again, or any girl without her consent for that matter, and next time you won't be walking away. Now fuck off."

Mark scrambled, muttering, "Fucking lesbian," under his breath, and I had to restrain Kieran from going after him again.

"You okay, love?" he asked.

"My hero," I whispered to him as he tucked my hair behind my ear and brushed his thumb gently across my cheek.

"Always."

CHAPTER NINE

KIERAN

"Ninety-eight, ninety-nine, one hundred. Now switch," Con said, calling out one-arm press ups. I changed arms without hesitation and continued in time with his count. When I'd done the same number on both sides, I climbed up the bars to start the hanging sit ups, even before he asked. I knew the routine; we both did. I'd been calling out these instructions to him for years.

"How we doin?' Danny asked.

"He's getting faster, and not a single fucking complaint all day," Con told him.

"That girl must be good for him," Danny said. Arms crossed, and a cigarette hanging out his mouth, he analysed my form.

"His tone is looking good, but I want to up the cardio," he said to Con. "Have him run midday and then before he finishes for the day." He studied me some more before shuffling his way to check on the other fighters, which was as close as Danny would ever get to telling me he was impressed.

"Still no complaints, fucker?" Con said, chuckling.

"Mate, I feel like I'm on top of the fucking world at the minute. Truth be told, we could do with stepping up the training, 'cause I know I've still got something left in the tank at the end of every day," I told him.

"That'll be the sex ban," he said. "Let's see how much energy you've got when you spend four hours a night fucking."

"Jesus, no wonder Em always looks tired," I said, earning a scowl from Con. "Oh, so you can give it but'cha can't take it."

"I don't like you thinking about Em like that, let alone talking about it," he admitted.

"Well, cool your jets, fucknut. I've got my own angel now."

"Makes you feel invincible, don't it?" he said, smiling.

"I am fucking invincible," I replied, making him roll his eyes.

He was right though. This feeling was indescribable. I wanted the fight to be tomorrow, because right now I felt like I could take on the world. The last four weeks had been amazing. For six days a week, I trained from dawn till long after dusk. It was probably just as well that it was Irish's busy season at the shop, because the times we saw each other were getting harder and harder. We couldn't keep our hands off each other. She was a fire in my blood, and the burn consumed me. When we did get together, we tried to see each other in public places. It worked at first, but last week we'd nearly been kicked out of the cinema. It started as an innocent kiss in the back row, and by the end of the movie, I was nearly on top of her.

The upside was that my testosterone and adrenaline levels were through the roof. I was fighting better than I ever had before. But when this was all over, and we were finally together, I was gonna have to jack off like fifteen times to makes sure I didn't split her in half. Funny thing was, after years of being a manwhore, I couldn't even get a twitch from looking at other girls. Irish was my drug of choice, and I was addicted. I was gutted that I wouldn't be seeing her tonight, but I called her every night when she went to bed. We'd talk for hours. She had the most beautiful voice and was kind of quiet, but when we were alone, she would tell me everything—stories about her family, plans for the future, all her hopes and dreams. I lived for those calls, and for the day that she'd be in my bed every night, having these conversations in person.

By four, when I was getting ready to do my last round of circuits, it occurred to me that I hadn't seen Liam for a couple of days. He came to the gym for at least an hour or two after work every night, so it must have been something serious for him to miss it.

"Hey, Con, you spoken to Liam at all?" I asked.

"Nah. I called him a couple of times, but he hasn't called back. I was thinking about paying him a visit after we've finished later actually. Albie's complaining to Em that he's becoming more and more distant. Cancelling dates and shit and not rearranging. Albie thinks Liam's getting ready to break things off with him."

"No way," I argued. "Shit, he looks at Albie like he hung the moon. There's no way he's calling that off. My money's on his piece of shit da making trouble somehow."

Just at that moment, the man himself walked into the gym. Hood pulled over his head and shoulders hunched, the guy looked defeated.

"Well, speak his name and he shall appear. How's things going, big guy?" I asked.

"What's up, Kier?" Liam said, acknowledging me with a nod, while avoiding showing me his face.

Con followed Liam into the locker room, and I wasn't far behind. From the look on Con's face, I knew this was serious.

"What's going on, mate?" I heard Con ask. Liam pushed his hood back, and his face was just fucked up. Bruised and battered, even cut in places, it looked like someone had given him a right going over.

"It's my own fault. I had it coming," Liam said.

"Son, you wanna explain to me how any of this is your feckin' fault? 'Cause this is a story I really need to hear," Danny said, having followed us all.

Liam sat down dejectedly on the bench and hung his head.

"I kissed Albie on the stage in front of a club full of people I forgot about everything and just kissed him. Up until that point, I'd kept us pretty private," he said.

"That was weeks ago," I pointed out.

"It took a while for the news to filter through, but someone filmed Kier's performance and caught the kiss at the end. The film made the rounds, and someone showed my da a couple of days ago," he said.

"He did this to you?" Con asked, his fists clenching and unclenching, a tell-tale sign that he was close to losing his shit.

"He and my brothers took turns. Said they were gonna beat the gay out of me," he admitted.

"How many of 'em did you put in the hospital?" I asked, knowing full well just how powerfully he could hit. He clasped his hands together and looked down.

"You didn't raise your hand to one of them, did you, son?" Danny asked. Liam shook his head slowly.

"Why the fuck not?" I asked him.

"Albie," Con said, knowing it was the only reason he wouldn't defend himself.

"They know who he is and where he lives. They gave me a choice. Either give him up, cut all ties, and take a beating, or they'll find him and kill him. They don't give a shit about me. They've kicked my arse out. But they don't want a 'gay boy' associated with the family," he said bitterly.

"What did Albie say to all this?" Danny asked.

Liam looked up at him and his expression was one of pure agony. "I can't do it, Danny. I haven't told him, because there's no way he'd stay away from me. I know I need to hurt him bad to make him leave for good. I just haven't got the fuckin' stones to do it. I can't be with him and keep him safe, but I can't let him go either." He ran his hands over his head and just looked fucking broken.

Knowing exactly what to do, I left Con and Danny to talk things over with Liam while I made a couple of calls. Ten minutes later, I came back to learn that Liam had been sofa surfing with a guy from his construction site.

"Why didn't you come to us first? Any of us would've had your back," Con said.

"I wanted Albie to have you guys. I knew he'd need you, and if I can't be there for him, then I needed to know you would be. He wouldn't have been able to come to you if I'd been there," he replied.

"That is the single stupidest thing I think I've ever heard you say. As if there's anywhere else I'd ever go but straight to you," Albie said. He stood in the doorway, his hands buried deep in his pockets.

"That was fast," I said.

"I was already on the way when you called," he replied. "I wanted to talk to you about this dumb-arse."

Liam was staring at him longingly.

"Why didn't you tell me?" Albie asked Liam gently.

Liam swallowed hard before answering. "I needed to protect you. Alb, I can take a beating all day, every day. It's what I grew up with it. But if you got hurt because of me, it would kill me." Liam's voice cracked at the end.

"If you let the fear of something that might never happen destroy something great, then they've already won. You can't control people filled with hate, Liam. Who knows why they are the way they are. All you can do is find your own happiness and leave them to their own misery," Albie told him.

"And if you get hurt?" Liam asked him. "I know my family, and this ain't no hollow threat."

"Brother, they ain't your family. We are. Blood doesn't make a family. Love and loyalty does. And nobody fucks with our family.

Right?" Con said.

"Right," Albie replied.

"Right," added Tommy and Heath. They moved passed Albie into the locker room, and I'd guessed they'd heard what was going down.

"Right," I added, and we all looked towards Liam, who hadn't taken his eyes off Albie.

Eventually, he stood up, and I swore to God the tank was near to tears. "Right," he said, making us all smile. Con was right, we were a family, and the fuckers who were lucky enough to share blood with Liam were about to lose some of it. There ain't no fighter more lethal than the one protecting his family.

"Right then, boys. This shite ends now. We ain't the animals they are, so we're going to give these feckers a chance to walk away, but they keep threatening my boys, they're gonna wish we brought Father Pat for the last rites," Danny said. "Tommy!" he called out. "Bring that truck of yours round. I'm too old to put my wrinkly arse on the back of a bike. Con, Heath, Kieran, you follow us."

"You're not going without me," Albie said. "There's no way I'm not standing up for you after what they've done."

"Albie," Liam said, his voice cracking again.

"Do you want Liam there for the shitstorm that's coming?" Danny asked him.

"Of course not," Albie replied, red faced.

"Then how d'you think he'd feel knowing you were that close to the people who threatened you without being able to do anything about it?" Danny asked, reasonably. Liam stood up and looked straight at Albie.

"They'll make you fuckin' hate me. They'll tell you all sorts of shit about me. And you won't want to believe it, but then you'll see the arsehole stock I come from and you'll know I'm not worth the trouble. Besides, there's no fuckin' way I'm letting you get anywhere near them. If a single one of them laid a finger on you, I'd kill them all," Liam said.

"Your job is to take care of Liam. Let us take care of the rest," Danny assured Albie. He looked frustrated, but nodded briefly, acknowledging that he would stay.

"When we get back, I'll move your stuff over to me Ma's. Since I got my own place she's got room to spare, and you know she'd love the company," I said. She'd known Liam practically all his life. When we were kids, he ate at our house more than he ate at his own.

"Thanks for the offer, Kieran, but he's staying with me," Albie said, not taking his eyes of Liam.

"It's cool, Albie," Liam said. "You have a box room in a house share and a single bed. Even if it was cool with your housemates, there's no way both of us could stay in that room."

"Then we'll find a new place together. I would have asked you to move in with me months ago if I didn't think you'd turn me down," Albie replied. For the first time in weeks, I saw Liam break a smile, and it was beautiful.

"You sure?" he asked Albie.

"Positive," he replied with an answering smile.

"Is it cool with you if I take up your offer for a couple of weeks, until we can find a place? You know, if it's okay with your ma," Liam said.

"I've already asked her, mate. She's probably making your bed and cooking your dinner as we speak. I told her to expect Albie for dinner too," I replied.

"Cheers, Kier," he said, still grinning.

"Right, ladies, now the dinner arrangements are sorted, let's get a feckin' move on. The Antiques Roadshow is on tonight, and I don't plan on missing it," Danny said, breaking the tension. We waited until Liam and Albie were both on their way to Ma's before putting on wraps. It was far from our first street fight, but splitting your knuckles got old fuckin' fast. Danny had me running back and forth to training every day, so we took Con's car. As we pulled up outside, I was pleased to see the driveway of the Murphy household full of cars. Liam told us they went to the Holy Cross Sports and Social Club after dinner every night, so it looked like we'd caught them just in time.

Danny led the way, and though I instinctively wanted to protect him, there was no telling him what to do. Walking purposefully up to the house, he knocked sharply, then crossed his arms while he waited for a reply. The door opened, and there stood Stuart Murphy. Though shorter, it was clear that he'd once been built like his son, but where Liam was pure muscle, Stuart had a significant middle-aged spread, another side effect of a lifelong drink habit.

"I see the spineless little poofter sent the old fart and his little arse kissers to fight his battles for him. Should've known the useless little queer wouldn't resist running his mouth off."

"Murphy," Danny replied. "I see ya manners haven't improved any since the last time I saw ya."

"Cut the shite, Danny. I said everything I needed to say last time was spoke. So tell me what the fuck you want and get the fuck off my doorstep," Stuart said.

"Very well. If ya going to be like that about it. I want you to leave Liam and Albie be. You've cut Liam off from the family for good, and while I think you're making a mistake, he's better off without ya. But I don't like this threat you've left hanging over them. I don't like it one little bit. So this ends now. They'll live their life, and you'll live yours and let that be an end to it."

"Who the fuck d'you think you are to be telling me what to do with my boy? I don't want any feckin' queers in this family. It's ungodly and it ain't feckin' natural. I should've hit him harder when he was a kid and beaten the soft outta him," Stuart replied.

"Since when do you give a fuck about God, you selfish bastard?" Danny barked.

"Problem, Da?" came a voice behind Stuart. His three other sons shared their father's beer belly and looked just as smug and in need of a fuckin' pasting as he did.

"Nothin' I can't handle, boys. Driscoll here was just leaving and so were the pissants with him," Stuart said. "Now you tell Liam he can do whatever the fuck he wants for all I care. But he so much as looks at a boy again, and me and the family will make 'em both wish they'd never been born." With that, he spat at Danny's feet.

I didn't see it coming, and I didn't think anyone else did either. With speed and skill that belied his age, Danny drew back his fist and gave Stuart a right hook to the jaw. I learned more in that moment about his former skill as a boxer than he'd ever let on to us. The punch wasn't powerful enough to knock out a man like Stuart Murphy, but it sure was enough to put him on his arse. Stepping forward to stand over him, Danny looked down at the piece of shit.

"Don't you ever threaten one of my boys again, Murphy. I've let too much slide over the years because your boy begged me to. Why he showed you any loyalty, I don't know, 'cause you certainly never showed him any, but this ends now. After today, the boy is free to be whoever he wants and see whoever he wants. He's gay. Live with it. Or don't, I don't really give a fuck. But you stay away from him and his. 'Course, if you ain't happy with that arrangement, then perhaps I need to speak to one of them 'cold case' coppers. Ya' see, boyo, I know what went down all them years ago," Danny said, leaning in closer to deliver the last part of his message.

"No one's gonna believe some crazy old fecker's word after all these years," Stuart said smugly.

"Well, that depend, don't it?" Danny replied.

"On what?" Stuart asked mockingly.

"On whether I've still got the feckin' gun," Danny said quietly.

"That ain't possible," Stuart whispered, turning completely white.

"Well, why don't ya test me and find out?" Danny replied. "As long as you leave 'em alone, I'll let things stay buried. You decide you want to continue this conversation, you know how it'll end."

"Fuck this. I don't know what you're talking about, Driscoll, but no one threatens my old man. I'm going to fucking nail you for this," one of Stuart's kids said. I forgot his name. They all looked the same to me. Con took a step forward and cracked the knuckles on each hand before rolling his shoulders, looking like the meanest fucker Hell ever spat out.

"Enough!" Stuart said, halting his son in his tracks. "You keep your end of the bargain, Driscoll, and I'll keep mine."

"Done," Danny replied. "And don't get up, Murphy. We'll see ourselves out." With that, he adjusted his flat cap, turned on his heels, and headed back to the truck. The boys and I looked at each other in shock, but followed behind him.

"What the fuck was that all about, Danny?" I asked, desperate to know what the hell kind of secrets he'd been keeping.

"Mind your own business, boys. What's done is done. Liam needs to get back on his feet again, and you have a fight to focus on. Now get me home, lads. Antiques Roadshow starts in fifteen minutes," he replied.

CHAPTER TEN

MARIE

Like every night for the last month, I'd gone to bed with a smile on my face. Although we didn't see each other nearly as much as we'd like, it only heightened the anticipation. Kieran was in my every thought. When I ate breakfast, I wondered what he ate. When I slipped on a lacy camisole, I imagined that it was Kieran's hands ghosting over my skin. The electricity forming between us was a beautiful seduction, and the most delicious of procrastinations. Even in the dark of night, when his voice on the phone hinted at the pleasure he would one day introduce me to, I couldn't bring myself to ease my own agony. Kieran had kindled a fire inside this body, and only he could put it out.

Restless and needy, I drifted into a fitful sleep, only to be woken by a tapping against the window. Although startled and a tiny bit freaked out, I rationalised that murderers and rapists were unlikely to scale two floors of my building to get to me. Besides, I was pretty sure they didn't knock. When I finally plucked up a bit of courage, I peeped out of the curtains to see Kieran throwing stones at the window.

"Rapunzel, Rapunzel, let down your hair," he mock shouted, when he caught my eye. I opened the window to whisper loudly back at him.

"Are you high?" I asked. "Why didn't you just ring the doorbell or call me?"

"I thought this would be more romantic," he said.

"If I ignore the fact that my nipples probably have frostbite, I am feeling romanced," I replied. He looked pained. "What's wrong?" I asked.

"You said 'nipples' and now I can't think of anything else," he replied, making me smile.

"Now I'm down here, what's the chances of seeing an accidental nip slip?" he asked.

"Depends," I replied.

"On what?" he asked.

"What's in the bag?" I said.

"Hot chocolate and warm doughnuts," he said, holding up the bag as if to barter.

"Well, I would have said slim to none, but fresh doughnuts might have just tipped the odds in your favour," I replied.

"Yesss!" he said, fist bumping the air in victory.

I closed the window and ran to buzz him in. He bounded up the stairwell, his heavy footsteps echoing loudly in the hallway. When he got to my door, he looked me up and down, taking in my short royal blue, silk pyjamas. Dropping the sack, he speared his hands into my hair and pulled me into a kiss that had me melting. Kier didn't kiss with just his lips; he did it with his whole body. Without shoes on, I was tiny in comparison, but inside of the cage of his huge arms, I felt protected and safe. Despite his size, his lips were so gentle. He didn't treat me like I was fragile, but like I was precious, as though every touch was one that he was experiencing for the first time and memorizing for later.

Feeling bold, I traced the seam of his mouth with my tongue, and when he parted his lips and touched his tongue against mine, I groaned. Every sensation was too much, and not enough. Breathless, he pulled away from me to nuzzle his face in the crook of my neck. I reached up and gently stroked the short hair at the back of his neck, making him sigh.

"Apples," he whispered to me, but as it seemed like he was talking to himself, I didn't reply.

"You okay?" I asked.

"I am now, love. Shit day is all. Sorry I woke you, but I couldn't wait until tomorrow to see you."

"Best surprise, ever." I grinned, but the chill from the hallway was beginning to seep into my bones.

"Come on, let's get you back to bed and warm. I'm gonna fill you up with my sweet treats and keep my eye out for that nip slip I've been hoping for," he said. With an effortless show of strength, he leaned down to place his shoulder at my stomach and rose to carry me, picking up the sack along the way. Kicking the door shut, he threw down the locks and walked into my bedroom.

"How did you know this was my room?" I asked him, as he set me down on the bed. His cheeks blushed red, and I was intrigued.

"I dropped Em over here once straight from the gym and asked her which one was your bedroom. She laughed her arse off, but she told me. You gonna make fun of me now?"

Sitting up on my knees, I cupped his face and kissed him in reply. Having him here in my bedroom felt just perfect. He smiled and nuzzled his nose playfully against mine before unloading his goodies. I climbed under the duvet and shimmied across the bed to make room for him. Sitting in my bed, we opened our hot chocolates and sipped as we nibbled on the delicious sugary treats. I told him all about the beautiful lace dress I was making for the loveliest girl.

"I try to make every dress special and unique," I told him. "Especially with my collection, because a little bit of me is in all of them. But I swear, the nicer the client, the more love I put into it. I don't mean to do it, but I think about the clients as I'm sewing, and I can't help going the extra mile for the people who you know are just special."

"What was it about this girl that you liked so much?"

"She and her partner just found out that they're having a baby. They were already engaged, but hadn't planned on having children this early. They wanted to get married before the baby comes, but that's not what I liked about her. It's the way she was when she saw my designs. I mean, she looked beautiful in all the dresses, but when I brought out my collection, she looked at me like I was some kind of magician. I guess I just want to give her a little bit more of that magic."

He smiled at me and kind of stared. "You're something else,

you know that, Irish?"

I smiled and shrugged. "I'm sorry for rambling on at you about my day."

"Baby, I could listen to you talk all night," he replied, and I wanted to kiss him all over again.

"Why was your day so bad?" I asked, thinking of how terrible I was for telling him all about my great day before asking about his awful one. He told me about Albie and Liam, and I felt a great swell of rage towards arseholes who always wanted to tear down and destroy anything beautiful they didn't understand.

"Are you okay?" I asked him, quickly checking him over for signs that he'd been fighting.

"Irish, I didn't even get to raise my fist. Con cracked his knuckles and got to swan about all manly, and I'm pretty sure Tommy didn't even get his face in the doorway. All I did was stand there and look pretty. Danny's the hero of the day. I don't know what he has over Liam's dad, but I sure as shit would like to find out."

"Will he tell you?"

"Hell no, darlin'. I love him like me own family, but that man is tighter than a duck's arse when it comes to secrets and money."

"Poor Albie and Liam," I said, handing Kieran my empty cup to throw in the bin and scooting down to cuddle into his shoulder.

"They'll either find a way or make one, but a love that's meant to be will last forever. No ignorant fuckers are gonna destroy the beautiful thing they've found together," he told me. I could tell from the reverent tone of his voice how in awe of these boys Kieran was and how deeply he wanted them to find their happily ever after, and I knew then that I was falling for him hard.

"Where are they now?" I asked.

"He's staying over at Albie's tonight, and to be honest, I think Albie needs it. Tomorrow I'll get him settled into Ma's place. She'll be fussing over him so much, he won't be able to wait to move out."

We chatted some more about our plans and how things were going, but eventually I couldn't hide my yawns anymore. I didn't want the night to end, but I wouldn't be able to stay awake much longer.

"Will you stay?" I asked, half asleep already.

"I can set the alarm on my phone and run to the gym in the morning, if that's okay with you?"

"I'd love that," I replied, then waited for him to shrug off his trainers, socks, T-shirt, and hoodie.

"You're not taking off your sweat pants?" I asked in confusion, having expected him to sleep in his boxers.

"I need the protection in case any randy little dressmaking nymphs get carried away in the night and start dry humping me in their dreams," he said, mischievously.

"Well," I said, as he lifted the duvet and pulled me into his chest, "it's always a possibility."

"Here's hoping. But fair warning, any accidental pyjama malfunctions in the night, and I'm totally eying up your boobs."

It was with one of his hands over my heart and the other just below my breast, that I fell headlong into the deepest, most restful night's sleep I'd had in a long time.

* * *

I woke in the morning, and I knew without opening my eyes that he was gone. Everything about him just exuded life, and I hungered to be a part of that. Without him, the room just seemed a little colder and emptier. That I was the solace he'd looked for after a bad day filled me with joy. I'd gotten so used to the idea that he would be the bright spark that lit up my dark places, that it never occurred to me that I might be his, that he might need me as much as I was coming to need him. Not willing to drag my lazy arse out of bed yet, I curled deeper into the duvet that smelled so deliciously like him. The ring of the alarm was interfering with a perfectly good daydream, but when I realised the noise was coming from the phone, I grabbed at it. None of my family called this early in the morning, so I worried it was an emergency.

"Hello?" I said down the phone, bracing myself for bad news.

"Tell me you were touching yourself in bed and thinking of me when I called," Kieran replied.

"You sound like some heavy-breathing pervert," I said, giggling.

"Irish, that's exactly what I am."

"Serious, what's with the heavy breathing?"

"I'm running, but I've got hands free."

"Doesn't it mess up your rhythm to talk while you run?" I couldn't imagine being able to run to the corner shop and back, let alone hold a conversation while I was doing it.

"Hell yes, but it's worth it to speak to you. Between my training and your work, I'm getting some serious withdrawals. Last night just made things worse. Now I want you in my bed every night," he admitted. I couldn't help my little groan as I imagined that too. "Seriously, baby, you can't be making noises like that when I'm not there. Running and talking is one thing, but even I don't think I can run with a hard-on."

I laughed as I imagined it, and just like that, Kieran had filled up the gloom with his light.

"Why are you running again?" I asked him. "Didn't you run to the gym this morning?"

"Usually I don't have to run again until lunch or the evening, but Danny's pissed."

"Why?" I'd met Danny a few times since I'd known Em, but I didn't know him well. Still, I couldn't see what Kieran could have done to wind him up already. He'd only been at the gym a couple of hours.

"Tommy shouted across the gym to ask me where I spent last night, because he called me at Ma's and I wasn't there. When I told him I spent it with you, Danny lost his shit. He thinks I broke the sex ban, and despite pleading my innocence, I don't think he's really buying it. He told me to 'feck off outta his sight for five miles.'"

"Poor baby. Do you think it would help if I wrote you a note confirming that my virtue's intact?" I asked him, giggling.

"Even if he didn't tell me to feck off, it wouldn't be entirely true. I mean, we might not have technically broken the ban, but I think about fingering you at least once every half hour," he admitted.

"Kieran," I whined, rubbing my thighs together, trying to ease the ache building between them.

"'Course, then I start think about touching my tongue between your legs, and how sweet you'll taste. And that gets me thinking what it'll feel like when I'm finally inside you, below with you above me, and behind with you bent over in front of me. Whether I'll have my hands on your tits, or whether they'll be in my mouth," he said. It might have been my imagination, but his breathing seemed to get much harder.

"You're going to give yourself that hard-on," I warned.

"Yeah, it's a bit late for that, Irish. Not one of my best ideas, calling you in the middle of training."

"Serves you right for getting me all hot and horny when you aren't here to do anything about it," I replied, laughing.

"Man, that is a fucking beautiful sound. I'll see you tonight, love, and I don't worry, I don't mind in the slightest if you touch yourself after I hang up as long as you're thinking about me," he said.

"Good luck training for the rest of the day with that visual in mind," I replied, making him groan as he realised what he'd done.

"It's gonna be a long day," he said on a sigh.

"Only twelve more hours, Kier, and just for you, I'll wear my favourite blue panties today to match the colour of your balls," I replied. The line went quiet for a second, and it sounded like he'd stopped.

"Irish, I think I've finally met my match," he said, breathlessly.

* * *

The morning flew by in a flurry of activity. As it was a Saturday, I had back-to-back appointments and fittings all morning. Lucas had popped in briefly to give me a hand shifting some boxes, and I managed to snag a packet of salt and vinegar crisps from the bag containing the enormous lunch he'd bought for himself. Perched on a stool, I was snacking on the proceeds of my pilfery and sketching out a new design that had been dancing in my head all morning. I was so engrossed in what I was doing, I didn't even register the opening door, or the man who walked through it, until my favourite chicken tikka baguette was placed on the counter next to me. I looked up to see Alastair leaning towards me on the counter, smiling.

"Now tell me I didn't make your day," he said.

"Ugh, that's really kind of you. I wasn't planning on stopping for dinner though. I've got another client in fifteen minutes," I lied. It was seriously beginning to creep me out the amount of times he just 'popped up' into my life.

"What are you doing here?" I asked.

"I was seeing a client in the area, and I had a feeling that you'd end up working too hard to eat. So I thought I'd take care of you," he replied, and I kind of felt bad.

"It's probably a good thing you stopped by," I said, hesitantly. "I think we need to talk about something."

"Talk and eat," he said, pushing my baguette closer to me. He removed his coat and jacket, placing them carefully over the wooden counter, before pulling up a stool, far too close to mine. Easing my legs as close to the counter as they'd go, I opened my lunch and started taking small nibbles. Not knowing how to break this gently, I figured that coming straight out with it was probably best.

"The thing is, Alastair, although we are friends, I'm not sure that us seeing each other like this can happen anymore. You see, I'm sort of seeing someone, and it feels wrong to be friendly with another man while I'm in a relationship." I braced myself for his reaction.

He slowly lowered his sandwich, his face as black as thunder. "You told me that you weren't in the right place for a relationship, so I waited. I've waited for all this time for you to be in the right place. And now you're telling me you're seeing someone else," he said, eerily calm but with an edge that had me twisting in my seat.

"I didn't lie to you. I wasn't in a place where I wanted a relationship, and I told Kieran the same thing, but he just swept me off my feet." In truth, I'd never felt about Alastair the way I felt about Kieran. Alastair had seemed so easy-going when I'd first suggested that we just be friends. I had no idea he felt so strongly. I felt terrible, but it was best that he knew where he stood with me.

"I see," he said, finally. "Well, if you'll excuse me, I have to get back to work. But I'm sure we'll see each other again soon." With that, he put on his suit jacket and coat, and after leaning in to kiss me gently on the cheek, headed out the door.

CHAPTER ELEVEN

KIERAN

I fucking hated running. I'm sure that's why Danny made me do so much of it. I wondered, if I spent more time moaning about how much I hated weight training, would he have me doing that instead. Knowing my luck, he'd probably just double up on both. Despite my bitching, I couldn't argue that he was getting results. I always thought I was fit, but his regime had taken my fitness to another level. It was totally old school of course. There were no machines to record how hard I could punch or how much I had increased my lung capacity. If we all had a talent, Danny's was the ability to look inside a fighter and know exactly what it would take to make him the best he ever could be. Apparently for me, that meant endless miles pounding the pavement.

At least these days, I had something to occupy my thoughts. With every step I took, Irish was in my head with me. Whether I saw her or not, the world was suddenly a better place. It was like I'd been handed this amazing gift, and every day, as I got to know her a little better, I'd get to unwrap another layer of it. I ran mile after mile wearing the dopiest smile, but I just didn't care.

"Shit, I'd never have guessed this was your third run of the day. I've been trying to catch you up for the last mile," Liam said, falling in step next to me.

"Why aren't you driving?" I asked, pulling out my ear buds and stuffing them in my pocket.

"I'm trying to keep a low profile," he admitted. "Danny is convinced that Da won't break whatever truce they've got going, but I wouldn't put it past one of my arsehole brothers not to key my truck if they saw it." Liam loved that fucking truck. It was the first thing he bought himself when he started making good money in construction, and it was a beast. It certainly fit the tank of a man driving it.

"I give it until it rains for the first time before you jack it in and decide to risk it," I told him.

"I don't even think I'll make it that long. I can train in the gym all day long, but I'm just not built for this."

"Stop ya bitchin'," I said jovially. "You've got a man to keep in shape for now. Speaking of which, how's the house hunting going?"

"Trying to get rid of me already?"

"Not at all, mate. You stay as long as you like. As long as you're there, Ma's more interested in your love life than mine."

"You told her about Irish yet?"

"She knew the minute I walked in the door with a smile. If there's a hint of romance in the air, she'll sniff it out like a bloodhound. She's already got me and Irish married off with kids, and she hasn't met her yet."

"Doesn't bother you, does it?"

"Hell no," I replied. "I just don't want Ma scaring her away. She's coming around for dinner tonight before we go out. It's the first time I've ever brought a girl home before, so I have a feeling Ma's gonna have a total freak-out and start talking grandkids or some shit. At least, if you're there, I can deflect."

"Ah, sorry, bro. I already told your Ma that we're going to see a house tonight, so we're grabbing food afterwards. It's just the three of you I'm afraid," he said, grinning remorselessly.

"Laugh it up, lard arse. One day soon you're gonna be meeting Albie's parents." I smiled as his face dropped.

* * *

"What if she doesn't like lasagne?" Ma said, patting her hair nervously to make sure no strands had come loose.

"Her ma is Maltese," I told her. "I'm sure she'll love it."

"What's that got to do with anything? Lasagne is Italian."

"They're both in the Mediterranean, aren't they? Besides, everyone loves your pasta."

Ma's food really was amazing, but she cooked like she was feeding a small army. Even after Da died, she never really got the hang of cooking for two. Luckily, I had more than one mate who never let anything go to waste.

"I hope she's here soon. Dinner is just about ready. Why aren't you picking her up from work?" she asked.

"She was going to the hairdresser's after her last appointment. I offered to collect her when she was done, but she told me she'd just meet me here, and I've learned not to argue with my girl. I think she's worried about me not having enough downtime to rest after training. Why are you looking at me like that?" I asked her, seeing the look on her face.

"Awww, you said 'my girl.' That's so sweet! Do you know how long I've waited for you to bring a nice girl home, Kieran Doherty?" she said, squeezing my cheeks together like I was a cute baby.

"Maaaa," I protested, squirming away just as the doorbell rang. Leaving her in the kitchen, I raced through the house to the front door. Irish stood on my doorstep, waving goodbye to the taxi behind her. She'd barely turned to face me when I bent slightly to pick her up and claimed her mouth mercilessly. Having no choice, she wrapped her legs around my waist and moaned as she speared her hands into my hair. I was completely lost, my body craving to claim her in every way possible. Her tongue brushed tentatively against mine, and I captured it before she could move away. Everything about that kiss was wild and primate. Her taste was so fucking addictive, I knew I'd never have enough. She pulled back just long enough for me to remember where we were.

"What if your Mum see us?" she whispered.

"If she didn't, I'm pretty sure the neighbours will fill her in tomorrow."

"Great," she groaned, burying her face in my neck with embarrassment. "Some great first impression I'll make."

"Irish, I'm pretty sure you could tell her you were a convicted criminal and she'd still love you." Reluctantly, I set her down but kept a gentle hold on her waist when she seemed unsteady on her feet.

"Why?" she asked, seeming confused.

I stared at her for a beat before replying, "What's not to love?" A blush spread from her neck to her cheeks as she smiled shyly. I wanted to tell her that it was because I loved her, but it was too soon. Six months ago, I would have called myself a pussy. But six months ago I didn't have Irish. Now I knew what I wanted, and I wasn't letting her go. She was it for me, and I thought Ma knew that too.

"For goodness sake, boyo, put the girl down and let me get a look at her," Ma said, as she barrelled down the hallway, probably fed up of waiting for me to bring her in. I rolled my eyes but moved from blocking Ma's view and stood beside Irish. Unable to keep my hands off her, I snaked an arm around her waist and pulled until she tucked herself gently into my side. Ma stopped in front of her and raised her hands to her cheeks.

"Oh, you two are going to make me beautiful grandbabies!" Ma exclaimed.

"Ma! I thought we agreed you were gonna cool down the crazy!" I said. Knowing Irish said she couldn't have kids, I worried that Ma had upset her, but she looked more amused, and maybe a bit bewildered, than anything else.

"Yes. Sorry. No more acting weird, I promise. But you are so beautiful!" Ma said. I rolled my eyes again, but kissed the top of her head affectionately. She was totally nuts, but she was my ma.

"Thank you, Mrs Doherty. It's lovely to meet you," Irish said nervously.

"Enough with the 'Mrs Doherty' as well. Call me Kathleen. Now, how do you feel about lasagne?" she asked. Pulling Irish away from me, she led her to the kitchen. Shutting the front door behind me, I followed, grinning all the way.

* * *

I eyed up the lasagne and wondered if I could get away with another helping. Mourning the loss of my usual portion, I knew Danny would pitch a bitch fit if he knew what I'd eaten already. I had a diet plan that I stuck to rigidly usually, but no way was I going to turn down Ma's food tonight. She'd been nervous enough as it was without me asking her to cook something different for me.

My girl was all lit up as she chatted to Ma about her dressmaking business. Knowing that Irish designed wedding dresses just added fuel to Ma's fire. If she looked at me and winked one more time, Irish was gonna think she had some kind of nervous tic.

"And how do you feel about children?" Ma asked Irish, out of the blue.

"For fuck's sake, Ma!" I snapped.

"Watch your language, Kieran Joseph Doherty," she replied, clearing the plates and stacking them up. Shit, every kid knew they were in trouble when their ma pulled out the middle name.

"You're gonna scare her away with your crazy," I whispered loudly.

"It's okay, Kier, honestly," Irish reassured me, before she looked despairingly at Ma.

"The truth is, Kathleen, I love kids. I'm from a big family, and I always wanted one myself, but I can't have children. I have a congenital heart defect and the strain of pregnancy would be too much for my body," she explained. I knew Ma's thoughts would jump straight to Da when she found out, and I wanted her to get to know Irish so she'd understand how I felt, but she had to push.

"I'm glad you told me, and I'm sorry that I was so pushy. But if there's anything I know, it's that there's no shortage of little souls in this world looking for someone to love them. Children don't care any less because you didn't birth them. If anything, they care more because they know you chose to love them. So, if you want a big family, you can adopt. I never had one son, I had four. The fact that I only gave birth to one of them didn't make them any less my kids."

I could see Irish's eyes well up. I wanted to say something, but I had no words.

"You're a very special woman, Mrs Doherty," Irish whispered.

"What did I say about calling me Kathleen?" Ma scolded gently. "Now, why don't you go and freshen up while I domesticate my son some more by getting him to clean up these dishes. The bathroom is upstairs. First door to your left."

Irish smiled broadly at her and left the table. As soon as she was out of earshot, Ma turned to me.

"Now, why did I have to hear that from Marie and not you? I would have kept my big trap shut if you'd given me some warning," she admonished.

"I looked up more about her condition on the Internet. Her projected lifespan isn't the same for most people. I know what you went through with Dad, and I didn't want you worrying over me and Irish, or trying to talk me out of making a life with her," I admitted, not catching her eye as I gathered up all the plates and carried them to the sink. There was always going to be a part of me that worried about losing her. Ma had survived Da's death, but I wasn't that strong. Losing Irish now would break me, unconditionally.

"Oh, Kieran, you silly boy. All I want for you is to find what I had. It doesn't matter whether it's for a few years or a lifetime. Nothing perfect lasts forever. But what your father gave me was a gift I wouldn't give back for all the world. It changes you in a way I can't begin to explain. The worst pain wouldn't be losing someone. It would be forgetting the way their love consumed you. I will live the rest of my life knowing that, of every woman on this earth, your father chose me. He loved me with his dying breath, and somewhere else he loves me still. How could I want anything less for you?"

I'd seen Ma broken in her grief for Da. Never in a million years could I have predicted that this was how she felt. She was the strongest and wisest person that I knew. I couldn't comprehend how experiencing such terrible pain would still leave her capable of feeling such unconditional love.

"Thanks, Ma. I had no idea you felt like this. I will never understand how a woman's mind works," I replied, feeling slightly choked up.

"You're not meant to understand us, love. Just thank your lucky stars for the complicated and wonderful beings that we are. Love is a gift. Always be thankful for it and you can't go far wrong." She patted my cheek indulgently as Irish walked back in. "So what are you kids up to tonight then?" she asked.

"Friday night at Seamus O'Donnell's," I said, rubbing my hands together, as though it was self-explanatory.

"What does that mean?" Irish asked, her face scrunched up in confusion.

"Karaoke!" I replied.

* * *

I walked behind her as we made our way to the back of the packed pub. More than one pair of appreciating male eyes roamed over my girl, until they saw my scowl and turn hastily away. O'Connell smirked at me from where he was slumped in his seat, like he knew what I was thinking. Irish kissed me, then went over to join Em and the other girls, so I pulled out the seat next to him.

"How do you fucking deal with it?" I asked him.

"Deal with what?"

"This feeling like everyone is out to steal your girl away. I've never had a quick temper, but I swear to God, five minutes in this place and I wanna knock out every fucker that even looks at her," I explained, making him chuckle.

"Most of the time, I don't deal with it. Anyone disrespects her and I'll be up in their face so fast, they won't have time to shit their pants. But Em explained to me once that I shouldn't get upset with other people for admiring what we have and wanting it for themselves. So, as long as they're only looking, I let 'em keep their teeth. 'Course it helps that she only has eyes for me."

Irish looked for me over her shoulder, smiling when our eyes met. As she turned back to chat to Em, I grinned wider, knowing just what he meant.

"What does Marie think about the fight?" he asked me.

"I only told her last night. I think she's nervous, but she didn't say much. She's never seen me fight before, so she has no idea what to expect. I want to show her what I can do, but I don't want to scare her."

"A fighter is who ya' are, Kier. You can't hide that any more than I can. She'll either accept it, or she won't."

"I could go back to what I was doing before though. You know, just stick with the training."

"Fighters don't stop being fighters. They just take off the gloves," he said, taking a sip of his pint. I knew he was right. I had boxed my entire life, not because I had to, but because it gave me a high like nothing else. It was a sport I loved. I'd give it up for Irish, but I wanted to know that she wouldn't expect me to, that she could accept all of me. To know that when I went into that ring, that she'd be with me all the way.

"Are you ready for this?" he asked. "Because if ya' head ain't in the game, you tell me now. I've seen this guy fight before. He's a nasty fucker that won't give you an inch. He smells weakness on you and he's gonna fuck with your head before you even throw the first punch."

I thought carefully before answering. It was something I'd been thinking about for a long time now, wondering if I had it in me to do what Con did. I might not have his wild temper or his sixth sense for gaps in his opponent's game, but I had a clarity of vision. I never lost my temper or allowed myself to be goaded into fighting another man's fight. It was why Con and I made such good training partners. In the ring, I was the calm to his storm.

"I've got this, Con. I'm in the best shape of my life, and I'm ready for this fight. I've seen him too, and I know I can beat this guy. I just don't know if I'll want it forever like you do."

"Well, boyo, a few more weeks and we'll find out. In the meantime, I'd make the most of ya' last night out if I were you. From tomorrow, you're training is gonna be on a whole other level. If you have the energy for anything other than eating and falling straight into bed when we're done with you, then we ain't doing it right.

"Fan-fucking-tastic," I replied sarcastically. I eyed up his pint enviously and felt tired at the thought of what they were going to put me through. Then I watched my girl walk gracefully up the steps of the stage, and suddenly I was wide awake.

CHAPTER TWELVE

MARIE

I wiped my hand nervously against my jeans as I gripped the microphone with the other. Already, I was regretting my stupid decision to allow Em to dare and goad me into doing this. It was supposed to be her turn at karaoke, but here I stood. When the opening bars to Nina Simone's "Feeling Good" played, I gave a small sigh of relief. At least I knew this song. Now all I had to do was pretend that the eyes of the whole pub weren't on me, waiting for me to mess up.

I closed my eyes, taking a deep breath against the nerves. When my voice sang out, it was true and clear, giving away little of the trepidation I felt at singing in front of such a large audience. My gaze found Kieran's across the room and it calmed me. Somehow it felt easier to pretend I was singing just for him rather than everyone else.

When it was over, you could hear a pin drop. Then Kieran stood up and applauded and the whole pub erupted, wolf whistling and shouting "encore." I might not be able to dance, but I knew I had a set of pipes. I just didn't have the balls to use them all that often.

"That was amazing!" Kieran said, hauling me into his arms when I walked down the steps of the stage. "I had no idea you could sing like that!"

"You're one to talk. You sang live with a band last week," I reminded him, happy that I hadn't made a fool of myself.

"Aw, Irish, I can hold a tune, but that was something else," he replied, capturing my lips in a sweet kiss.

"Nice work, darlin'," Con told me.

"Thanks, O'Connell. Are you singing tonight?" I asked curiously.

"I don't sing," he replied.

"That's a step up from the 'fuck off' you gave me when I asked," Tommy said. "Em must be teaching you some manners."

"Fuck off," Con replied, making me smile. Tommy and Albie's names were called next, but Liam didn't move from his seat in the corner. Instead, he took a long sip of his pint and watched Albie possessively.

"You aren't joining them?" I asked him.

"I don't sing either," he replied.

Heath sat by his side. He was nowhere near as quiet as Liam or as sullen as Con, but he wasn't quite the extrovert that Tommy was either. I suspect that Albie was more of an innocent bystander, caught between them all. Despite their differences, they all looked happy, this eclectic band of brothers that was Kieran's family. It warmed me to think that they would always have his back. No matter what happened to me in the future, they would be here for him.

Following Em's lead as she sat down on Con's lap, I let Kieran pull me down and cuddled into his side. When I traced the tip of my finger down his tattoo, he shivered.

"Ticklish?" I whispered.

"That's not tickling. It's foreplay," he answered quietly, so only I could hear. Tommy and Albie were belting out the lyrics to Queen's "Don't Stop Me Now." They had all the right notes, just not necessarily in the right order. The pub loved their enthusiastic rendition though.

Kieran was looking their way but didn't seem to be paying them any attention. His hand was on my leg, and his thumb was slowly tracing a pattern on the inside of my thigh. My skirt wasn't short, but he'd found the small patch of exposed skin and used it to teach me that my body had erogenous zones in places I'd never dreamed of. I swore, if he bent down to kiss the patch of flesh he'd been stroking, I'd have come then and there. To anyone looking on, there was nothing erotic in what he was doing. We were just like any young couple, sitting together and enjoying the entertainment. But in reality, we were inside our own bubble, one where Kieran was slowly seducing me, tearing down my walls, making me hotter with each stroke.

I didn't know how much more I could take, but his touch was addictive. I wanted to change positions to ease the ache building inside me, but his hand held me firmly. The callouses on his hands only sensitised each stroke. I squeezed his arm, warning him to stop, but that only made him chuckle. He knew exactly what he was doing to me. Playing him at his own game, I carried on tracing my finger down the length of his tattoo. Knowing that only he would hear me, I moaned gently into his ear.

"Fuck," he muttered under his breath as he adjusted his tightening jeans. "Come with me," he whispered in my ear before abruptly standing up and pulling me towards the back of the club. Walking down the corridor to the toilets, he took a sharp left and started climbing a flight of stairs, clearly marked "Private." I followed him through two more doors before he tugged me into a large, empty room with a stage at the back.

"What is this place?" I asked.

"It's a private room the landlord's hire out for functions." He pushed my jacket off my shoulders, dropping it to the floor. The air rushed from my lungs as he speared his hand into my hair, pulling my lips against his. What we were doing was too explosive to be called just a kiss. It was like he feasted on me, drawing every moan and every breath into his mouth and making it his own. It was wild and tempestuous, and I wanted more. I wanted so much more. I wanted him buried so deep inside me that I would feel the echo of his lovemaking for weeks.

"I didn't think you were allowed to do this," I gasped, as he used his free hand to cup my arse. Heat pooled at my core as he slid his calloused hand down the length of my thigh and wrapped my leg around his hip.

"I'm bending the rules a little, love, not breaking them," he replied between kisses. His hand left my hair and he slipped it under my top instead. When his thumb brushed over my beaded nipple, I couldn't help but throw my head back and close my eyes in pleasure.

Desperate to find some relief, I rocked my hips against the bulge of his erection, making him groan. I wanted him to feel as on fire as I did.

"Sorry, baby, you do that once more, and I won't last," he said. Before I could even register what he was doing, he'd dropped down on one knee, lifting my leg over his shoulder.

"Kier, what are you doing? Anyone could come in and... Holy Shit!" I exclaimed. Without even stripping off my panties, he moved them aside to touch me with his tongue.

"Kieran," I begged without knowing what for. I teetered on the edge of orgasm, knowing that I couldn't take this exquisite torture much longer. When he slipped his calloused finger inside me, not missing a beat with his tongue, I was lost. Stars exploded behind my eyes as I threw myself head first into the abyss.

By sheer force of will, I stopped myself from sliding down the wall. Easing my underwear back into place, Kieran ran a gentle hand down the back of one thigh, while kissing his way up the other. When I finally gained some composure, he rested his forehead against my midriff as he tried to regain his. I slid my fingers through his hair slowly, and the moment was intimately tender.

"Let's do that again," he said finally, making me laugh.

"Next time, I'll go down on my knees," I said.

"Can we talk about something that doesn't make me think of your lips around my cock?" His groan made me giggle again.

"Is it worth it?" I asked him curiously, thinking of all the sacrifices he'd made for this fight.

"It's worth it," he replied with certainty. "Knowing that you'll be there at the end of it as well is everything. Just a few more weeks, and all of you will be mine."

With a contented sigh, I leaned down to kiss him gently.

"Kieran, I'm already yours."

* * *

A week later, I was still walking on air. After a packed schedule of back-to-back dress fittings and appointments, I was glad to turn the shop over to Mum for the day. I yearned to spend it with Kieran, but Con hadn't been joking about stepping up the training. He pushed himself from sun up to sun down. I had never seen such single-minded focus in anyone before, and I couldn't be prouder. I was more than a little nervous about the fight, but Kier promised me that he wouldn't lose. With everything in me, I believed him.

We snatched small pockets of time together whenever we could, making it work. He had invaded my thoughts so completely, it was hard remembering what life pre-Mr Doherty was like, much less why I'd resisted his charms in the first place.

I wandered leisurely down the aisles of the supermarket, taking my time just because I could. So consumed was I by thoughts of Kieran and how finely he'd trained my body to respond to his touch that I didn't feel him coming up behind me until it was too late.

"Fancy meeting you here," Alastair said, so close in my personal space that I could feel his breath on my neck. I dropped the peach that I was holding, and he caught it. Bringing it slowly to his mouth, he bit into it, sucking on the juice to stop it from dripping. To say that

I was creeped out was a massive understatement.

"Um, hi, Alastair," I replied. I couldn't bring myself to spout out the usual pleasantries. It wasn't nice to see him, and I knew exactly what he was doing here. This supermarket was five minutes from my apartment and more than half an hour's drive away from his home across London.

"Hello, Marie. I wonder if you might spare me a few minutes to talk?" he said, looking at me intently.

"Umm," I said, glancing around and trying desperately to think of a reason why I had to be somewhere else just then. "Sure, I guess, but I can't stop long. I have an appointment in a little while that I need to get to."

"Of course," he said, smiling broadly in a way I was sure he thought was charming. "Look, I don't really want to talk in the aisle. There's a little coffee shop in the back. Why don't we grab a coffee? Then I can leave you to get back to your day."

I really felt awkward that, even after our last conversation, he still wasn't taking the hint. It felt wrong to be doing this, but the fact that he was here meant that I needed to put him straight. Hiding from him wouldn't accomplish anything. My basket was empty, so I left it by the door and followed him to the coffee shop. At this time of day, the place was pretty packed, which made me feel a little better. It wasn't that I was uneasy about Alastair himself. I wouldn't have continued our association in the first place if that had been the case. It was more his persistence that a relationship between us could work that made me uncomfortable. Surely I wasn't the only one to see that we had nothing in common and that there was no chemistry between us.

I sat down at a table, worrying over what I would say. When he joined me, Alastair brought a pot of tea and a blueberry muffin. I didn't particularly like blueberry muffins, but now that I thought of it, he often took it upon himself to order for me.

"This is nice," he said, pouring tea for us both. "I'm so busy at the office most days that I don't often get to sit down like this, rather like you I expect."

"I'm so sorry if I sound rude, Alastair, but what are you doing here? After our last conversation, I wasn't expecting to see you again." I hated to be so blunt, but it needed saying.

He stirred his coffee and dropped his spoon a little sharply. I sensed that he wasn't particularly impressed with my directness. "I must admit you took me by surprise the last time that we spoke. I wasn't prepared to hear that you'd abandoned any idea of a relationship between us and taken up with another man, especially without giving me a chance to plead my case."

"Alastair, you shouldn't have to plead your case. If I thought that there was enough spark between us to make things work, I would have said. We're friends, but I'm not the kind of girl you need at all."

He leant his elbows on the table and steepled his hands together while staring at me in a way that made me feel a little uncomfortable.

"Marie, the very first time I saw you, I knew you were the one for me. Call it love at first sight if you will. I knew then that I'd do whatever it took to get to know you and for you to get to know me."

"But... our first meeting was completely random, wasn't it?" I asked.

"Of course not. I don't leave things like meeting the love of my life to chance. I am the master of my own fate."

"How can you believe we're meant to spend our lives together from one look? You didn't know anything about me."

"There are somethings you just know, Marie. I never forgot about you. Never stopped engineering a way for us to meet. When we finally did, I was sure you would feel the same magnetic pull that I did. I was terribly disappointed when you didn't, but I knew that, given time, once you could see the real me and understand the life I could give you, you'd come around. I know all about your heart. I know everything about you, and still I want you. This chemistry that you're so worried about is there. You just need to get to know the person I am now to give yourself a chance to see it."

I took a deep breath, but for the first time in a long while, breathing wasn't that easy. I told myself to calm down, knowing it must be the stress of the situation causing my heart to beat so fast.

"Honestly, Alastair, I'm not sure how to feel about all this. The fact that you went to such great lengths to get to know me is flattering, but I feel uncomfortable that you won't accept that I don't feel the same way. Whatever compelled you to get to know me, I think it best to end things here and leave it at that." I wanted Kieran so desperately right then. I knew if I called him, he'd come. But this was my battle to fight.

I got up from the table, and he looked shell-shocked, as though he couldn't believe I'd walk away after everything he'd told me.

"Goodbye, Alastair. I hope that someday you'll find what you're looking for." I leant down to give him an awkward hug.

Abandoning any thoughts of food shopping, I headed home.

My head throbbed unbearably, and as I willed one foot in front of the other, I wondered if I could keep going long enough to face plant in the middle of my bed and sleep the rest of the day away.

CHAPTER THIRTEEN

KIERAN

Meeting Stella Kelly was hands down the scariest thing I'd ever done. I felt like I was on one of those game shows where you put one foot wrong and you fell into the water, disqualifying you from the game permanently. Irish loved her family fiercely, and from what she'd told me, they were all very close. It only took five minutes for me to see where she fit into the family dynamic. She might have been the first-born child, but her Ma and brothers cosseted and protected her as though she was the youngest. Something told me that, with her heart condition, it was something they'd always done. They all still respected her though. In a loud family, she was by far the quietest, but when she had something to say, everyone listened. Still, I wondered if she liked me well enough to keep me if her family didn't approve. My palms were sweating as I worried on it. I'd never given a shit about whether anyone liked me before, but I never had my heart riding on anything like I did then.

"Why don't you like me pasta then, Kieran?" Stella asked me, as she piled green vegetables on her plate and then passed the dish to me.

"It's not that I don't like pasta, Mrs Kelly. I'm sure that yours is delicious. It's just that I have a professional fight coming up soon, and my trainer will skin me alive if I eat anything that isn't on my diet plan. But if you'll have me, I'd love to come over and try some when my fight is done," I replied.

Tristan snorted in amusement at my sucking up to his ma. She caught him, gave him a filthy look, then smacked him on the arm before turning back to me. I tried not to look smug, 'cause Irish's other brothers were all still staring at me like they'd like to drag me down into the basement and take turns beating the crap out of me. Sensing my tension, Irish slid her arm under the table and squeezed my thigh, leaving her arm resting there. I was sure she meant it as a gesture of affection and support, but damn if it wasn't making my dick jump. If I didn't get this fight over with soon, I was going to end up walking around with a permanent hard-on. No doubt it would have given my boys a laugh, but here? Walking around with a hard-on was likely to get me castrated.

"Of course you are invited to come back here and eat," Mrs Kelly said. "As long as you and my Marie are courting, you are always welcome here. And please call me Stella. I feel too young for you to be calling me by my mother-in-law's name, God rest her soul." Stella did the sign of the cross as she said it, and I paused to look at what everyone else was doing before deciding whether I should too.

"So, Kieran," said Luca, "what are your long-term career plans?"

I held back a smile at the serious, almost condescending tone in which he said it. Then I remembered that Luca was only asking questions that Irish's da would have asked me if he'd been there. I knew all about stepping in for the man of the house, so I decided to answer with the respect I would given if her da had still been there.

"I've worked construction since I left school. It's what my da did before he died," I explained. "But I've been fighting since before that. I enjoyed building, but unless I open me own firm, I was never gonna earn a great wage. So when me best friend Con became a professional fighter and asked me to come on board as his full-time trainer, I knew that's what I wanted to do. I love boxing, and I'm good at it. Plus, the money is a lot better, so I'm actually getting to put some away now."

It was like being at an interview for the most important job I'd ever applied for. My profession likely wouldn't be as impressive as if I was a doctor or a lawyer or something, but I wasn't ashamed of what I did. I was bloody good at it.

"And where do you boys all work, if you don't mind me asking," I said. Of course, Irish had already told me, but I was hoping to deflect the conversation away from me.

"Wow, Marie can't like you that much if she hasn't told you about us," Matt said. Of course I'd shortened Matteo's name in my head. It was pretty much the only way I could pay back the dick while he sat round a table with his ma. Turns out that Stella had my back, and she gave Matt a smack to the head this time.

"Stop intimidating him, boys. Kieran is a nice boy, and you'll scare him away," Stella said.

"If he scares away that easily, then he's not good enough for

Marie," Luca pointed out, making me smile. I was beginning to like this guy more and more. I could see where he was coming from too. They'd been protecting Irish their entire lives, but it was my turn now. Her heart was in my hands, and it was mine to protect. There was no one on this earth that could protect her and care for her like I could.

"Luca," Irish chastised. It was a gentle rebuke though because she knew what they were doing. She'd warned me that, as she'd never brought a guy home before, she expected them to be pretty much feral.

"Cool your jets, little sis. We just want to make sure this one's an improvement on the string of douchebags you've dated in the past," Tristan said.

"Well he is. He's the most wonderful man I've ever met, so I'd appreciate it if you wouldn't terrorise him," she said, and I couldn't hold back a smile any longer. The twins rolled their eyes, making us all chuckle.

"I'm sure our sis has already explained, but we're roughnecks. We work on an oil rig out in the North Sea. Two weeks on the rig, two weeks off," Luca explained.

"That's pretty intense," I said, wondering how I'd feel if I had to go away from Irish every two weeks.

He shrugged like it was nothing, before answering. "We're used to it. We're all engineers, but the money on the rigs is far better than we'd get anywhere else. We're all single, and although none of us have bought a house to live in, we've all invested in buy-to-let properties that are tucked away for our retirement. Two weeks hard work followed by two weeks hard partying while loading up on Mum's food isn't a bad life," Luca explained.

"It's a dangerous job though, isn't it? More dangerous than fighting even?" I asked.

Luca frowned and gave me the big brother stare down.

"Yes it is. Very, very dangerous. I have one girl with a heart condition and three boys who are trying to give me one. It's a miracle they haven't put me in the grave by now with all the worrying I do," Stella protested dramatically.

The twins launched into their reasoned arguments about how dramatically health and safety measures have improved to make it a safer working environment and how she had no need of worrying. Amidst all the noise and banter, Stella winked at me, and I smiled as I carried on eating my meal, knowing exactly who wore the trousers in this family. The wink told me that Stella had shifted the focus of the boy's inquisition to allow me to eat my meal. Stella Kelly was indeed a legend.

The guys laid off after that, and it was kind of fun listening to them tell stories of their time on the rig. I ate my chicken and vegetables, looking on enviously as everyone heaped on potatoes and mushroom and white wine sauce. When all the guys opted for seconds of dessert while I stuck to water, I knew they were likely doing it to fuck with me. But when this fight was done, I was gonna come back and eat Stella out of house and home. Maybe I'd wait until they were back on the rig, then text them selfies on me ploughing into their ma's home-cooked meal just to fuck with them back. The thought was little comfort when the warm chocolate fudge cake smelt so friggin' amazing.

After the meal was over, Irish and her ma cleared the table. I stood up to help until Matt stopped me.

"Give us a hand carrying Ma's spare chairs back downstairs, Kieran?" he asked. I sighed, knowing I was better off getting this over and done with. There were two chairs to be taken down, and Matt could have carried them both one handed. Lifting the one he left behind for me, I followed him down the stairs to the basement. Seconds later I heard footsteps behind me, and the door closed with a gentle click.

"So what's the deal then? You looking to fuck around with our sister then drop her? Because we go back to the rigs tomorrow, and I'd hate to have to spend the next two weeks worrying about which part of the North Sea to dump your body," Tristan said.

Both he and Matt stood legs apart and arms crossed in an attempt to be intimidating. They weren't small guys and even looked like they'd be handy in a fight. But I'd trained every day for over ten years with a world-class fighter. Odds were I could take them both and be on my merry way. I didn't think Irish would appreciate that much though. Before I had a chance to say anything, the door open and shut again and Luca walked down the basement stairs.

"We've got this, bro," Matt said to him.

"I have no doubt," Luca replied, relaxing against the counter, "but it amuses me watching you give the 'big brother speech.'"

"You mean you've done this before?" I asked, kind of glad that Irish had so many people looking out for her.

"She never brought anyone home before, so we never needed to. The fact that she brought you over when she knew we were home tells us this is serious. For her at least," Tristan said.

"It is for me too. From the minute I met her, she knocked me off my feet. I don't know what she sees in me, and I know that she's too good for me, but you won't ever find a guy that wants her as much as I do or will take care of her as well as I can," I replied.

"That's fine and dandy now, but what happens if the shit hits the fan? Do you know what it takes to watch someone you love get put to sleep, knowing that they may never wake up again? Or that if she exercises too hard, her heart might give out if she can't get medical assistance fast enough? Marie's had seven surgeries. Seven surgeries since she was a kid, and two of them were open heart. There's only so much her little body can take, and if her last treatment fails, then a valve replacement or transplant might be the only option left open to her. Now, if we get on that helicopter tomorrow and leave her to fall in love with you, then we need to know that you're going to be there when the chips are down. Because she can't fight for a heart if it's broken. If you kick her when she's down, it will kill her, and then I will be fucking dumping your body at the bottom of the North Sea," Matt said passionately.

He was breathing kind of hard from his outburst, but other than that we were quiet while we thought over what he'd said. Tristan looked as pissed as his twin, but Luca just stared as though he was trying to get the measure of me.

"I know what it's like to watch someone strong and healthy getting sick, to watch their body wither and die in front of you, knowing that you'd give your own life to swap places with them. That you'd give anything, promise anything, to have them with you for just one more day. I know all of that. So don't take what I say next lightly. For as long as she'll have me, I will never leave her side. Whether it's a year or fifty, she's it for me. So you can warn me off or try and scare me. Shit, you can take a shot at me if you're feeling brave enough, but there's only three of you, and it's gonna take a fuckload more than that to keep me away from my girl. Now don't get me wrong, lads, I ain't meaning to get on your bad side. Hell, if I had a sister, I'd be doing exactly the same thing, but the fact is that we're gonna be seeing a lot more of each other in the future. For Marie's sake, I'd like for that to be on good terms," I argued, holding my hand out to them.

The twins looked at each other and nodded curtly.

"That's good enough for me, brother," Tristan said, shaking my hand.

"You've got one shot. Don't fuck it up," Matt said, grasping my hand briefly. I looked towards Luca. He was the hardest one to read. He was only fractionally older than the twins, but he had a quieter, more calculating manner about him. If I had to worry about any of them shanking me in my sleep, it would be him.

"I'm not going to make hollow threats about the safety of your genitals if my sister gets hurt, because I'm pretty sure that's implied. Marie's old enough to make her own decisions about who she wants to date. Worrying about her heart has made her put her life on hold for far too long. I've been telling her for years that it's bullshit, but it took you to make her listen. If she's prepared to go balls to the wall with this relationship, then I'll be right behind her. Maybe things between you will work out, maybe they won't. Nobody goes into a relationship believing it will fail. I will ask one thing of you though.

Come tomorrow, me and the boys will be back on the rig. If she needs me for any reason, because she gets sick, because you guys didn't work out and she's heartbroken, whatever it is, you call me. I'm not asking you to be responsible for her, that's our job, but you leave her in a world of hurt without letting us know, and you and I are going to have a problem," he said. His calm, even tone didn't fool me. Luca was not a man to be crossed.

"It's not something you ever have to worry about, but I appreciate you looking out for her. If she needs you, I'll call. You have my word," I reassured him, offering my hand. He shook it, grinning.

Behind us, the door opened and my girl stood at the top of the steps, hands planted firmly on her hips.

"If you boys have finished measuring your dicks, can I have my boyfriend back please?" she asked, making us all chuckle.

"I'm telling Mum you said dick," Tristan told her, smirking.

"Go ahead, and I'll tell her you got drunk and had your arse tattooed," she replied, sounding bored.

"How can you possibly know that?" he asked, outraged.

"I came to the house for breakfast and you were sitting around in your white boxers eating cereal, despite the fact it grosses everyone out. When you took your bowl out to the kitchen it looked like you had skid marks in your underwear. When Lucas finished laughing his arse off, he told me what you'd done," she explained, looking a little smug at her brother's disgruntled expression.

"Sisters are a pain in the arse," he grumbled.

"What's the tattoo?" I asked.

"None of your business," Tristan told me.

"Ignore grumpy guts," Irish replied. "It's Jessica Rabbit blowing him a kiss."

"That's not bad," I reasoned. "Jessica Rabbit is sexy as fuck."

"I know, right?" Tristan said, suddenly pleased that I was standing in his corner.

"Yeah, I'm sure it would be a lovely tattoo if he didn't have a hairy arse," Matt said.

"You ever imagined what Jessica Rabbit would look like with a beard?" Luca asked me, smiling. Simultaneously, we all looked towards Tristan's jean clad behind and burst out laughing.

"Fuck you all," he replied grumpily. "My arse is a work of fucking art."

"Show Mum then. I'm sure she'd love to see your canvas," Marie baited.

"Forget what I said, Kier. That little punk is a menace. She seems all sweet and innocent, but turn your back and she'll own your arse," Matt warned me.

"She already does," I answered back as I walked up the stairs and slung my arm around my girl.

"Wow, whipped sure is a good look on you," Tristan said, smirking.

"Says the boy hiding his ink from his ma," I taunted back. "I bet you've all got tattoos that you're keeping quiet about," I guessed. All three of them avoided eye contact, looking around the room sheepishly.

"Why didn't your ma have a problem with my ink?" I asked Marie curiously.

"Because your tattoo is beautiful. Whereas, she worries that this lot lack the mental capacity to permanently brand their skin," she replied.

"Yep, total fucking menace," Tristan mumbled.

"Good luck, my friend," Luca said. Patting my back consolingly as he and his brothers walked past us. "'Cause in this family, you're going to need it."

CHAPTER FOURTEEN

MARIE

"You look tired," Nat said. Having spent more of my teenage years in a hospital bed than I did in school, I didn't leave with many close friends, but Natalie was one of them. Although quiet, she wasn't at all shy. Most of the time, I thought she just preferred books to people. At least that was until the library assistant tried charging her damages for dog-earring a book. After ranting at the imbecile for ten minutes about how she would never defile books that way, she realised he was teasing her. They were getting married next month.

"You'd be tired too if you realised how crazy wedding season is," I mumbled from the floor. Taking pins from the cushion wrapped around my wrist, I worked my way slowly around the bottom of the dress until I had it pinned at the perfect length.

"Now I feel guilty for asking you to make my dress on top of everything else you've got to do," she said.

"Nat, you're my best friend. I would be devastated if you hadn't asked. I want you to feel like a princess on your special day, and no one else is going to put as much love into your dress as I will," I reassured her. Standing up, I made some adjustments and moved her to look into the mirror. "Now, what do you think?" I whispered.

"It's so beautiful. I can't believe that's really me." She covered her mouth with her hands. "Thank you so much."

Twisting from left to right, she stared at her reflection in awe. This was by far and away the best part of my job. That magical look in her eyes. That knowledge that, on her special day, she would be mesmerising. That she would put on that dress and feel like the most beautiful woman in the world. To know that I was responsible for that, made all the late nights and calloused fingers worthwhile. I met her eyes in the mirror as I hugged her from behind.

"You're welcome, lovely. Now, I distinctly remember you promising to feed me."

* * *

Forty minutes later, I'd shut up shop and was stuffing my face full of maple syrup covered pancakes with strawberries. I adored pancakes. Only a healthy fear of having an arse the size of an elephant's kept me from eating them morning, noon, and night.

"Jeez, for someone so tiny, you sure can pack them away," Nat said, staring at my rapidly depleting stack in awe.

"You can talk," I mumbled between mouthfuls. "That double cheeseburger you're holding probably weighs more than you do."

"Do you know how long it's been since I've had a burger?"

"I have no interest in knowing how regularly you get your meat." I grinned childishly.

"Very mature." Nat poked her tongue out at me.

"Why the fast then? You love anything you can barbeque," I asked, shovelling another fork full of gooey deliciousness into my mouth and resisting the urge to groan in public.

"My dream wedding dress is out of this world amazing, but it's also fitted, and burgers go straight to my hips."

I leaned around the table to take a look at her physique. As I suspected, she was as slight and elfin-like as the last time I saw her.

"Nat, you've been exactly the same size the entire time I've known you. And I've seen you put away more food than men twice your size. I really can't see your metabolism changing radically between now and the wedding," I rationalised.

She rolled her eyes at my observation and ploughed into her burger, as though someone was going to snatch it away from her any second.

"So speaking of meat, how's that man mountain of yours?" she asked. The twinkle in her eye told me she was looking for juicy details.

"Mmm, edible. Totally edible," I replied, dreamily. I had a clear picture in my head of him shirtless, throwing punches at a bag in the gym. Despite my surroundings, and the fact that he wasn't even with me, just thoughts of him were getting me a little hot and bothered. Nat giggled at my reply.

"I've never seen you all starry-eyed like this. He must be some guy."

"I've always dated guys who I thought I had things in common with, you know? I've gone for friendship hoping that things progressed into something more. But Kieran.... He's just a force of nature. When I'm with him, I don't think about whether things will work out between us long term, or whether we have enough shared interests for a lasting relationship. It's nothing that calculated. Being with him is like getting caught in a riptide. It's pointless fighting against the current. The only way to survive is to let it carry you along. Only I don't want to escape. I want to drown. I want to bury myself against his six pack and never come up for air. I want his arms around me, keeping me afloat. And I want his deep, delicious, sexy-as-fuck voice whispering in my ear all the reasons why I'll only ever be the girl for him and he'll only ever be the man for me."

"Holy shit! That's fucking intense."

"I know, but it's how he makes me feel. I don't think around him. I don't worry or overanalyse, I just... feel. I've been concerned about my health my whole life, but it's like Kieran takes that weight off my shoulders—and it's not because he's detached or indifferent. It's because he's so calm. He makes me safe and protected, as though nothing will ever hurt me. With him, it's like I'm the only girl in the room. It's as though every woman disappears and there's just me, sitting there in his spotlight. When I talk, he listens to every word, like he's hungry to know everything about me." When I'd finished daydreaming, I looked at the ridiculously big grin on her face.

"And his kisses?" she asked, wiping up the ketchup on her plate with the last of her burger.

I thought of the way his firm, plump lips teased mine gently, making me groan before hungrily pushing me for more.

"Time standing still, fireworks, explosions, just... everything. Okay, so you know how some guys kiss like a fish out of water, floundering for air?" I asked. She covered her mouth to hold in her food as she laughed.

"Yeah, I've kissed a few boys like that," she finally replied, still smiling.

"Kieran kisses so hot and so deep that you feel it in every part of your body. He gets inside your head, and for at least half an hour afterwards, I struggle to formulate sentences, let alone remember my own name. He's a bad boy with really, really good lips."

"You know the sex is going to be over in, like, five minutes, don't you?"

"Really? After everything I've just told you?" I said sarcastically.

"Apart from the abstinence thing and the fact that he'd probably be ready to pop a load if you so much as sighed near his cock at this point, you've built it up too much in your head. I'm telling you, a few fumbles in the dark and it'll be over in five minutes."

"Maybe. But man, what a five minutes they'll be," I said with a wistful sigh, and we both burst out laughing.

* * *

The oak door creaked as I closed it behind me as stealthily as I could.

"Are sure it's okay, my being here?" I asked Em for about the millionth time.

"Don't worry, it's totally fine. It's probably best to try and stay out of Danny's way though," she warned, making me even more nervous.

"Is that fresh paint I smell?"

"Yeah. Liam just repainted the hallway for Danny. It's been a pretty successful year for the gym, not just with O'Connell, but for other fighters as well," she told me proudly. "Since Heath joined us and started promoting professionally, the place has become more successful than it's ever been. I spend more of my time fielding phone calls every day from suits looking for the London version of 'fight club' than I do running the books lately," she said with a chuckle.

"How does Danny feel about that?"

"Well, I let him answer the phone for a couple of hours the other day. He told the first two callers to 'fuck off,' and after that, he would just pick up the phone when it rang and put it straight back down again."

"He scares me," I admitted.

"Danny scares everyone," she replied, smiling.

"It's great news for the gym though, right? I mean, all the success you've had."

"As a business, it's fantastic. Bit by bit, we're replacing all of the outdated equipment and doing repairs that the building really needed. Danny will always be old school, so there's nothing here that you'd find in any of the modern, fancy gyms, but we're not short of anything anymore, and there's a heathy balance in the company account for unforeseen contingencies. It also means that we can help out the younger ones coming through. Some of them are really talented young fighters, but their parents can't afford the expense of travelling to fights. This gives Danny the means to help them out," she explained. She talked a lot about Danny, but the pride and passion in her voice told me how much a part of this place she was, and how important these guys were to her..

"Do you think he'll move to bigger premises as the business grows?"

"Never," she replied adamantly. "This is Danny's home. Years of blood, sweat, and tears line the walls of this place. Moving somewhere else just wouldn't be the same." She looked around reverently, and I could see that this wasn't just a building to her or any of them. It was something infinitely more important. We reached the top of the main stairs, and as she opened another door, I could hear the smack of gloves hitting bags and the grunt of guys hard at work.

My plan was to follow Em to the office and keep her company while I waited for Kieran to finish training. I scanned around, my eyes searching for my man in a sea of lean, cut torsos, until I found him standing, feet apart, on the canvas of the raised ring at the back of the room.

Staring at me.

Willing me to see him.

It was though he had radar, like he could feel my presence in the room. My skin tingled with the need to be near him, to touch him. I could see from the rapid rise and fall of his chest that he was as breathless as I was. It had only been days since we'd seen each other, but it felt like weeks. Months even. Outwardly I was calm, but inside my heart was beating erratically. His sculpted torso was tanned from training outside, and the sheen of sweat made him seem more ethereal. His low-slung shorts sat lazily at the base of the most perfect external obliques I had ever seen. And I wanted to touch him there.

So very badly.

My mouth was dry, and I wet my bottom lip with my tongue before biting it. His eyes narrowed, and I knew exactly what he was thinking. He wanted to bite it too. We might as well be alone for all the fighters there, because right then, there was just the two of us. He looked at me so intently that I shivered, suddenly a little afraid, not of him, but of how it would feel when he finally took me, when he peeled away my underwear and moved inside me. I wondered if he would be slow and gentle, or hard and powerful. Either way, I knew he would consume me, that the experience would consume us both.

"Wow, you two give off some serious sparks," Em said, her eyes darting back and forth between us both. "I wonder if O'Connell and I were like that when we first met."

"What do you mean? We're still like that," Con replied gruffly. He stood behind Em. Holding her hips, he pulled her into his huge body and, dipping his face into her neck, inhaled deeply before gently kissing her jaw. He didn't look away from her once, and I knew he didn't see anyone else in the room either. Nobody but her.

"Jesus, baby, you frightened the life out of me. You were in the ring when I walked in. How did you move so fast?" she asked, her hand over her heart in shock. He shrugged lazily in reply, then went back to kissing her neck. I turned towards the ring, but Kieran was gone. Before I could even look for him, my arm was nearly wrenched from the socket as I was pulled into the locker room.

Backing me into the lockers, he ran his hand along my thigh

before lifting it to wrap around his waist. Fitting snugly between my legs, his cock brushed gently against my core. And then he devoured me. It was the only way to describe how it felt. It was all too much to process at once. The feel of his tongue penetrating my mouth, demanding more of my kisses until my lips were raw. The rough, scratchy wraps on his hands as they rubbed along the sensitive skin of my thigh, sending darts of pleasure straight to my core. I was lightheaded and breathless, but still we didn't stop. I didn't want him to ever stop. I was so in love with the way that he kissed. He rocked his hips against me, and I pressed back harder. Looking for some relief from his delicious torment. He moaned into my mouth, and it only made me wetter. I was on fire. We both were, but neither of us cared.

"Spend the night with me," he whispered, his forehead pressed against mine. His eyes closed with the strain of his arousal. "Just to sleep, nothing else. But I need you in my arms tonight. I need to wake up tomorrow and know that this is real."

"Will there be kisses?" I whispered back, giving him a shy smile.

"Hell yeah there'll be kisses. More than your pretty little body can handle."

I nodded in reply, seeing his happy smile, before I threaded my hands in his hair and pulled his lips back to mine.

The bang of a locker door slamming shut had us jumping apart. In front of us stood a cranky-looking Irish man with a cigarette hanging precariously from his lips.

"Didn't I say no bloody shenanigans in my club? Well, didn't I?" he barked. We hung our heads like chastised school children, though I could sense Kieran was fighting a smile.

"Now then, girlie, I like you, but you've got my fighter all riled up, so what are you going to do about it?" he said. I didn't know whether he expecting me to apologise for kissing my boyfriend, or finish what we'd started. My horror must have been mirrored all over my face, because Kieran burst out laughing.

"Think it's feckin' funny do ya, ya little shite? Well, just for that, I'm gonna run you ragged this afternoon. I'm gonna make you hurt so bad, you won't even care that you've got a dick, let alone whether it works. By the time I'm finished with you, the only thing you'll be worrying about is whether you'll live long enough to make it to your bed," Danny said. With his hands on his hips, he stared gleefully at Kieran, and Kieran's smile started to slip as he realised what he was in for.

* * *

"I don't see why not. It worked for me," Con said. He and Danny looked almost comical with their identical poses. Both stood with their arms crossed, legs braced, and head tilted slightly to the right as they observed Kieran doing his hanging sit ups. Only Con was about six foot five and Danny about a foot shorter.

"You had a quick trigger though. Sunshine just being in the same room as you just about set you off," Danny replied quietly.

"She still does," Con answered with a rare chuckle.

"I'm not sure whether it will work as well for Kieran. He's too happy. I'm not sure we can get him riled up enough," Danny said.

"Are you fucking kidding me? Have you seen the way he looks at her? Anyone so much as sneezes too close to his girl, and he's about ready to put their lights out. The closer to the fight it gets, the worse he's becoming. He'd pretty much mounted her when you caught them in the locker, hadn't he? And I'd been working him hard going on eight hours now," Con replied passionately.

"Okay, let's give it a go?" Danny replied.

They'd both been chatting amongst themselves as I eavesdropped shamelessly. But at Danny's pronouncement, they both look towards me. "What's going on?" I asked nervously.

"Kieran doesn't want you to leave, but he's nowhere near done for the day, so we're going to put you to work," Danny barked at me. I used to jump every time Danny did that, until Em explained that he wasn't mad at me; it was just the way he spoke to everyone. Or maybe he was just mad at the world, but not at me in particular.

"Put me to work how?" I asked cautiously.

"If it's okay with you, they're going to make Kieran bench press continuously for half an hour. If he can do it, he gets to go home with you. If not, Con gets to choose which of the other lads will take you home" Em said, handing me a cup of tea.

"But I don't want to go home with anyone other than Kieran," I protested.

"Don't worry," she replied. "There is no way Kieran will let you walk out of here with another guy.

Danny passed her another cup, and she sat next to me, sipping on her own drink as she explained. "When a fighter gets to this stage of his training, he kind of hits a wall. He feels too tired to push himself any harder, so he needs some motivation to empty the last of his reserves left in the tank. He needs to finish each day of training having given everything he's got. In Kieran's case, his level of testosterone is ramped so high, he'll push himself further to impress you."

"And when that stops working, we'll start fucking with his head to make him go even further," Con said, lifting Em up and sitting down with her settled into his lap.

"Fuck with his head how?" I asked, completely alarmed.

CHAPTER FIFTEEN

KIERAN

Irish smelled fucking amazing. Every time I raised the bar, I inhaled. The clean scent of apples was nearly enough to drown out my stink after a day of blood, sweat, and tears. She didn't seem to mind though. When I first started lifting, she looked nervous, and I held back a smirk. As if I'd ever let anyone else take her home! When Danny suggested this, I was all for it. The thought of getting her alone was all the motivation I needed. Our kiss wasn't enough to slake my thirst. Now I craved her with every cell in my body.

"You're slowing down, boy," Danny taunted. "Maybe one of the other lads should take a turn."

"*Nobody* touches her except me," I said emphatically. Keeping Marie directly in my eye line, I kept up the repetitions.

"Time," Con called out. Slowly, I lowered the bar to see her smile of relief. I was far from done for the day, but knowing that I she was coming home with me, made me feel like a fucking God. Moving behind her, I gripped her waist and pull her into my body. She inhaled sharply, and I knew she felt this as much as I did. It was hard to believe that I'd avoided this connection for so long. It wasn't lust or anything you could attribute to a chemical imbalance. This feeling was deeper. It was binding. It was so totally fucking addictive that I forgot about the pain and the fatigue. I forgot about everything except showing this woman that I was the strongest man in the room. That I would be her protector. The only man who could give her what she needed.

Finally, reluctantly, I released her.

"Gloves on, lover boy. You've got three full rounds with me to go before you can get to her. That's if someone doesn't replace you first," Con taunted as he nodded his head towards Tommy. The fucker was leant against the ropes, chatting up my girl.

"Back away, Tommy," I warned.

"We were just talking," he protested, holding his hands up in the air innocently. No doubt he was telling the truth, but I was in full-on caveman mode. I'd never been this ramped up before. She was mine, and I didn't want her in the vicinity of any other alpha males.

Seeing the look on my face, Tommy rolled his eyes, but moved away from Irish.

"Fucking hormones when they fall in love. Makes normal guys fucking crazy," he muttered, under his breath. I relaxed a little when she winked at me, knowing that my possessiveness hadn't upset her. Luckily for me, Tommy turned his attention to Em. Showing how comfortable their long-standing friendship was, he threw his arm around her shoulders and hugged her to him. To my amusement,

Con dropped the smirk and now looked as fierce as I did.

"Not as much fun anymore, is it?" I said, baiting him.

"Right then, ya fucker. Game on," Con said, moving towards his corner to glove up. Tommy had pissed him off, and he was looking for someone to take out his bad mood on. Lucky for him, I had a few frustrations of my own that I wanted to vent.

"That's your girl down there, and just you remember it," Danny whispered in my ear.

The sneaky fecker had come out of nowhere, but I listened to him as I kept an eye on Irish.

"O'Connell is gonna pick you apart a piece at a time. That boy is in peak physical condition. He's in his absolute prime. Nothing and no one is going to make him look bad in front of his wife. But you see, that's your girl down there. She's never seen you fight before. She doesn't know you like we do. She thinks that Con is the most dangerous person in this room. She's probably worrying right now how you'll walk away from this. Right now, he ain't your best mate. You ain't pulling your punches. You go out there and you show her that you're stronger, fitter, and faster than anyone has ever seen. You make her forget that there's any other guys in here, and you make sure *you're* the one she's going home with."

My blood was pumping, my heartbeat roaring in my ears. I was electric. I was on fire. I was alive. There was nothing between me and the girl I wanted to spend the rest of my life with, except him. He might think he was the best in the world, but I was better. Why? Because he might have been fighting his entire life, but his entire life I'd been watching him. I knew his tells. I knew his weaknesses. I knew how to win.

There was no biding our time and dancing around. We knew each other too well for that. He was in this ring to hurt me. To make me work for the win. He threw combination after combination at me relentlessly. I blocked repeatedly, so used to his style that my moves were instinctive. I'd had a lifetime of dodging that famous right hook of his. It was time that I unleashed what I was truly capable of.

Every one of our punches was brutal. We were both giving it everything we had, without reservation. By the end of the first round, I'd cut his eye and my lip was bleeding. The fucker smirked at me, so I decided to make him hurt some more. Spitting out a mouthful of blood, I beckoned him towards me. The second round was equally as vicious, and by round three we were both breathing heavily. Changing southpaw suddenly to throw me off my game, he came at me.

"You're mine, little man," he taunted.

"Laugh it up, Con, but my girl is watching every move I make right now. She's imagining how much stamina I've got to train all day and still kick your arse. And your girl? Your girl is hanging off the arm of Tommy Riordon, the most notorious fucking skirt chaser this side of the Irish Sea," I replied calmly.

And there it was. Con's tell. His strength and ultimate Achilles heel. His wife. He couldn't resist a quick glance at Tommy to see if I was right. Feinting left, I dodged his automatic right hook and gave him mine. His blow glanced my shoulder as I turned. Mine hit him square in the face and put him on his arse. I wasn't his easy-going best friend. I wasn't the life of the party. I was a fighter. A champion. I was Marie's champion, and there was nothing and nobody who was going to take that away from me.

Con looked up at me from the floor, and to my surprise, he was grinning from ear to fucking ear.

"What you smiling at?" I asked him, confused. He was a world-class fighter, number one, at the absolute top of his game, and I'd put him on his arse. He should be devastated, not smiling like a fucking lunatic.

"You, ya fucking legend," he said to me, as though that answered my question at all.

"I told you it would work," Con told Danny.

"I've gotta hand it to ya, kid. I didn't think it would, but I underestimated how bad he has it for this girl," Danny replied with a rare chuckle.

"Oh shit," Con muttered. I followed the line of his stare to Irish. Watching the ring from below us, she was white as a sheet and shaking. *Fuck!* I completely panicked, standing there, frozen like a deer in the head lights. We'd all been boxing our entire lives. This was every day bread and butter to us. But she'd only ever seen my softer side. The side that was hers and hers alone. Inside of those four ropes, I had become an athlete. A stone-cold killer. Focused. Driven. Hungry for victory. I'd revealed my most basic self, and she was terrified.

I took a step forward, and instinctively she took one back. I froze again, fearing that if I moved she'd bolt. Em looked towards Con worriedly, but I couldn't see him. I couldn't turn my eyes away from Irish. If I did, she might leave, and I didn't know whether she'd ever come back.

A hand came down on my shoulder, and Con whispered in my ear, "I've got this." Moving ahead of me, he took off his remaining glove and dropped it on the canvas. Parting the ropes, he jumped down.

"Marie, why don't we go for a walk? Get a bit of fresh air," Con suggested.

Irish looked towards me, for guidance I guessed. Her eyes pooled, and I willed those tears not to fall. I willed a lot of things in that moment. Most of all, I prayed that I hadn't lost her, that her glimpse of my dark side hadn't sent her running for the hills. The idea of fighting professionally didn't faze me, but the thought of her seeing me unworthy had me scared. I couldn't lose her. Not now.

I stared, immobile and petrified, as Con pulled on a hoodie, then guided her out the doors towards the street. All I could do was watch her leave. The sound of the closing door echoed through the gym like a death knell.

"You can't hide it from her, Kier. You're a fighter, and that's not going to change. She needs to see all of you, not just the bits you want to show her," Em said. She walked up the steps to the ring, but instead of getting in, she leaned on the ropes to talk to me.

"Did you see the look on her face? That wasn't eve three rounds. Nowhere near as bloody and brutal this battle is going to get, and she was destroyed," I replied forlornly.

"Kieran," she said gently. "You have no idea what it's like watching someone you care about take a beating, to stand there and knowingly watch then take hit after hit without being able to do anything about."

But Con's my best friend. She must have known that he would never seriously hurt me. If she can't handle that, what hope have I got?" I asked earnestly.

"I hate to break this to you," she said with a chuckle, "but neither of you were pulling your punches. All she saw were two of the best fighters in the world knocking the stuffing out of each other. It was the first time she's ever seen you raise a hand to someone, so you're going to have to give her some time to adjust."

"What if she never adjusts? You're fine with Con being in the ring, but she looked terrified."

Em stood up a little straighter, her gentle expression becoming a little more serious. "I am not, nor will I ever be, fine with my husband being in the ring. When he stands on that canvas, I fake it. I put on this veneer of serenity, and I stand there and be who he needs me to be. Every time, I have faith that he will kick arse and bring home a victory. But my fear, that one stray punch will hurt him badly, is every bit as strong as my faith."

I swallowed hard, my throat completely dry. I had absolutely no idea that she felt that way.

"Why do you do it then? Why do you go with him to fights and let him do what he does?" I asked, confused.

"Because it's who he is. It's who he was born to be. I want him to hang up his gloves when he's ready, not because he wants to please me. So, for however long that takes, I'll be there for him. I think Marie loves you, and if I'm right, she'll do the same. Today was a shock, but I'd bet good money that by tomorrow, she'll be the happy-go-lucky girl we all know and love."

"You think she loves me?" I asked quietly, not quite able to stop a small smile.

"Who doesn't?" Em replied.

* * *

I rubbed my clean-shaven jaw and sighed, my stare unwavering from the door.

"She'll be here," Con assured me with a pat on the back. I wished I could have shared his optimism, but it had been twenty four hours. She sent me a text apologising that she'd left, and explaining that she was tired and that she'd see me tomorrow. When I called, her phone had been switched off. I spend the night tossing and turning, fighting the urge to go to her instead of giving her time.

"I'm sorry, Kier. We have to leave now or we might not make it to the weigh-in on time," Heath said sympathetically. They all knew who I'd been waiting for, and with every passing minute, their faces began to mirror the desperation I was feeling. Reluctantly, I stood, put on my leather riding jacket, and grabbed my helmet. There was nothing I wanted more than to climb on my bike and track her down. To make up for the days and nights that I hadn't been able to spend with her. To finally make her mine. I couldn't do it though. No matter what. Every man here had invested something in getting me this far. They'd invested something in me, and I wouldn't let them down.

Irish meant the world to me, but deep down in my gut was a burning need to climb into the ring, open myself up, and see what I could do. Con's problem was containing himself, keeping control of himself long enough to make magic happen. My problem was releasing that control. I needed to know, once and for all, what I could do, whether I was good enough to make it. I didn't want to be an old man lying in my bed and wondering what I could have been if only I'd taken a chance.

And I was taking it.

That didn't mean that this was an either-or situation though. Irish was mine, whether she knew it or not. There might be a million guys more deserving of her than me, but I knew how rare and precious she was, and I wasn't letting her go. If a million worthy guys wanted her, they'd have to get through me. Because no one would take care of her, fucking worship her, like I would. Tomorrow I was going to own the fight, and when I was done, I was coming for her. If it took the rest of my life, I was going to make her fall for me as hard as I'd fallen for her. With that binding resolution and determination in mind, I followed the boys confidently out the door. What I found outside almost brought me to my knees.

"Hey, I was beginning to think I'd missed you," Irish said quietly. Her cheeks were flushed pink with the cold, her hands stuffed deep into the pockets of her short, leather jacket. Honestly? I'd never seen a more fucking beautiful sight. The weight I'd been carrying on my shoulders all day lifted as she spoke. Without saying a word, I strode over to her. Holding onto the soft woollen scarf that rested around her neck, I pulled her to me and rested my forehead gently against hers. My eyes drifted shut as I inhaled deeply, drawing the apple scent deep into my lungs. Hungry for more, I nuzzled her neck, my lips desperately close to her smooth, peachy skin. I was millimetres away from seeing if she tasted as good as she smelled, but if I started, I'd never stop. She giggled, my cold nose tickling her. The sound was music to my ears.

"You came back," I whispered to her.

"I never left you," she replied.

"I was worried I'd scared you off. You know, seeing how violent the fighting can be. Seeing how violent I can be," I admitted.

She thought carefully, her brow furrowed in concentration, before she answered. "I'm not stupid. I knew you were all fighters and what that meant. I knew you weren't a choir boy. But I never realised how it would feel to watch someone try to hurt you. I wanted you to win, but I was petrified you'd get hurt. The look on Con's face was just... terrifying," she replied.

Tilting her chin up with my knuckle, I looked her deep in the eyes.

"The world around us, whether it's in the gym or between the ropes, I've got that. I can control that. But I need to know that this," I said, gesturing between the two of us, "is rock solid. Without you, I can't breathe anymore. When I think of doing this without you, there's a pain in my chest that won't go away. I can fight anyone you put in front of me. I will defeat any man who tries to stand against me, but I need you with me."

"I'll always be with you, Kier," she whispered. "Always." Wrapping her hand around my neck, she pressed her lips against mine. Reaching around her waist, I pulled her tightly against me, not wanting a breath of air between us. She opened her mouth to me, and I lost the ability to think. One of us moaned, but I had no idea who. I didn't care. Her tongue slid against mine, and I lost it. I wanted to be gentle, but she was an addiction I was desperate to feed. She shivering as I moved my hand under her jacket and sweater to stroke the naked skin at the base of her spine. Her hand wound around my hair and gripped my hair with urgency. She was as consumed by the kiss as I was, oblivious to anything else.

"What the feck did I say about feckin' shenanigans going on in my gym?" Danny shouted, making us jump guiltily apart.

"Ah, leave 'em alone," Tommy replied. "They're not inside. They're on the doorstep. Besides, we're enjoying the show."

Irish buried her face into my chest in embarrassment. I would have worried, but I caught her shy smile before she hid. Looking over my shoulder, I could see the fuckers all lined up, watching us with amusement. Tommy was even tucking into a bag of crisps as he spectated.

"Fuck off," I told them jovially, wrapping my arm protectively around my girl.

"All of you feck off," Danny said as he locked the door to the gym. "He's on stage in an hour, and we're already feckin' late!"

CHAPTER SIXTEEN

MARIE

We made it to Kieran's weigh-in by the skin of our teeth. Following Heath through the back door of the arena, we passed through dozens of burly security guards in black caps and T-shirts, who all nodded at Con and Kieran like they knew them. Finally, we were herded into a dressing room. It was pretty basic with a mirror and a few chairs, but from the way the guys were standing around, I didn't think we'd be in there for long.

"Well, this is exciting, isn't it!" Em exclaimed.

"You act like you've never been to one of these before. You must have done dozens of them," I remarked.

"I've never been to a weigh-in before," she explained. "At the fights, I sit with Nikki if she comes, but all the boys are with me. Only Kieran and Danny are in O'Connell's corner. But at the weigh-ins, all of the boys go on stage with him. I don't want to be in the media photos, and O'Connell doesn't like me being unprotected, so I usually stay at home or the gym with a babysitter," she said, rolling her eyes at Con's overprotectiveness.

"I won't have to go on stage, will I?" I asked in horror.

"Not if you don't want to, love," Kieran said, wrapping his hands around my waist and pulling me to stand snugly between his legs.

"I'm good just watching from the sidelines, as long as that's okay with you?" I said to him.

"As long as you're here with me, I don't care where you stand," he said.

"Come and stand with me, baby girl. I'll take care of you," Tommy said, winking at me.

"I changed my mind," Kier said, giving Tommy a death stare. "I do care where you stand."

"Where's Albie?" I asked Liam. He answered with a shy, secret smile that he always wore when he was thinking about his boyfriend.

"He's having dinner with his family tonight. His mum and sisters have been shopping for stuff for us. You know, bedding, towels, and shit. They wanted me to come too so they could show us everything, but your old man needed me more," he said.

"You should have said, mate. I would've understood if you wanted to go there instead," Kier told him.

"Nah, you're all right," Liam replied. "Albie's mum understands how important this is. Besides, I have a feeling that dinner with his family is gonna be a pretty regular thing from now on," Liam replied.

"She's cool then, about you boning her son and all?" Tommy enquired.

Kieran jumped in before Liam got mad and hit him. "You still looking for a guy, Tommy boy? Liam and Albie are solid, and I know you've had a torch for me all these years, but I'm off the market too. Somewhere out there is the guy for you though."

"What the ever-loving fuck!" Tommy protested, sounding pissed. "I wasn't asking if he was gonna be single any time soon. I was just asking if Albie's family is cool with him being a friend of Dorothy. Besides which, for the millionth time, I ain't fuckin' gay!"

"Whatever you say, Tommy," Liam said, joining in their fun. "But anytime you feel the urge to experiment, you just call."

Tommy leaned away from Liam, looking absolutely horrified. "You follow that offer up by touching any part of my body, and I will knock you the fuck out," Tommy warned. If their messing with him hadn't been funny enough, watching a guy of Tommy's size threatening Liam, who was big enough to squash him like a bug, made me giggle.

Suddenly, the door opened and one of the organisers, wearing an ID badge from a lanyard around his neck, said to Heath, "It's time."

Kier kissed the side of my neck, then let me go. "Heath is going to lead you to your seats in the front row then join us on stage. When we finish, he'll come and get you and bring you back here."

"Okay, love. I'll try not to jump on you when you start getting your kit off," I replied. Threading his hand into my hair, he kissed me hard before letting me go again.

"You can jump on me anytime. But if you do it in front of a couple of hundred people and a television audience, then be prepared for them to get a show," he whispered.

"Best keep my appreciation of your washboard abs until after the fight then, when I can show my admiration privately," I whispered back, making him groan.

"Shit, you really want me going out there with a hard-on?"

"Only if it's for me."

"Always." He kissed my neck playfully, making me squirm and giggle.

"For fuck's sake, Earnshaw, separate Romeo and Juliet over here and let's get this show on the road," Danny barked to Heath. We grinned at each other as I followed Heath and Em out of the room, listening to Danny mumble, "I'm too old for this shit," under his breath.

* * *

"Seriously? Of all the cool names you could have picked when you registered me, 'The Storm' was the best you could come up with?" Kieran said to Con.

"What? You don't get it? A storm is a baby hurricane, you know, like you're the smaller, less-powerful version of me," Con answered, chuckling at his own cleverness.

"Very fuckin' funny, arsehole," Kieran replied. But I knew he wasn't mad about it. Kieran had weighed in at two hundred and twenty pounds. Apparently that was exactly the same weight as Con when he'd fought for the same title. The boys had taken it as a good omen and had been in great spirits ever since.

"Where on earth are we going now?" I asked, chuckling at

Kieran's exuberance. I expected that we'd go straight home, but to my surprise, we followed the convoy of guys straight passed Kieran's place and kept driving for another ten minutes.

"We're following tradition," he replied. His fingers threaded through mine as we climbed the steps of an old church. It was surreal to have gone from the media circus that was the weigh-in, to the calm serenity that was a Catholic church at night, but then nothing about my time with Kieran had been normal. Everyone looked comfortable as they found a seat in the back pews, so I followed Kieran's lead and nestled in close when he wrapped his arm around me. Feeling a little tired, I rested my head on his shoulder as I listened to the guys analyse the evening, jumping when the sound of a closing door echoed loudly.

"Well, lads, are ya' all ready for the big night then?" the priest said, rubbing his hands together excitedly as he walked towards us.

"We are indeed, Father Pat," Danny answered as he stood up to shake hands.

"That's grand news," Father Pat replied. "And what odds are Ratray's giving him, would you happen to know?"

"Twenty to one, on account of his ranking," Tommy replied. I looked from him back to Father Pat in shock.

"Bloody hell, we'll make a killing," Father Pat blurted out. It was clear the comment had fallen out of his mouth, because he made the sign of the cross and muttered, "Bless me, Father, for I have sinned," under his breath straight after.

"So, how much shall I put you down for then?" Tommy asked him.

"Let's say two hundred pounds," Father Pat replied. "The pew cushions need replacing, and at twenty to one, that would about do. Mrs Gilbert, who does the flowers, has asked if you can put her down for twenty pounds as well. She would do it herself when she does the Irish lottery, but her arthritis has been playing her up lately."

"Right you are," Tommy replied, taking a pencil and paper from his back pocket to mark down the odds.

"No pressure to win then, Father," Kieran commented wryly.

"My boy, you have this in the bag," Father Pat replied. "Besides, when there are pew cushions involved, God is always on your side. Now you're starting to look a little nervous over there. No doubt that look will better your odds, but at two hundred pounds, you're not doing anything for my nerves, so we'd best be having you first."

Kieran squeezed my hand, then stood up to follow the priest into what I assumed was the vestry. Seconds later, Em slid into his empty seat.

"Do you have any idea what's going on, because I've been Catholic my whole life and this has never happened to me in church before?" I asked her.

"Don't worry, I was just as shocked when Con brought me here before his first big fight. Father Pat likes to have a flutter on all the boy's bouts, but he can't be seen betting when there's big money involved. Then again, he considers anything over ten pounds to be betting big," she explained.

"Isn't it wrong though? Don't they feel the pressure of letting him down if they don't win?"

"I think it's the opposite for them. They see it as a show of faith. That he believes in them enough to bet church money on them."

"He's betting church funds!" I exclaimed.

"No, it's his salary he bets, but he puts all of his winnings back into the place," she reassured me, which did seem slightly less scandalous. Noble even.

"What did Kieran mean when he said this was tradition?"

"The night before any of the boys, young or old, have a big fight, everyone from the club goes to confession. It's Danny's way of making sure whoever is fighting has a clear head. All of the guys join him because we're a family. Only one of us goes into the ring, but with us behind him, he's never alone."

My heart warmed at her words, and I realised how special a moment this was. Kieran was making me a part of his family, and the bond between them all couldn't have been stronger. When he finally emerged, his cheeks were flushed. Whatever was said, it must have been pretty scandalous to make him blush, but I never got to find out because Father Pat called my name.

Dutifully, I stood and followed as he led me to a small antechamber. When the door closed behind us, he turned to face me.

"Right then. Cup of tea?" he asked.

"Um, that would be lovely. Thank you," I answered politely. I stood awkwardly, unsure of myself and what to do. I'd been to confession many times before, but tea and betting had never been involved.

"Take a seat, my dear. I think I've got some chocolate biscuits in here somewhere, but I can't be sure. If not, I've definitely got some lovely custard creams. I usually get Tommy in first as his list is the longest, but the cheeky little bugger can devour a packet of biscuits in less time than it takes me to say a Hail Mary."

I smiled as I took a seat. He had a way about him that made you feel less like a stranger and more like a friend.

"Bingo," he called out and popping out from behind the curtain of what I assumed from the sound of a boiling kettle was a little kitchenette. He lobbed a packet of chocolate fingers at me. Thinking it would be rude not to, after all his efforts to hunt them down, I opened the packet and took one. Five biscuits later, he handed me my cup and I pushed the packet guiltily towards him.

"This is nice," he said, dunking two in his tea and sucking off the chocolate before dipping them again and finishing them off. I couldn't help but laugh at his childish antics.

"Best way to eat them," he told me. "Now, I hear that you have a weak heart."

"Wow, that's direct. Um, yes, I had a lot of cardiac surgery when I was younger."

"I'm sorry if I've offended you with my abruptness. I'm afraid that old age and too many years with the Driscoll's boys have robbed me of all tact. I'm used to plain talking," he answered, sheepishly.

"I'm not offended, Father. I guess I'm just not used to people wanting to discuss it."

"That's understandable. But I think it's good to talk about the things that worry us. Worrying doesn't take away our troubles. It just robs us of the strength we need to deal with them."

"Has Kieran been sharing his worries with you?" I asked. He seemed to favour directness, so I didn't think he'd find my question rude.

"Of course. It's what I'm here for, especially tonight of all nights. Better that he gets anything off his chest that he needs to, rather than take it into the ring with him," he explained. "Of course, what ails him isn't what you'd imagine. I think it's fair to say that he's avoided long-term relationships because he's experienced the pain of watching his mother lose the love of her life. He's grown up believing that love is like a fire that will burn you. Now that he's met you, he sees not what the fire can burn, but what it can forge."

I paused, my cup raised halfway towards my mouth, and stared in shock at his profoundness.

"Goodness, that was very deep, wasn't it? I should write some of this down. Perhaps less people would fall asleep in my sermons if I actually wrote them in advance." He chuckled.

"You don't prepare a sermon for mass?"

"Not usually, dear. I've become very adept at winging it, depending on my audience and whether I've had the odd pint of Guinness the night before. Although I do find that my congregation donates a little more generously to the collection if I keep it short and sweet. So perhaps my pearls of wisdom are best revealed over a cup of tea and some nice biscuits."

He held out the packet of chocolatey temptations, and it took all of my will power to refuse.

"So, if Kieran isn't worried about my heart, then I'm guessing you must be, or we wouldn't be having this conversation." I waited for his condemnation, for him to give me all of the reasons that I gave Kieran about why we shouldn't be together.

"My girl, you couldn't be further from the truth. No matter how long or briefly your path will lie alongside his, love doesn't change the destination. It just makes the journey all the sweeter. He is with you all the way now, no matter what. Once he makes a decision, he's not one to worry about the what-ifs or the maybes. What does concern him is *your* fears. He doesn't want your anxiety to blind you to the great things that lie ahead for you both."

"Of course I worry about these things. How could I not? And if you were in my shoes, you would worry too."

"Perhaps," he replied. "But one day we'll all leave this world behind. The only thing that's important is that you live a life you will remember."

"I've heard that before. Is that a famous quote?"

"It's Avicii. Great song. I have a laptop now thanks to Tommy, so I get all sorts of music through that YouTube."

"Well, it's a great philosophy, but I've agonised over this stuff for most of my life."

"All the more reason to let it go, child."

* * *

By the time we made it home, I felt a kind of peace I hadn't ever felt before. On the back of Kieran's bike there was nothing in the world that existed other than the two of us. There was nothing but open road ahead of us and a future that we were travelling towards together. I was almost sorry when we came to a stop.

"When your fight is over, can we take a day off and just ride as far as we can?" I asked him wistfully.

"Baby, we can do anything you want." He kissed the tip of my nose as he helped me remove my helmet. "It kind of makes me horny that I've turned you into a biker chick."

"Everything makes you horny." I laughed at his almost permanent state of arousal.

"You're not wrong, love." Bending down, he hoisted me over his shoulder in a firefighter's lift. With one hand holding our helmets and the other halfway up my denim-clad thigh, he opened the front door and bounded up the stairs.

"Kieran! Put me down! You're supposed to be resting. What if you pull a muscle or something?" I admonished.

"Please, have you weighed yourself lately? I curl more than you weigh."

"What's so urgent that you can't wait for me to walk up the stairs?" My voice stuttered as he took the steps two at a time.

"In less than twenty-four hours, you'll be riding my love train all the way to paradise, and I need a treat to tide me over until we make it to the station."

I burst out laughing as he set me down gently, then ushered me in through the door as soon as it was open.

"Love train?" I asked, still smiling.

"What? I thought it was more poetic than cock."

CHAPTER SEVENTEEN

KIERAN

"What are you doing?" she asked breathlessly.

Stripping us both at the same time, I couldn't get her clothes off fast enough. Feeling her body pressed against mine on the long bike ride home had my testosterone levels skyrocketing. I was amped. I was primed.

I was ready.

It was a euphoria I couldn't begin to describe, knowing that my body was in peak physical condition. I was fitter, faster, and fiercer than I'd ever been. If Irish asked me to conquer the world for her tomorrow, I could do it. But it was more than that. In this game, fitness was only half the fight. The other half was mental. My friends. My family. My girl. All of them had a hand in creating the man who would climb into that ring tomorrow. The man I had become.

The smell of her perfume, the touch of her skin, every single thing about her had every one of my synapsis firing. My need to claim her, to possess her, was almost violent. She owned every part of me, and tonight I was going to show her.

Reaching behind me, I pulled my T-shirt over my head and threw it on the floor with the rest of our clothes. Desperate to mould her body to mine, I pushed her gently up against the door and kissed the ever-loving fuck out of her. The taste of her sweet, plump lips was addictive.

I feasted.

Spearing my hand into her soft curls, I devoured her. Our lips parted for the briefest of time. Our need for each other was stronger than our need to breathe. I knew this wouldn't end how I wanted it to, with me buried so deeply inside her that I couldn't tell where she ended and I began, but just when I was about to pull away, she touched her tongue tentatively against mine. It was like adding fuel to the fire. She moaned into my mouth and the sound vibrated straight to my dick. There was no way I could possibly get any harder than I was then.

Torturing myself some more, I slid my hand up her thigh and pulled it up to wrap around my hip. Grinding my hips against hers, I pressed the seam of her jeans against her core with every thrust I could tell by the hitch in her breathing that she was close, and she wasn't alone. Easing her back down from the edge, I gave her lips one last peck, then dropped her leg and picked her up bridal style.

The street lamps outside illuminated the room enough that I didn't need to waste time turning on the lights. The animal in me wanted to throw her on the bed and rip the rest of her clothes off. The man in me wanted to revere and nurture her. The look she gave me, so full of love and tenderness, satisfied both. Laying her down gently, I hovered over her, putting my weight of my forearms, and I couldn't help but stare. The contrast of her pale, soft skin against my own fascinated me. I had no idea why someone so pure and so beautiful, inside and out, would choose me, but I would never take her for granted.

"I love you," I whispered, so quietly that I wondered if she heard me. She stilled beneath me, and after a moment that went on for eternity, she tilted my chin so that my gaze met her own.

"I love you too," she replied, and just like that, all was right with the world. Grinning with pure, unadulterated happiness, I kissed her. Something between us had shifted. Not only was there a knowing of myself, of what I had trained my body to do, now there was a knowing of us and of who we could be together.

I undid the top button of her jeans and slid them down legs that I fantasised about. Regularly.

Her hands moved to my belt buckle, but I stopped her.

"Not yet. Tonight is about you, and I'm barely keeping it together as it is. Tomorrow night you can get me naked before we even leave the locker room. But if my cock so much as touches any part of your body tonight, I'm going to come, and I really don't want Danny making mincemeat of my balls."

"Maybe we should stop then," she suggested. "It doesn't seem fair that you keep pleasuring me when you can't get anything from it."

"Trust me, Irish, I get plenty from it. Now, I've got some pent-up energy to burn off, so just relax and enjoy the ride."

"Yes, sir," she replied, and fuck if that didn't make my dick twitch.

Her lacy underwear looked black in the half light and so delicate against my big, clumsy hands as I slid the straps of her bra down her shoulders. She finished what I had started and removed it completely. When she was done, she reached for her panties, but I stilled her hand. Almost reverently, I peeled them down her legs, feeling the tremble that belied her confidence. Nothing had ever compared to that moment. Making love to someone I loved so completely fulfilled me in a way that nothing else ever would. It was possible that the tremble wasn't hers, but mine.

I moved to lay down beside her. Kissing her softly, I traced circles on the small of her back until she shivered and buried herself in the heat of my body.

"Tell me again," I whispered.

"I love you, Kier," she replied, knowing instantly what I meant. It was all I wanted to hear, all I *needed* to hear for the rest of my life. She parted her legs as my touch moved closer to her core. Her lips left mine as she arched her back in delicious anticipation, and I gave her what she craved. She moaned as my fingers traced gentle circles across her folds. I'd never seen anything more beautiful than her body in the throes of ecstasy. Even her surgical scar was flawless. It was the badge of honour that made my girl a warrior. Leaning forward, I ran my tongue along it before peppering it with kisses.

Irish was so close that she gripped my arm fiercely. The ache to shed my jeans and sink my body deep into hers was almost unbearable. Knowing that I wouldn't last much longer, I slipped two fingers inside of her and flicked my thumb against her clit. Her grip was almost painful as she cried out. Her body bowed in orgasm before she melted boneless against me. The whole time she stared deep into my eyes, her gaze unwavering. It was the most intimate moment I'd ever experienced. As I tucked her exhausted body against my own, I wondered how three little words would ever be enough to convey just how this felt.

* * *

Every fighter brought something different to the ring. Some carried rage and looked to harness it. Some took fear and tried to overcome it. Fewer still, like Con, made magic. Each man brought what he needed to in order to give himself that edge to win. I brought pride. Pride and pain. Before any fight, I would look out across the ring, imagining that my da was standing in the back somewhere, a pint in his hand, talking the ear off his mates about how I was his boy and how proud he was of me. It didn't matter whether I won or not. I knew he'd love seeing me fight. He was gone, had been for a long time now, but that didn't stop me from imagining his voice shouting my name from across the room, cheering me on.

I came into the ring with pride, and I left with it. But the pain? That I gave that to the man I left behind. The rage at knowing my da wasn't watching from the front row, just where he should have been, that I bottled up each and every day. When that bell sounded, all of that anger and frustration went into every hit. Inside those ropes, I became the man I needed to be. Losing a loved one was a pain you carried with you, but one day, if you're lucky enough, you meet someone who takes your pain and makes it their own, who makes you feel such overwhelming and powerful things that you find yourself forgetting to be sad. That was how it was when I was with Irish. After what we'd done together, after the words we'd spoken, I wanted nothing more than to wrap her in my arms and love her for as long as she'd let me.

It was why I had to go.

She looked so peaceful, that I couldn't resist bending to kiss her soft, plump lips. She woke with a start and, looking me over, clocked the fact that I was dressed.

"Where are you going?" she asked.

"To get my head in the game, love. If I spend one more hour in bed with you, I'll forget my reason to fight. This time tomorrow, I'll be all yours, but I owe the boys tonight."

Grabbing the front on my sweater, she pulled me forward slightly.

"You owe it to yourself as well. Now go do what you've got to do and make me proud. I'll be the one in green waiting for you in the front row," she replied with a lazy grin.

"You're wearing green?" Nothing sexier than seeing my girl sitting front row and wearing my colours. Shit, I just about came every time she walked round wearing any of my clothes. I had a particular preference for seeing her in nothing but plain white panties and one of my hoodies.

"Of course I'm wearing your colours. That's how they'll know I'm your girl. Besides, you can wear an England shirt on St George's Day and we'll call it even."

I shuddered at the very thought.

"Everyone will know you're my girl by the guard ring I'll have round you," I said, making her roll her eyes.

"Honestly, what do you think is going to happen to me? It's a professional boxing match."

"Have you ever been to a boxing match before, love?"

"Well, no."

"There'll be men and beer, and you with the sexiest arse I've ever seen. If even one fucker tries chatting you up or starting something while I'm ramped up and in the ring, I'm likely to lose my boxing licence for life."

She gave me that long-suffering look that said I was overreacting, but cupped my jaw as she leaned forward to kiss me gently.

"Then I'll stay in your circle of friends until you've won yourself a title, because there's only one man I'm starting something with tomorrow," she said, talking me down from my over-possessive ledge.

"Hold onto your knickers, Irish. There's a storm coming." With a cheeky grin, I gave her one last, lingering kiss before picking up my training bag and walking away.

"Cheesiest line ever," she hollered after me.

"But it made you wet though, didn't it?" I called back and closed the door to the perfect sound of her giggle.

* * *

As I made my way out of the building, I clocked Con's car parked by the curb with the engine running.

"Are you fuckin' psychic then?" I asked him, jumping into the passenger seat.

"I don't need to be, dickhead," he replied with a chuckle. "I just think exactly the same way you do. Nowhere I'd be the night before a fight 'cept with my girl. Nowhere I need to be the day of the fight than as far away from her as possible. Can't get your head in the right place for a fight with a woman who makes you soft."

"Why the lift then?"

"I was feeling generous, dickhead. I'm pretty sure Em's bet money on you. Last thing I need is you falling off your bike because your head is somewhere else and losing me good money."

"Wow! I'm feelin' the fuckin' love over here, brother. So where we goin?"

"Where we always go," he replied as he pulled away from the curb. "Home."

* * *

Turns out that home is exactly where I needed to be. It was a Saturday, so a lot of the younger kids were in Driscoll's gym, training with Danny and Liam. When Con was in the country, he pitched in with Saturday training as well. The kids stared at him in awe, like he was some kind of rock star. I guessed to them he was. Maybe someday they'd look at me like that.

"Kier, will you help me with the bag again?" Pete asked me. He was about ten years old with the spindliest little arms and legs you'd ever seen, but the kid was all heart. No matter who was here, he always came to me for help first.

"Sure thing." I walked over to hold the bag for him. He didn't need anyone really. It hardly moved when he hit the thing, but I'd never damage his pride by pointing that out. After an hour of coaching, I could see he was getting tired.

"That's it for today, but you're doing great. You've really improved over the last few weeks. Just remember to keep practicing that jab combination. Speed is every bit as important as strength and accuracy."

"You really think I'm doin' good?" he asked with a hopeful smile.

"Definitely. I don't think you're gonna have to worry about the heavy-weight division anytime soon, but you're a solid fly weight. You keep up the hard work, and I might be able to talk Danny into letting you fight next year."

"Thanks, Kieran." He looked like he was struggling with his gloves, so patting the seat next to me, I waited for him to sit down before pulling off the Velcro tabs for him.

"Can I ask you something?" he said curiously.

"As long as it's about boxing. I don't fancy any questions where I'd have to explain my answer to your ma later."

"Fair enough," he said with a smirk.

"Are you scared. You know, about tonight?"

I took a deep breath then leaned back against the wall and let it all out.

"I'm not scared of who I'm fighting, and I'm not scared of losing, and I'm sure as hell not afraid of getting hit. Am I nervous? Sure. My girl's gonna be there, and I'd prefer not to make an arse outta meself and get knocked down on live TV. But no, I'm not scared. I'm taking everything I need into that ring with me, and I'll be walking right back out with it as well. Title or no title, that ain't gonna change."

"Maybe I need a girl too," he said, making me laugh.

"Just focus on finding some solid mates, ones who'll always look out for you before they look out for themselves. If you're lucky, the girl will find you." I ruffled his hair. "Now bugger off," I said jovially. "Your ma's probably outside waiting for you."

"Good luck." He grabbed his drink bottle and ran out the door. When I was a kid, you had to be sixteen to fight here. Now, from the age of ten you could box at Driscoll's on Saturdays. Maybe Danny had seen how it had turned mine and Con's lives around. Or maybe he was getting soft in his old age. Whatever it was, his change of heart was a good thing. Kids enjoy sports for the love of the game. It was adults who took something pure and beautiful and twisted it into something commercial. Having them around taught us a lesson it was good to remember.

When the place emptied, I spent a couple of hours with Con in the office, running over and over footage of my opponent's fights. I'd seen it all before, but running through it again kept me sharp. He was a big fucker. If I let him get too close because I was slow on my feet, I was gonna be in a world of hurt. My foot work needed to be instinctive.

"Do you think I can beat him?" I asked Con.

He scoffed and went back to fast-forwarding the tape. After a few seconds, he turned to see me watching him.

"I'm sorry, were you waiting for an answer to the stupidest

fuckin' question I've ever heard?" he asked sarcastically. "I don't *think* you can win. I *know* you can win. You know why?" He didn't wait for me to answer. "Because I can beat him, and I know you can beat me. Some of the time. Very occasionally, when I'm having an off day," he added, making me roll my eyes. "But none of it counts if you don't know it too," he added. I nodded, knowing he was right.

"Enough with the fight tapes," he said and, reaching across the desk, grabbed my iPod and chucked it to me. "Go and get in the zone."

Patting him on the back in thanks, I walked out and found a bench to sit on at the far side of the gym. Sticking in my earbuds, I closed my eyes and focused on my breathing, letting the music wash over me. The smell of hard work and victory that was unique to this place permeated my nostrils and grounded me in the present. With every beat of the song, I saw the bout play over in my head. I saw how I was going to step, how he was going to punch, and how I would react. A few hours later, I saw him go down and I opened my eyes. It was time.

CHAPTER EIGHTEEN

MARIE

I'd never seen anything like the media circus that was a professional boxing match. Heath was flat-out networking with television networks and potential new sponsors, so Kier had Tommy pick Em and me up for the fight.

"Do I look okay?" I asked her nervously as I smoothed down the front of my emerald green wrap dress.

"You look beautiful," she assured me.

There was nobody in this room right now who knew how I was feeling better than she did. I didn't even have to ask her to come over and get ready with me. She knew I needed her, and she was there. I cursed the stupid medication that wouldn't let me have a shot of something for my nerves though. Lord knew I could have done with it.

A huge queue of people was patiently filtering their way into the arena when we arrived, but we were taken around the back. I expected the hallways around the locker rooms to be empty, but the place was packed. Tommy explained that they were a mixed bag of reporters, promoters, and staff. Lots of them were hoping to get a quick interview with the guys, but I doubted that either camp would allow that this close to the fight.

"I don't even know who he's fighting," I said to them both.

"Konstantin Schmidt," Tommy replied. "He's an up and comer like Kieran. His old man was a heavyweight boxing champion, and his kid brother is working his way through the light heavyweight rankings. Schmidt has a bit of a chip on his shoulder though. His old man set up the fight, and Schmidt doesn't think our Kier's a worthy opponent. He's pissed off at Kier trading on Con's name."

"I just assumed that Kieran had lots of fights before that put him in contention," I said.

"It works differently for different fighters. Con worked his way up the ranks. He could have tried trading on Danny's old title, but that was so long ago I don't think it would have worked. A lot of this is about the connections you have and how good a match you'd be for the other fighter. If you haven't got a lot of experience under your belt, it can make the fights harder to put together and promote, because people aren't going to buy tickets for a shit fight. Lots of people will come because Con's camp is promoting it, but your boy is about to become an international heavyweight fighter in his own right. It's up to Schmidt how he wants to come to terms with that," Tommy said, shrugging indifferently.

"He sure has a lot of support here," Em said worriedly.

"So does Kier," Tommy replied. "Trust me, support for both

of them is a good thing. If this thing plays out like I think it's going to, your boy's going to be offered big things after this. It's gonna be a hell of a show."

He pushed open the changing room door, and I let out the breath I didn't even know I was holding. Kieran was sitting with Con knelt on the floor in front of him, taping up his knuckles. They both looked up at our entrance, and Kier's face lit up with a smile.

"Hey, love. How's our boy doing?" Em said to Con as she placed her hands on his shoulders and leaned down to kiss him.

"He's good, Sunshine. His eye's on the prize," Con replied.

Kieran didn't say anything to me, so I stood awkwardly at the door. The second Con was done, he tapped the back of Kier's hands to indicate he was finished, and Kier launched himself from his seat. Grabbing my hand, he pulled me into the bathroom. I was so shocked I didn't even have time to worry what everyone must have thought. Pushing me gently against the closed door, he stroked his calloused fingertips down my cheek.

"You're so fuckin' beautiful," he whispered. "I can't believe you're here with me."

"Always," I whispered back. "No matter what."

"Even if I get my arse kicked tonight and completely embarrass myself?"

"That won't happen, but even if it did, then yes, even then."

He closed his eyes briefly and moved his lips against mine. His kiss was so breathtakingly perfect that longing and excitement raced through me, chasing away all of my nerves and doubts. The violent maelstrom of fear and worry that had always existed between us, about my health and his fight, all of it was gone. In its place, the air was electrically charged with excitement, longing, confidence, and love. When he rested his forehead against mine, I felt them all. There was no other word for it than magic.

"I'm going to ask you to marry me one day, you know that, right?" he told me.

"One day I might say yes."

"One day...," he whispered.

Three hard knocks sounded on the door.

"Enough shenanigans," Danny hollered out. "Kier, get your arse out here."

"Time to go to work, baby," I said to him.

"Bring it on." He smirked before giving me a quick kiss. We opened the door to a room full of grinning friends.

"Shame, shame, know your name!" Tommy teased, wagging his finger at us.

Kier laughed, and I buried my face in his side with embarrassment. I walked over to sit down by Em and watch the guys do their thing. Liam and Tommy talked quietly amongst themselves, while Con helped Kieran with his gloves before holding up some pads. I loved watching him. He moved so gracefully and fluidly, it was almost like he was weightless.

"We ain't practicing now, kid. This is for real," Danny murmured to Kieran as he fired into the pads. "Now, when you get out there, you know what to expect. The lights, the TV cameras, all of its nothin' but a feckin' circus. You gotta ignore it, you hear me? You focus on the dickless wonder in the ring. This guy is mean. He's cutthroat, and he wants nothin' more than to leave you on that canvas bleeding and broken while he walks away with your girl. So you tell me, are you gonna let that happen?"

"Hell no!" Kieran shouted.

"I can't hear you, kid. Are you gonna let that happen?" Danny asked again.

"Hell no!" Kier shouted louder.

"That's real good, kid. I'm proud of you. Now I want you to make everyone else proud, and you show 'em what we know you've all got," Danny said, slapping Kier on the back.

Kieran shadowboxed for a bit until Heath walked through the door, just before one of the officials.

"Mr Doherty, it's time," the official told Kieran before closing the door behind him.

"All good?" Kier asked Heath.

"All good," Heath replied. "You just focus on winning. I've got the rest sewn up."

Seemingly satisfied with his answer, Kier turned back to Con, who was holding out his robe.

"Bloody hell. Bit fuckin' fancy, ain't it?" Kier commented. The robe was silk, but it looked as though it had been made from the Irish flag.

"Courtesy of your sponsor for the fight," Heath explained.

Kier looked up at me. His predatory eyes narrowed, and I knew he was thinking about me wearing it later. I tried to suppress my smile, because I was thinking the exact same thing. I couldn't wait to see his face when he saw the emerald green underwear I was wearing under my dress. I'd even replaced the tiny bow in the middle of the bra with a bow in the colours that matched his robe. He was going to have a coronary when he peeled it off later.

Liam and Tommy both gave Kier a man hug, then touched their heads to his, in what I assumed was a gesture of good luck. Em hugged him and kissed his cheek, which earned a scowl from Con. After telling him to "kick some arse," she walked into O'Connell's arms to soothe his ruffled feathers.

"What are you thinking about?" he asked me. His gloves gripped either side of my waist as he rested his forehead against mine. I laid my hands on his rock-hard abs and sighed.

"I'm wondering how long it's going to take for you to knock him out, so you can do bad things to me," I answered, making him chuckle.

"Well, now I have extra incentive to hurry things up," he told me with a quick kiss.

Liam and Tommy walked Em and me to our seats, and I was more than a little overwhelmed. The arena was packed full, and the ring was surrounded by cameras, suits, and scantily clad ring and sponsor girls.

"Are you ready for this?" Em asked me.

"Is there ever any way to be ready for all of this?" I asked.

"Sure there is. After they've kissed you goodbye, they get into the zone, and they make themselves the biggest, toughest badarse in the room. The only thing that can mess with that is us. If they think we're hurt or worried or upset, it messes with their heads. So you get in the zone, just like they do. You take all your fear and anxiety and that feeling like you're going to vomit every time they take a hit, and you hide it behind a mask. The only thing you show the media vultures is how proud and confident you are that your man is going to completely kiss arse. That you know it, and soon they'll know it too."

"And if I actually think I am going to vomit?"

"Then swallow it and think of anything else, but do not leave your seat. If they see your empty seat, the fight's over for them."

I imagined my big guy hopping over the ropes to come and hold my hair back when I puked, and I knew she was right. Kieran had promised to stand by me, despite all my shit. The least I could do was hold my head high for him. Standing a little straighter, I pushed my shoulders back and walked confidently towards my seat. I was relieved to see Albie and Kieran's mother in the seats next to ours.

"You look beautiful," she told me.

"You too," I complimented back. And she really did. Her long-sleeved, fitted black dress, coifed hair, and understated jewellery were the epitome of Grace Kelly elegance. It seemed such a tragedy that she'd been widowed so young and had never remarried. But after meeting Kieran, I understood. Sometimes two people have a love so profound, that when one dies, the other has no choice but to wait for them in the next life.

"I'm practicing my 'proud and happy' face so that nobody realises I'm trying not to vomit or burst into tears," I confided in her.

"Thank God." She put her hand over her heart. "I thought I was the only one!"

She slipped her hand in mine and gave it a squeeze before we joined in with the applause as the MC made his way to the stage.

"Ladies and gentlemen, welcome to the main event of the evening. I am proud to present twelve three-minute rounds of heavyweight boxing, sponsored by Red Bull and MB Promotions. It is the IBF Heavyweight Championship, being broadcast around the world by Sky Sports Pay-per-view. Let's meet the fighters. Coming to the stage first and fighting out of the red corner, with ten victories, two by knockout, and only one defeat. With head coach Danny Driscoll. His official weigh-in being two hundred and twenty pounds. From Killarney, Ireland and trained here on your very doorstep, Kieran 'The Storm,' Doherty!" the MC hollered through the microphone. The crowd erupted in cheers as Kanye West's "Stronger" belted through the speakers.

"Did Kieran pick this?" I asked Em, standing up and clapping with everyone else.

"Tommy picked it. Kieran owed him a favour for fixing his mum's heating, and Tommy called it to pick his theme music. Mind you, Tommy has a thing for power ballads, so Kier could have done a lot worse," she shouted back to me.

The boys began to emerge through a walkway covered in Sky Sports and Red Bull banners. The powerful beat vibrated through the floor, and I could totally see why Tommy had chosen the soundtrack for their entrance. Con strutted confidently, his hoodie pulled over his head and his face a mask of concentration. I suspected it was his automatic game face for his own fights. Danny looked just as mean and stern, wearing his usual scowl, but Heath was all business.

The man who made my heart beat faster emerged and the crowd

went nuts. Unlike Con, he looked totally relaxed and in control as he searched for me. Meeting my eyes, he winked cheekily, making me laugh. God, that man made me melt just with a smile. He swaggered up the steps and into the ring like he didn't have a care in the world.

My smile turned to a frown as I watched the Red Bull ring girl move to his side. In tiny booty shorts, an over-sized red bull belt, and a crop top that made her huge tits look like a volcano about to erupt, I felt strangled by the tendrils of jealousy wrapping themselves around me. Standing as close to him as she possibly could without actually touching him, she put her hand on the hip she'd cocked out and pouted to the crowd as she pushed out her chest towards Kieran. I honestly didn't think he noticed until he followed my line of sight. Grinning at my affront, he moved to put his sponsor between them as they stood for a photo.

"I didn't like the ring girls either," Em said to me, grinning as she saw the expression on my face. "They have them at the fights too, along with round girls. But then I met one of them in the corridor before a fight. Her feet were killing her, but if they take those killer heels off or drop the plastic Barbie smile, then they get shit from the promoters. Her mum was sick, and she was trying to help out with the bills in between school. The money isn't great, but it's better than waitressing, so she could fit it in around college."

"Well, now I feel like a jealous bitch," I admitted.

"Don't worry, there's plenty of women out there who would happily run you over to be on the arm of a professional fighter, and you're going to have to grow a thick skin to deal with them. But as long as you remember that he's only got eyes for you, you'll be fine."

"Doesn't it bother you, watching the women throwing themselves at your husband?" I really wasn't trying to be a bitch, but she and Con were the most solid couple I'd ever met. There must be some secret to her taking all this stuff in stride.

"Of course it does, but the only thing I know with more certainty than how much I love him is how much he loves me. The people he cares about are the ones who were there for him when he had nothing. Anyone that sucks up to him now just pisses him off, women included."

I followed her gaze back to the stage where Con and Kieran were chatting as they kept their eyes fixed on us. Eventually, they both turned to Danny, and I knew he was getting them back in the zone.

"And for his opponent, fighting out of the blue corner, let's welcome to the stage the champion. With twenty-seven victories, ten wins by knockout, and zero losses. With head coach, Kris Van Der Berg. His official weigh-in being two hundred and thirty pounds. From Düsseldorf, Germany, the unbeaten Konstantin 'Bone Breaker' Schmidt!" the MC called out.

Schmidt's supporters erupted as the strains a familiar Red Hot Chilli Pepper's song boomed through the arena. The hairs on the back of my neck rose as the spotlight focused on a titan that materialised from the darkness. Unlike my man, who'd put his family first, this guy walked out with an army behind him. Dressed in matching tracksuits, two men held a belt each high in the air. I didn't think it was possible to make men much bigger than Kieran and Con, but I'd bet that Schmidt even had an inch or two and a couple of pounds on Liam.

As he got to the ring, Schmidt deliberately looked over and caught my eye. Remembering Em's words, I met his stare and tilted my chin in defiance. That was *my* man up there, and if Schmidt thought I'd let Kieran see fear on my face, he was sorely mistaken.

CHAPTER NINETEEN

KIERAN

"Man, your Marie's got some balls. Did ya see that look she gave Schmidt?" Con commented.

"Yeah, that fucker's gonna pay for eyeballing my girl," I replied.

"Is that a poncho he's wearing?"

"It's the wrong shape," I answered. "It looks more like one of them tabard things the three musketeers wear."

We both stared at him again, trying to work out if that's what it was.

"Either his sponsors made him wear it or he lost a bet," I remarked.

"Whatever it is, it's a fuckin' weird fashion choice if you ask me."

"They probably couldn't get a robe to fit him. Look at the size of the fucker."

"Do you know why Em won't buy anything other than them little baby tomatoes?" he asked me.

"Why?" I asked, confused as to where he was going with this.

"It's because she says the giant ones are all genetically modified and full of water. This fucker ain't no different. He's full of water, piss, and wind most likely. Big means heavy. Heavy means slow. He gets you on the ropes and you're gonna be in a world of hurt. So you stay mobile. You stay light, and you wait out the rounds until you wear him down. He goes for the knockouts 'cause he can't last the twelve rounds. You do what you need to do to get to the end of the fight, and then you go to work on him. Remember the plan and stick to it."

"Don't worry, mate. I've got this. But if I get caught and slapped around a bit, remind me of the plan between rounds. You know, in case I'm a bit concussed."

"Sweet Jesus," he said on a sigh. "You are such a candy-arse sometimes. Just get in there, knock him out, and let's go party. I plan on getting laid tonight, and if you don't get knocked out, you might get some action too."

"Is that an offer, big boy?" I teased.

"In your dreams, dipshit." He shoved my gum shield into my mouth as I grinned.

"For feck's sake, do you boys ever take anything seriously? Kier, you listen to Con now and stick to the plan. Your girl and your ma are down there watching. Make 'em proud," Danny added.

I bounced up and down and shook out my shoulders as I took it all in. All the pageantry and bullshit fell away, and just like that, I was a teenage punk, scrapping with my best friend in some spit and sawdust ring. I knew in my heart that I could take this fucker down. It wouldn't be easy by any stretch of the imagination, but I wasn't afraid of the fight, and I wasn't afraid to lose. I was going to give him absolutely everything I had, and if he was still standing at the end of it, then I'd shake his hand. After I kneeled him in the balls for disrespecting Irish of course. There was no shame in losing if you gave it all you had. Trying and failing takes courage. The real tragedy is in failing to try at all.

Schmidt was terrified of losing. I could see it in the clench of his teeth as his father shouted out rapid instructions in German, accompanied by angry hand gestures. By the way he kept looking at his promotors and the ridiculously huge entourage he'd brought with him, if he lost this title, he imagined there'd be more than a few angry words from papa Schmidt tonight. The referee signalled us both, and we moved to the centre of the ring.

"Right, boys, I want a good, clean fight tonight and protect yourself at all times. Now, touch gloves and move back to your respective corners," the referee said. He moved back, leaving Schmidt eyeballing me.

"I like your girl. She needs breaking in a little bit, but she looks like she'd enjoy it," he said with a thick German accent.

"Well, she told me to tell you that she liked your cape. Said it goes with your pretty eyes. She's a designer, so maybe I can introduce you when you get out of hospital, and you can exchange fashion tips," I replied, channelling *Deadpool*. Fuck, I loved that movie.

"You are a comedian. You think you are funny. Let's see you laughing when the fight is over." Clearly, I'd hit a nerve.

"You put that cape back on big boy, and I promise you I'll

laugh," I responded, making him sneer.

"Fuck you, arsehole!" He bashed his gloves down on top of mine before going back to his corner.

"Well, now I'm hurt," I retorted as I walked back to mine.

Danny and Con had already climbed out of the ring, and in the final seconds I glanced at my girls. Ma and Irish both sat ramrod straight and so serious they almost looked like they were in pain. They caught my eye, and I winked as I grinned. They both smiled back, though Ma rolled her eyes. Schmidt's little show of bravado had cut the cord of tension between us. I might take a beating, but I'd taken a beating before. At least now I was having fun.

The bell rang, and I did what I do best. I pissed him off. He came at me straight out of the gate, probably hoping to get me on the ropes for a first-round knockout. As if I'd have made it that easy for him. I danced and weaved around the canvas like I was born to it. I might have been big, but I was also fuckin' fast. I had to be growing up in the ring with Con. A few minutes of this and the crowd was getting restless as well. There was only one thing an audience at an international bout wanted, or at any boxing match as it happens, was blood. I'll bet Schmidt didn't think I'd be the one to give it to them first. He caught me in the ribs with a couple of glancing jabs as I was on the move, but made the mistake of glancing past me to see if the judges had clocked the hits. Dodging to the left, I left a clear line of sight between him and the judges as I threw all of my weight in a right hook to his face. They say that light travels faster than sound, which is probably why I noticed the splatter of blood before I heard the crack of his nose breaking. The referee moved in, just as the bell signalled the end of round one.

"Well, I certainly wasn't expecting that," commented Con with a chuckle as he swilled out my mouth. I spat the water into the bucket and wondered how long it would stay clear.

"Do you think this means he won't want to be friends?" I asked.

"Don't worry. I'm sure when he gets a few more of those ribs shots in, he'll feel better about himself," he replied. "There best not be any rib ticklin', ya hear me? He's got eleven pounds on you, and I want you to make him drag 'em round every inch of that canvas. You spent most of ya life shakin' your arse. Don't see any reason for you to stop now."

The bell rang just as Con shoved my guard back in my mouth. If I thought Schmidt would be intimated by the fact that I'd broken his nose, I was wrong. His old man had let it rip in the break, and I was guessing that Schmidt blamed me for it. For seven rounds, I wore him down, but this fucker knew what I was about. He'd learned his lesson in round one, and he wasn't making the same mistake twice. Darting to the right, I threw a left-right-left combination to his face, making the fatal mistake of leaving my liver unguarded. The fucker had me. He pounded a jab into me so hard, I figured I'd probably be pissing blood for a week. I was falling to my knees when he came in with a right uppercut and I saw stars. My head flipped back so far it felt like my back was breaking, but with my knees already buckled, I sprang forward and fell face first onto the canvas.

The crowd around me erupted, and the lights blurred together. The ringing in my ears was so loud. At first, all I could hear was the crowd, then the counting. By three, I heard Danny's voice.

"Get up! Open your eyes and climb those feckin' ropes!" he screamed.

I did it instinctively. I wasn't even sure what I was doing, but Danny rarely screamed. So when he did, it was instinct to do what I was told. Grabbing onto the first ropes, I pulled myself to my knees. By the count of seven, I was on my feet and had come round. That fucker had me seeing stars, but he hadn't knocked me out. It was a close call, but I'd made it to my feet before the count. I spent the last few seconds convincing the referee that I was fine. When he let us go, Schmidt flew at me. Determined to capitalise on my mistake, he threw combination after combination. I did well to fend them off, but I was literally saved by the bell.

"How ya doin', kid?" Danny asked, as he examined my side. Con filled my mouth with water, and it took a strength of will to lean to the side to spit it back out. My face was bleeding heavily, and I was a little shocked that uppercut hadn't knocked loose a few teeth.

"I'll be honest, Danny. I've been better." I was heavily winded, and if he caught me like that again, I wouldn't just be knocked out, I'd be hospitalised.

"If you could avoid getting knocked down again, I'd appreciate it. Your ma's been givin' me evil looks since the bell went, and I don't fancy havin' my balls busted all night."

"Ah, Danny, good to know that you care," I said, wheezy and laughing, fuck knows why. I was getting my arse kicked.

The bell rang out again, way before I was ready. During the next round, I guarded so well that Schmidt wasn't landing any body shots. Minute by minute, I was slowly wearing him down, but that last round had definitely taken the edge off my speed. The game plan was all for shit if I was knocked out before the twelfth round. Slumping back down on my stool as the bell rang, I had to face facts. I was losing, and losing badly. There was no way I was winning this thing on points. It was a knockout or nothing, and Schmidt had never lost, let alone been knocked out.

"Marie's ex is here," Con told me.

"What the fuck!" I said, my gaze finding her in the crowd.

"She has no idea what he's doing here, but she thinks he's come to check you out. Tommy passed the message on," he explained.

I searched the crowd, but it was pointless. I had no idea what he even looked like.

"Now don't go stressing yourself out. Liam, Tommy, and Albie ain't letting her out of their sight. But you can't lose, Kier, not in front of Marie and not in front of her fuckin' ex either. You go back in there and you do what you do best with me. You look for Schmidt's tells. Look for his weakness, and then you knock him the fuck out. You show Marie's ex just how fuckin' badarse you are, and you make sure he knows you ain't to be messed with," Con said, pumping me up with every word.

Adrenaline coursed through my veins, and this wasn't about me and Schmidt anymore. It was about a man standing between me and the girl I loved. If her ex was here, she needed me. And if I had to go through Schmidt to get to her, so be it. The bell rang out and I stood, invigorated. Jumping up and down, I rolled my head around my shoulders to loosen up the muscles and went to work.

I ducked and sidestepped as he chased me around the ring.

Throwing punch after punch that didn't connect was tiring him, and I could see his frustration with each jab that sailed past me. He'd convinced himself that he'd won, but that weakness was back. He needed reassurance. From his coach, from his father, and, to his detriment, the judges. His gaze flicked to them briefly as I narrowly dodged a killer right hook. And there it was. My opening. Distracting him with a solid left hook to his liver, I followed it up with a right jab to the ribs. When his hands dropped to protect his body, I delivered the same uppercut that he'd given me. He fell hard against the ropes. I hadn't knocked him out, but on the ropes was exactly where I wanted him.

I used his face like my personal punching bag. He tried to defend himself, but I deflected blow after blow with ease. Con was right. This guy didn't have twelve rounds in him. He was worn out. I was seconds away from a knockout when the fucking bell rang. He staggered back to his corner as I slumped down hard on my stool, pissed off and frustrated.

"That's more like it," Danny said, swiping the sweat off my face with a towel, then salving up the worst of my cuts.

"I didn't knock him out," I said, panting.

"He's got nothing left in the tank, Kier," Con told me. "Keep focused, stay moving, and when he drops his guard again, make him kiss the canvas."

I nodded in agreement, and I knew he was right. I needed the knockout, and he knew that. All he needed was to stay on his feet for two more rounds. The eleventh round was bloody and brutal. My face was a mess, but so were his ribs. He was exhausted, we both were, but he was content to wait out the round blocking and staying off the ropes.

Danny sorted my face out as I sat down again.

"This is it, kid. One more round. This is the round that's going to define the rest of your life. The round that your da would 'ave given his heart and soul to see. You push away all that tired and hurt and you focus. This is your fight. Your moment. You define what happens today, not him. Get this done and let's go home," Danny told me. He squeezed the back of my neck in support, then moved out of the way to let Con come in and hydrate me.

"How's my face?" I asked him, knowing it was a mess.

"Still pretty, but not as pretty as mine," he answered, making me chuckle.

"My girl doin' okay?" I asked.

"Oh yeah. Tommy's taking great care of her," he answered, smirking.

"Fuck he is," I said, leaning over to try and see them.

"Take it easy," he replied. "That girl is head over heels for you. You knock this fucker out, and she's gonna be here kissin' it all better. Just remember, you got three minutes, Kier. That's it. Three minutes. So ask yourself, how badly do you want this? There ain't nothing in this world stronger than us."

He grabbed onto my neck as he touched his head to mine in a gesture of solidarity.

"You hit him and keep on hitting him until it's done, you hear me?" he whispered before letting me go.

Round twelve was just as fierce. Schmidt had this sewn up on points, but that didn't mean he wasn't afraid of me. For two minutes, our roles reversed as I chased him around the ring. We traded punch for punch, but he could barely lift his arms. He hit the ropes and took a second to rest before moving his feet, but that was all the time I needed. Keeping out of range of those body shots of his, I jabbed repeatedly to his face. I had a long reach and I was quick, too quick for him to get a decent hit in before I went back to pulverising what hadn't been the prettiest of faces to begin with. His nose was well and truly fucked, and he could barely see out of the black eyes I'd given him. When he relented and raised his hands to protect his face, I pounded into his ribs as hard and as fast as I could. Hours and hours on the speed ball had burned this into my muscle memory. When he dropped his hands to his body, I went to work on his face again. I had no idea how long it was until the bell, but I was determined to make him feel every second of it.

I barely registered the pull on my arm. It wasn't until the referee moved between the two of us, and pushed me away as he waved at the judges, that I realised the fight was over

Stumbling back to my corner, I barely reached it before Con climbed between the ropes and lifted me off my feet.

"You did it! You fuckin' did it, you crazy bastard! You've won!" Con screamed at me. I swore, he never looked this happy when he won his own fights.

He put me down, but kept his arm around me. It was pretty much the only thing keeping me up at this point. I looked over as Schmidt's camp started pouring into the ring to see that the ref had Schmidt on his feet and was telling him the score. He looked battered and dazed, and I'd hazard a guess that I probably wasn't looking much better. When Danny finally made it to my side, his eyes looked suspiciously wet.

"I'm so feckin' proud of ya, kid. So feckin' proud. You did it, son," he said.

"We did it," I replied and pulled him in for a hug.

I tried to see Marie and the guys, but camera crews, officials, and sponsors had swarmed the canvas. Finally, the referee called Schmidt and me to the middle, where he held onto our wrists.

"Ladies and gentlemen, after two minutes and forty-six seconds, in the twelfth and final round, and by way of technical knock-out, your winner and new IBF heavyweight champion, Kieran 'The Storm' Doherty," the MC called out my name and held up my arm to the crowd who went absolutely nuts. I closed my eyes, not believing that I'd actually done it, and when I opened them, I swore I could see my father's proud face in the crowd.

CHAPTER TWENTY

MARIE

As his name was called, I couldn't stop the tears from streaming down my face. Watching the match was one of the hardest things I'd ever done. Win or lose, I couldn't stand to see him take any more hits. But this was his fight, his moment, and I wasn't going anywhere.

Cannons streamed confetti down on the ring as the song "Hall of Fame" boomed out through the speakers. When the referee had waved off the fight, Kathleen and I had hugged each other so hard I'm surprised that neither of us had broken a rib.

"I'm so glad that's over," I admitted to her.

"Me too. I don't think I could take another three minutes," she replied.

Tommy had disappeared when the bell sounded, leaving us with Liam and Albie. He emerged back through the crowd with a big smile on his face.

"The ring's too crowded. We won't be able to get to them, so

Con wants us to wait back at the dressing room," he explained and ushered us all towards the back of the arena. Every aisle was heaving with people cheering and dissecting the rounds, so it took us a while.

"I hope you're ready for a good party. The boys are going to be buzzing for weeks about this one," Em said as security let us pass. We were all staying together at a hotel in London tonight, and Con and Kier's friends who hadn't been at the fight were all meeting us there for a drink later.

"Well, I'll stay for a stiff gin and tonic or two, for my nerves, and then I'm going home to bed before the boys get too rowdy. I'm absolutely exhausted after that. I'm so pleased he won, but honestly, I think I'm going to be having nightmares for weeks seeing my little boy getting hit like that," Kathleen replied.

"Are you sure he'll make it to the party?" I asked worriedly. "He looked pretty banged up.

"This is Kier, Marie. Hell will freeze over before those boys aren't ready to party after a fight," Em said. "No matter how drunk he is tonight though, try and get him to take an ice bath. It will help ease the stiffness tomorrow. If he won't cooperate, run him a warm bath tomorrow. He's going to struggle to get up in the morning."

Celebrations were already in full swing when Con, Kier, and Danny strolled in a little while later. After his mother fussed over him and he'd accepted congratulations from everyone, he saw me. I hung back to give his mother some time and to take it all in. But when his gaze found mine, I knew that look in his eyes meant trouble. I was leant against the wall as he stalked towards me. Lacing his fingers with mine, the wraps on his hand scratching against my palms, he closed his eyes and rested his forehead against mine.

"I love my brothers, each and every one of them, but there's no amount of money in the world I wouldn't give for this room to be empty right now and for you to be naked up against this wall with your legs wrapped around my waist. Or lying down with them wrapped around my neck. Either works for me," he whispered in my ear. The noise of the guys' revelry slipped away, and with Kier surrounding me so completely, it felt as though we were in our own little world.

"I feel like Little Red Riding Hood. You look like the big bad wolf who's come to eat me," I told him.

"Give me an hour and a locked door, and I just might." He buried his nose in the crook of my neck and inhaled deeply, making me whimper. "Now who's bad, getting herself all wet while standing in the same room as my mother," he said, chuckling.

"Oh my God, it's totally not my fault. It's like a proximity alarm in my knickers that goes off every time you're near." I whimpered, making him burst out laughing. The laughing turned to coughing, followed by a little wheezing.

"Let's go and see the doctor, baby. I really don't like the sound of that," I said. I knew it was bad when he didn't argue with me, letting me lead him by the hand back to the guys.

Turned out that Kieran was banged up pretty good, bruised ribs, severe cuts, and swelling to his face. It looked like he'd strained or pulled a muscle in his shoulder as well. The doctor didn't think that anything was broken, but ordered bed rest until the bruising on his ribs went down.

"Best advice I've had all day," Kieran remarked with a wink at me.

"Jesus Christ, I'm rich!" Tommy exclaimed.

"What do you mean, Tom," Kier asked.

"Shit! Me too," said Liam, looking at his phone.

"What are you doing?" I asked.

"We're checking online to see what our winnings are," Tommy explained.

"You bet on me?" Kieran asked incredulously.

"Hell yeah," Tommy replied. "You were a sure thing. Seemed stupid not to make a profit out of it."

Kieran grinned broadly, pleased that he'd made the boys some money, but more likely touched by the fact that they'd believed in him enough to bet against the odds.

"How much did you win?" Kieran asked them all.

"Me and Albie didn't have much to spare, because we just got our own place, but we scraped together a hundred-pound bet. We got back two thousand," Liam said.

"Five hundred quid for me," Tommy piped up.

"I may have made a little money too," Kathleen said, as she sheepishly patted her hair.

"How much, Ma?" Kier asked.

"Same as Liam," Tommy said. Your ma didn't think it was seemly for a lady to go into the bookies, so I put the bet on for her," he said.

"Good for you," Kier replied, smiling at her.

"How much did you make, Con?" I asked. I figured he was used to the betting, because the boys must have put down some money on his fights in the past.

"Don't ask me," he replied, crunching down on an apple. "Ask my banker. Em takes care of the money in our house."

Em was busying herself around the room, doing anything she could to avoid looking people in the eyes.

"Em, love, how much did we make?" Con asked suspiciously. "I saw a betting slip on the notice board and figured you'd put down some money on Kier, but I didn't look to see how much."

She mumbled something that none of us could hear.

"Come on, Em, confess. How much of the green stuff you taking home?" Tommy pushed.

We all knew that Em was a brilliant mathematician. She was also one of the most fiscally cautious people I'd ever met. Finally, she turned around and put her hands on her hips as though expecting confrontation.

"I said we made twenty thousand pounds," she admitted. Con choked on his apple, and Em rushed to slap him on the back until he could breathe again.

"Holy fuckin shit, babe. I figured you'd put down twenty quid. Not....," Con said, stopping to try and calculate how much she would have bet for the return.

"A thousand. I bet the last of the waitressing money that I had left. I've been trying to give it to you for the best part of a year, but seeing as you won't take it, I decided to invest it. Are you mad?" she asked him quietly.

"No, Sunshine. It was a good bet," he said. They gave each other puppy eyes as he shared his apple with her. I swore she could have bet their life savings, and he wouldn't have batted an eyelid. He was that crazy for her.

"Well, it looks like Father Pat won't be the only one celebrating then. Drinks are on Con and Em tonight," Kier announced as he slung his arm around my shoulders. Con rolled his eyes, but smiled. The man was nothing but generous to his friends with his money, and I knew he probably would have paid for tonight's party with or without their windfall.

"I'm going to clean up. Ma, we're going to catch a lift with Con and Em, but there's cars booked outside to take everyone to the hotel, so Liam and Tommy are going to take you and Danny now if that's okay," Kier said to his mother.

"Are you sure you're okay? What if you get dizzy and fall in the shower?" she said.

"Don't worry, Marie is coming in with me for that very reason," he answered, wearing a sexy smirk.

"To much information, Kieran. Well, don't take too long, because I'm only staying for a quick drink," Kathleen said, putting on her coat. "I really am so proud of you, son," she said, cupping his face gently.

"Thanks, Ma," he replied and kissed her on the cheek.

Within minutes, the room emptied and it was just the four of us. Em and Con cosied up on the sofa, while Kier led me into the bathroom. I'd resigned myself to turning up to the party with wet hair and no makeup, but when I considered all of the delicious things we could do to each other in that shower, it seemed totally worth it. I was more than a little shocked when he lifted me onto the bathroom counter and... left me there.

"If you're imaging right now that I don't want you, you'd be wrong. I am so hot and hard for you, Irish, that you'd pretty much only have to sneeze next to me and I'd come. But I want us to remember our first time together for the rest of our lives, and I'm not settling for a quickie in the bathroom. I want long and slow, then deep and hard. I want it every which way I can with you, and then I want it all over again. So consider tonight foreplay. We're going to relax and have fun. Then Monday I have a surprise for you," he said cryptically.

I let out a huge sigh of frustration, but I knew he was right. We'd been building up to this for a long time. Half an hour in the shower wouldn't do anything to take the edge off. We needed time and privacy, and tomorrow we'd have it.

"The shop is shut tomorrow, and I have somewhere I have to go on Monday morning, but then I'm free all day Monday as well," I told him, wondering how I could find the act of him unwrapping his knuckles so sexy.

"I know. You have a hospital appointment for a check-up. I saw it on your calendar. I'm coming too," he told me.

"You don't have to do that," I said. "Em said you're going to be in a world of hurt for at least a couple of days. The last thing you want is to be dragging yourself out of bed to sit on a crappy plastic hospital chair with me."

"You're going to be there, which means that's *exactly* where I want to be. The *only* place I want to be."

"I'd like that, if you're sure. Mum covers the shop for me, so I usually have to do the appointments alone, although Luca takes me if he's home," I said, rambling nervously as the shower started to steam up the room. "I hate hospitals," I whispered as he walked towards me.

"I know," he replied. "Which is why I'm coming too."

Kissing the end of my nose, he walked to the shower and, yanking off his shorts and whatever was underneath in one go, climbed in. I crossed my legs, then uncrossed them. Hoping, fruitlessly, that the friction would help the ache. The view of my man from behind was so fine that I was literally sliding forward on the counter as he showered. It was like he had some magnetic connection with my vagina. Through the steam-filled haze, hot water sluiced down the most beautiful body I'd ever seen. His tribal sleeve only emphasized his ridiculously huge biceps. Strong, powerful shoulders and a broad back tapered into indents at the top of his hips. I wanted to touch those indents so badly. Scrap that, I wanted to kiss them, then run my tongue over them. I'd just worked my way down to his phenomenal gluteus maximus when the water shut off abruptly and he slung a towel around his hips. Tutting with amusement, he chuckled.

"Hold that thought, Irish," he said. "I fully plan on eyefucking you in the shower tomorrow. Unless you want to blow off my family and have some fun?"

I sighed as I contemplated whether that was actually an option, but he was already dressed by the time I'd run through the ramifications of going straight back to the hotel room.

Kieran looked good in pretty much anything, but in dark grey tailored trousers and a fitted black shirt, he was breathtaking. I wondered why he hadn't put on sweats and gone to the hotel to change, but when we arrived, I realised why. The crowd at the hotel bar was so big, they'd spilled out into the lobby, and Kieran was accosted as soon as we made it through the door.

"I'll get the drinks in, Marie. What do you fancy?" Em asked.

"I'll give you a hand and let Kieran catch up with everyone," I replied.

"No you don't," Kier said, wrapping his arm around my waist and yanking me back as I went to walk away. "The next few weeks are about me and you, and that starts tonight. I need to do the rounds and say thank you to everyone for their support, but tonight I don't want to be apart for any longer than we need to be. I've missed you the last few weeks, and I don't want to miss you anymore."

"Aww," Em said, "you guys are so cute. Con and I will get the drinks in, and we'll come and find you," she said, walking over to Con who was already at the bar.

"You don't mind, do you? If you're feeling tired and want to grab a seat, I understand," he said, looking worried that he was being selfish.

"If you're there, then that's where I want to be," I said, echoing his earlier sentiments back at him. He kissed me gently, then held my hand as we worked our way around the room.

Getting him to have an ice bath before bed wasn't a problem, because we never actually made it to bed. The party literally went on all night. The hotel must have made a killing, and as Con had all the drinks charged to his room, they were happy to keep the bar open for as long as we wanted. By 6.00 a.m., I was curled up in Kier's lap with my shoes off, sharing a bag of salt and vinegar crisps with Em who was sat the same way on Con's lap. Tommy was completely passed out in bucket seat, and Liam had discreetly slipped upstairs around 3.00 a.m., hand in hand with Albie.

"Tired, Sunshine?" Con asked Em, as she finished eating and tucked her face under his chin.

"Yep, but right now you're soft and warm, and I'm too tired to contemplate even walking to the lift," she answered sleepily.

"You sleep, love. I've got this," he answered, and I was pretty sure she was out before he'd finished his sentence. He bumped knuckles with Kier then leaned over to kiss my cheek.

"'Night, guys," he said and lifted his wife up as though she was weightless and carried her to the elevator.

"Ready for bed, Irish?" he asked, and I nodded with a yawn as I climbed off his lap and gathered up my shoes.

"What do we do with Tommy?" I asked Kier, and he sighed.

Standing up with a groan, he patted down the pockets of Tommy's jeans until he found what he was looking for and pulled out a room key.

"Can you hold this?" he asked and handed it to me. Pulling Tommy by the arm, he managed to hike him over his shoulders in a fireman's lift and we followed after Con and Em.

"If he pukes on me, I swear it's the last thing he'll ever do," Kier said, as Tommy burped in his sleep. We got him safely tucked up and put a champagne bucket by the side of the bed as a precaution. Though by the heavy snores as soon as Kier laid him down, I figured he'd be out for at least a good few hours. As we walked back towards the elevators, Kier lifted our joint hands to kiss the back of mine.

"Are you still on cloud nine after your win?" I asked.

"It wasn't the win, Irish," he replied. "It was knowing that you were there with me. Best feeling in the world."

CHAPTER TWENTY-ONE

KIERAN

I woke up warm and happy, then realised the reason for that was wrapped around me. Her body was pressed against my side, her hand rested over my heart, and her leg tangled with mine. Careful not to wake her, I just lay there completed contented and inhaled the smell that was uniquely her. A combination of her subtle perfume and apple shampoo, it smelled like home. Lying there I knew, without a shadow of doubt, that I wanted to wake up like this, every day for the rest of my life.

She wriggled a little in her sleep, burrowing deeper into my warmth. I held my breath as she brushed against my painfully hard erection. I wondered how it would feel when I no longer had to hold myself back. For months, I'd dedicated myself to training. Now I planned to dedicate myself, with the same single-minded focus, to worshipping her body. It was more than that. I relished in the idea of being able to be a normal boyfriend, of taking her out to dinner and other dates, knowing that this angel, who could have any guy she wanted, had chosen me. I wanted to pick her up from work and cook dinner for her and take care of her in a thousand ways that the training hadn't allowed. Most of all, I just wanted to love her. The greatest gift of all was that she'd let me.

Unable to take this blissful torture anymore, I reached down to stroke the creamy skin of her thigh.

"Arghhh," I cried out, unable to contain the almost pathetic squeal of pain. Every muscle in my body screamed out together in protest.

"What's wrong?" Marie said, sitting up sharply. Her hair was rumpled and an adorable pillow crease ran down one cheek. Disorientated and sleepy, her face was a mask of concern.

"I'm pretty sure Schmidt broke every bone in my body last night, then ran over me a couple of times afterwards," I whimpered.

"I'll go and run you a warm bath," she replied. "Em warned me this would happen and said that if you missed your ice bath, I should run you a warm one in the morning."

"Not yet," I said, lying down and dragging her back into my arms. "I want five more minutes. I'll be all right as long as I don't move." She laid her head on my chest, and all was right with the world.

"Move in with me," I whispered to her.

"You want to move into my place?" she asked, bolting up to look me in the eyes.

"No, I mean give up your place and let's find somewhere together. No offence, but your place is a little small, and I have a chunk of money saved, especially when I add in last night's winnings..." I trailed off, not sure if I was selling her on the idea. We'd known each other for years, but we'd only been together for a few months. Maybe we should wait, but every minute I spent away from her was a minute too long. I craved the intimacy of seeing her toothbrush next to mine every morning and knowing it was there to stay.

"Do you mean it?"

"Of course I do." I laughed when she jumped on top of me and planted kisses all over my face. That was until my body cried at the contact.

"Fuckin' Schmidt. I hope he feels as bad as I do," I groaned.

"I imagine he feels worse, given that you walked away with the belt and the girl," she pointed out, smiling.

"Yes I did," I replied with a smile on my face. My girl was so goddamn beautiful, it made my heart hurt to look at her. "So, just to be sure, do the kisses mean that's a yes to moving in together then?" I asked her nervously.

"That's a hell yes," she replied with a grin as she shuffled down the bed.

"What are you doin', baby?" I asked in confusion.

"Kissing it all better," she said.

She carefully peeled my boxers down my legs and leaned forward to kiss the tip of my penis. I closed my eyes as she tortured me with each stroke of her tongue. When I couldn't take any more, she took the whole of me into her mouth and I knew what heaven felt like.

Two hours later, I sat in a tub full of bubbles and girlie-smelling shit with my arms wrapped around my girl. It hadn't taken much convincing for her to join me. The steam from the bath was curling tendrils of her hair that had slipped from the elastic into ringlets. I was playing with one when I suddenly remembered something.

"What was your ex doing at the fight?" I asked her. She stiffened, and I almost regretted ruining the moment by bringing it up, but I wanted to know.

"I have no idea," she replied. "You can't even call him my ex. We only went out a few times. I explained to him when he asked me on a date that I didn't want a relationship, so we agreed to just be friends. But he became intense pretty quickly and I could see that he wanted more, so I broke it off completely. After that, he used to stop by the shop, or run into me in places that I go to regularly, telling me he was just passing by. It was starting to get a little uncomfortable, and when we got together last, I explained that it was best we didn't see each other anymore. He wasn't happy that I had a boyfriend, considering I'd told him I didn't want a relationship, and to be honest, I felt a little guilty because he had a point."

"Irish, I'm a force of nature. I was prepared to hunker down for the long haul and wear you down until you gave into me. Wanting a relationship or not, I didn't give you much of a choice," I said, trying to reassure her. She hadn't misled this guy. She really hadn't wanted a relationship. Thankfully, true love was both deaf and blind to reason.

"Falling for you was the easiest and most selfish thing I've ever done," she said.

"It wasn't selfish."

"Yes it was, and you know why."

"We'll agree to disagree, love," I said, kissing her temple. She leaned into the kiss for comfort, and I held her a little closer.

"He was a few rows back from the ring, sitting with a bunch of guys in suits. I didn't notice him until Tommy asked who the guy staring at me was. Then Alastair waved and went back to talking with the suits. Maybe he was entertaining clients. Lots of companies take important clients to sporting events," she said, like she was trying think of a reason for him to be there that wasn't fucking creepy.

"Sure. Of all the sports, he chose boxing, and of all the events, he chose the one your boyfriend was fighting in. I don't like it, Irish. Maybe I need to have a word."

"Don't," she implored. "He hasn't really done anything wrong. I'm making him sound like a stalker, but maybe he's just as determined as you were. I've told him honestly how I feel, so if he shows up randomly again, then I'll tell you, I promise." She turned in the bath and the subject of Alastair was forgotten.

With her tits level with my eyes, I struggled to remember my own name. I certainly didn't remember my aching joints or how I'd planned to wait until my surprise to take things further between us. In fact, I couldn't remember a single reason why capturing her nipple in my mouth and suckling wasn't the best idea I'd ever had, and so I did it. When I held her other breast in my hand and rubbed my calloused thumb over her nipple, she cried out in ecstasy.

Before she had time to register what I was doing, I lifted her tiny frame until she was straddling me. When I switched breasts to even the love, she rocked back against me. It was an instinct as old as time to reach between us and settle myself in the right position. When she rocked back this time, the tip of my cock slid inside her, making her shiver. As she reared back to take me in deeper, water sloshed over the side of the bath. Neither of us could give a shit. There was nothing outside of this moment but the two of us, and it was just as perfect as I imagined it would be.

"Ride me, baby, as hard and as deep as you can," I growled. Being inside her was nothing short of nirvana. Her nipples were puckered hard, and I blew over one gently to make it even harder. The water made her slippery, but my grip on her hips was firm as I lifted her up and down, encouraging to move faster.

To ride me deeper.

Her rhythm was nothing short of flawless as we moved together effortlessly. I thrust to meet her bounce, and every time I caught that magic spot, she clenched me tightly. I knew I couldn't hold on much longer. No sane man could in the face of such perfection. When her back bowed in ecstasy, I wet a trail of kisses along her exposed neck all the way down until I could feast on her nipple.

"God, Kieran, please," she cried out. Her thighs trembled the closer she came to orgasm. I'd never experienced anything like this. Having sex, even good sex, didn't come close to the way it felt to make love. To know that she'd given me her heart, along with her body, was nothing short of humbling. Having her friendship was a gift, holding her heart was a miracle, and if I had to spend every day for the rest of my life doing it, I'd prove to her that I was worthy of that miracle.

"Make me come," she pleaded. Knowing I could never refuse her anything, I bit down gently on her nipple as I rolled my thumb over her clit. Watching her fall apart was the most beautiful thing I'd ever seen. She rode the wave of tremors as she clenched and tightened around me helplessly. Wrapping her tightly in my arms, I buried my face in her neck and held on as the fiercest orgasm I'd ever had ripped through me. She lay down on my chest as our boneless bodies melted into each other.

"I love you, beautiful," I told her, and I could practically feel her smile against me.

"I love you too, Kieran," she replied. "It would be impossible not to."

* * *

"Where are we going?" she asked.

"It's a surprise," I replied, smiling. I had weeks to plan this. Weeks of running mile after endless mile, deciding how I would spend my time when the fight was over. A sunny vacation where she'd spend all her time in a variety of tiny bikinis was my first choice, but I knew she'd never leave the shop for long. Instead, I was taking her to my second choice, and if I was lucky, she'd spend the next three days naked to make up for the bikinis.

"I feel like a weight has been lifted off me," she said, leaning back against the headrest with her eyes closed.

This morning I'd taken her to the hospital for a check-up on her heart condition. After all the visits to hospitals I'd made with Da, I fucking hated them. But you would never have known that from my face. Marie's body had been wracked with tension as we ate breakfast in the hotel and then checked out. I'd still felt like I'd been run over, but a good night's sleep with my girl tucked into the side of me had definitely helped.

The whole time we were at the hospital, she had a death grip on my fingers. People stared as we walked hand in hand through the corridors. There was no hiding the fact that my face was fucked up. It would be weeks before I even resembled the man I was before. Irish didn't care though. She loved me regardless. I sat patiently for hours while she went through test after test until, finally, she was called to the doctor's office.

"Can I come?" I'd asked her.

"Do you want to?" she replied, and I'd nodded. If it was good news, I wanted to be the first to hear it, and if was bad, then she needed me.

"Okay," she agreed easily. Besides, going in alone meant letting go of my hand, and I wasn't sure she could do that.

"Dr Austin, this is my boyfriend Kieran," she said, introducing me.

"Hello, Kieran. Pleased to meet you," the doctor said. "Please take a seat."

We sat, still holding hands, while he got straight to business.

"Look, I know that you've had some concerns this last month about headaches and general fatigue, but I think that's because you've been working yourself too hard. You have to remember that your body is an engine. If you overwork it, it's going to pack up on you," he explained. So the headaches and fatigue were news to me, but we'd discuss that later.

"As far as I can see from the tests, everything is looking good. The aortic valve repair is still holding nicely. As long as you don't put your heart under unnecessary strain, there's no reason it won't hold for a very long time," he added reassuringly.

"And long term?" she asked quietly, squeezing my hand a little harder.

"One day at a time, Marie," he replied. "Cardiothoracic surgery has come a hell of a long way in the last twenty years, and will probably advance exponentially in the next twenty. There are any number of factors that can determine whether a transplant is absolutely necessary, but with the risk of organ rejection, it's often our last resort. I would want to explore further surgeries if it came to that point. For now, rest a little more and keep doing what you're doing. If you start having any problems or symptoms, don't wait for the review, contact me immediately. Other than that, plan on having a long and happy life, and I'll do my best to get you there."

Looking at her then, her eyes closed in relief and happiness, I couldn't believe how happy I was. Knowing that Irish was as healthy as she could be was the best news. It was the perfect end to the weekend and the perfect start to the week ahead.

"Are you ever going to tell me where we're going?" she asked me, smiling.

"You'll see soon enough," I replied, with a grin of my own.

"Won't Liam miss his truck?"

"Nah, I didn't think you'd be up to riding all this way on the bike, so we swapped for a couple of days."

"That's nice of him," she said, settling down.

"You tired?" I looked over at her sleepy expression.

"A little," she admitted. "I've been so anxious about the fight and my appointment, that I feel exhausted now that there's nothing to worry about any more."

"Why don't you nap for a bit then. I'll wake you up when we get there."

"That's okay," she replied. "I'll bet you're just as tired as I am." I smiled at her stubbornness, then flat out grinned when she was asleep five minutes later.

Hours later, and she was still out cold. The key to the cottage I'd hired was in the numbered lockbox, exactly where it was supposed to be. The owners had even been kind enough to leave a picnic basket of food, which I figured would come in handy. I'd just taken in our bags when she woke.

"I'm so sorry I fell asleep," she said, as she jumped out of the truck and shut the door. Rubbing her arms at the brisk breeze, after the warmth of the truck, she looked around. "Oh, Kieran. Is this where we're staying? It's beautiful," she said in awe.

The one-bedroom stone cottage was tiny, but stunning. A winding path led through a garden, which I'd bet would be full of flowers in full bloom come summer. The inside was pretty basic. The kitchen and bathroom were both tiny, but the wooden canopy bed in front of an open fire had me sold on the place.

"Yeah, I'm afraid there's only one bed and limited heating in this place, so we're both going to have to cuddle naked for warmth while we're here." I wrapped my arms around her waist and rested my chin on top of her head.

"Well, if it's for the sake of our survival, we really don't have a choice," she replied. Fuck, I loved this girl. "Wait, what am I going to do about the shop?"

"Don't worry," I answered. "I had a chat with your mum, and she's covering for you. She said you've got a fitting booked in for Friday though, so we need to be back by then."

"But that's three whole days away," she replied, turning in my arms and wrapping hers around my neck, "and I plan to make the most of each and every one of them."

Leaning down, I met her halfway and kissed her, just as the heavens opened.

CHAPTER TWENTY-TWO

MARIE

It rained every day for three days, but they were the best three days of my life. Despite the terrible weather, every morning we explored the coast, discovering quaint little seafood restaurants and cosy pubs. But that afternoon was our last, and we wanted it completely to ourselves. The cottage was pretty isolated along the coast, so when a tiny window in the weather allowed, we walked down to the beach and ate a fish and chip supper as we watched the tide go out.

"I don't care how rich either of us ever get. No fancy restaurant will ever be able to top the taste of good seaside fish and chips," I told Kieran.

"After months of egg whites and protein shakes, I reckon I could eat this every day for weeks and not have enough. Sorry, baby, but you might have a bit more to hold onto soon," he said, patting his rock-hard abs. There wasn't an ounce of spare fat on his body. He didn't sit still long enough to put on weight.

"I don't think you have anything to worry about, but I'd still love you, even if you were a chunky monkey."

"Plenty of sex will keep me trim," he assured me seriously.

"Ah, well, you definitely don't have anything to worry about then," I said with a giggle.

"Never can be too careful. I think we should work out at least twice a day, every day. You can't take your health for granted."

"What are you doing now?" I asked as he started on my half-eaten bag of chips, having devoured his own.

"The more I eat, the more I have to burn off," he replied with a cheeky grin.

He threw the empty bags away and grabbed my hand as we walked on the sand.

"Warm enough?" he asked as I shivered.

"There's something ethereal about walking along an empty beach in winter, but the wind is arctic today."

Letting go of my hand, he wrapped his arm around my shoulders and tucked me into his side. Instantly, warmth seeped from his body into mine.

"I *really* don't want to go home today," I told him.

"I do," he said, and I pulled away slightly to look at him. He laughed at my expression and pulled me straight back into his arms. "I want us to look for our own place. The next time we go somewhere, I want us to be going back to our home together. The sooner we get back, the sooner we can make that happen."

"I love the way your mind works."

"Baby, let me show you how something else of mine works. I promise you'll love it just as much," he replied, walking back to the cottage a little faster.

* * *

"Jesus Christ!" I screamed out. He hadn't been lying. I had loved it.

"Are you praying, Irish?"

"Don't stop!" I pleaded, and he chuckled as he lowered his head and went back to making me scream. How I wasn't hoarse by this point I didn't know. There should be a law against bringing someone to the point of orgasm and not letting them come. This was the third time, and if Kieran didn't end this exquisite torture soon, I was going to jump on him and finish the job myself.

He peppered the inside of my thigh with gentle kisses, then worked his way along my belly and ribs, stopping to kiss every surgical scar along the way. He was shaking himself as he reached my lips.

"I love you," he whispered as he slid inside me. I was speechless. Hell, I was completely breathless. I couldn't even remember how to formulate words. The feeling of holding him deep inside of me, filling every inch of me, only to retreat and slide back in again. It was perfect.

"I love you," I replied. It wasn't enough. It wasn't nearly enough, not to define how important that moment was or how I felt about him. Not enough to explain how meeting him had changed the course of my life forever. Those three little words weren't enough, but they were all I had.

His trembling hand slid along my thigh as he moved a little harder and deeper. I squeezed my thighs, desperate for everything he had to give. His lips brushed against mine, but they only stoked the fire even hotter. Our tongues collided as we devoured each other, desperately edging closer to that blissful release. We broke apart, and he bent his head to rest in the crook of my neck.

"Tá grá agam duit," he whispered in my ear. I didn't understand the Gaelic, but it didn't matter. I felt its meaning in Kieran. His huge hand engulfed my breast. His hand was capable of such violence, but he caressed me with such care and devotion. My body was liquid beneath his touch. No matter how much he gave me, I only craved more. If it were even possible, he grew thicker and harder inside of me, and I arched my back, desperate for what he alone could give me.

"Irish," he groaned into my mouth. He withdrew, sweeping his thumb across my nipple as he impaled me. His heated breath met mine as I nipped his bottom lip. Without warning, he lifted me, dragged a comforter off the sofa, and threw it down on the rug beside the open fire he'd lit. Hastily, he flipped me on all fours. Sympathising with his desperation, I clutched the fabric tightly and laid my head down. He groaned at the sight of me lying prostrate and ready for him. I shivered as he traced a gentle path down my spine with his fingertips. When he reached my arse, his touch became more urgent. Gripping my hips firmly, he thrust inside me to the hilt, and it was my turn to moan. It was so deep, so full, and Kieran's rhythm was relentless. As he pounded into me, I begged him for more.

Wrapping an arm around my waist he pulled me up, my back

flush against his chest His bearlike paw swallowed my breast, emphasizing the difference in our size. As his other hand travelled down my body, I reached back to clutch his neck, squeezing a little with excitement and anticipation. Pleasure darted to my core as he rubbed and tweaked my nipple. Surrounded by his strong, hard body, he consumed me, and I had never felt so cherished and protected. His thumb teased confidently at my core, like he owned it.

And he did.

He owned my body like no man ever had or ever would. Not because I was a virgin. I wasn't. But because I'd given him my body and my heart. Both were Kieran's in equal measure. What made sex so phenomenal was that he treasured me as much as I treasured him. Never had I surrendered myself to someone as I had to him.

"Kieran...," I moaned.

"Fuck! I love the way you say my name," he replied as he drove in deeper and deeper. I knew I couldn't hold out much longer. He bent his head to nip my shoulder, tilting his pelvis slightly. Pleasure sensors all over my body cried out simultaneously, and the strongest orgasm I'd ever had ripped through me. Kieran jerked violently, every muscled tensed and strained. Our shudders eventually stilled, and we both collapsed to the floor, his dick still buried deep inside me, like he couldn't bring himself to lose that contact.

"I think you fucked me so hard, I've gone blind," I told him, making him laugh.

"That was beyond epic," he said, tracing lazy patterns on my abdomen. The fire bounced light and shadows across his tan skin, and I was mesmerised. Limp and completely sated, I cuddled in closer and let him wrap me in his arms.

"I'm going to give you everything you ever dreamed of. You know that, baby?"

"Kieran," I sighed sleepily, "you already have."

* * *

Going back to work after a holiday sucked. It was official. Most days, especially since they featured Kieran, I loved my life. Every day was a gift I tried never to take for granted. That morning though was just the worst. After getting caught in the rain, having forgotten my umbrella, a thirty-minute fitting appointment for an alteration had turned into a two-hour ordeal with a bridezilla from hell. I wasn't particularly confrontational, but I was anything but a pushover. After barking all of the alterations she wanted at me, I calmly explained that what she was looking for wasn't alterations but a new dress. A huge row ensued, during which I held my ground until the bride-to-be burst into tears. Three glasses of prosecco later, and it turned out that the dress wasn't the problem at all. It was the groom.

"Why do people insist on marrying someone they know isn't right for them? She's got serious doubts about whether he's the man for her, and she's going to marry him anyway," I asked Mum about bridezilla.

She handed me a cup of tea, then added about three sugars to her own.

"It happens more than you'd think. Some women get scared that they'll end up alone, or they want children before they're too old, and they settle. For some people it works, and they have a long and happy marriage. For others, they don't realise their mistake until it's too late."

"I just can't imagine marrying someone without that certainty of knowing they are the one person I want to spend the rest of my life with," I told her.

"Ah, but marriage is rarely about certainty. It's about love, hope, and faith. When you love someone more than you've ever loved anyone else, even yourself, you hope for a long life together, and you have faith that both of you will compromise and sacrifice when times are hard to make that life a happy one."

I smiled at her wisdom, as I thought back on all the wonderful memories I had of Mum and Dad together.

"And sex," she added as an afterthought. "It's important to have a bit of chemistry in the bedroom. It's all well and good marrying your best friend, as long as they stoke your fire. Of course, a bit of the passion fades when you find yourself knee-deep in nappies and dirty dishes. But, Lord... your father could make my knickers take themselves off with a single raise of his eyebrow, right up until the day he died." She looked wistfully into the distance as she did some reminiscing of her own.

"I love you, Mum, but that's too much information. I do not need to think of you and Dad getting down and dirty."

"There was nothing dirty about it. Although, there was that one time—"

"Maaaa!" I protested, squirming. She laughed at my expression until I ended up giggling with her.

"It's good to see you so happy," she said to me softly. "You know, as a parent, that's all we really want for our children. Health and happiness. Kieran is a good boy, and he makes you smile. That makes me happy."

"Umm, so on the theme of you wanting me to be happy, you wouldn't feel too freaked out then if we decided to move in together?" I asked her, biting my lip as I waited for her reply. She stared at me hard, probably trying to decide whether I was being serious or not, then finally shrugged.

"You are a sensible girl and you know what you are doing. If this feels right to you, if you have *faith*, then so do I."

Abandoning my stool, I walked over to give her a big hug.

"Thanks, Mum," I whispered in her ear.

"You're welcome, love. Now drink your tea before it goes cold. Bridezilla'a maid of honour is in this afternoon, and if you thought the bride was a piece of work...."

* * *

The streets were dark by the time I was done for the day. Mum had left a little earlier than usual to get her hair done, and knowing that Kieran would be there to pick me up soon, I turned out all the lights and locked up the shop. Dropping my keys into my handbag and turning around, I jumped as I saw something move in the shadows.

"Jesus," I said, putting my hand over my heart in shock. Alastair stood there wearing a long woollen coat and expensive looking leather gloves.

"You're moving in with him?" His expression was a mask of disbelief.

"How could you possibly know that?" I asked, too furious to be freaked out.

"I saw you. You've been going into estate agents with him, getting listings for places. I saw you," he repeated.

"Have you been following me?"

"I *saw* you," he said, not really answering my question. I stood there completely shocked. He was acting like he had a right to be upset, as though we were in a relationship and I had somehow cheated on him.

"Alastair, this is nothing to do with you. Kieran is my boyfriend, and what we do together is absolutely none of your business. I've tried being nice and asking you to keep your distance, but enough is enough. Now I'm telling you. Stay away from me and out of my life or I'll get a restraining order."

"Why would you do that? We're friends. I'm just looking out for you. You've known this guy for five minutes, and now you want to move in with him? It's too soon. You haven't even given the idea of us a chance!"

"There is no us!" I cried in frustration. "I hoped we could be friends, but that wasn't enough for you. I don't want to hurt you, but you need to let this go. Whether you've been following me or not, I know you being at Kieran's fight wasn't accidental. This is becoming an obsession and it's poisonous. Do both of us a favour and move on. I love Kieran, and I know that out there somewhere is a girl who will make you happy, but that's not me. And you're never going to find her, not like this."

"I can't believe that you think you're in love with him. I can give you everything you ever wanted, you know that?"

"I don't need the world, Alastair. I just need him."

"You think you need him, but you don't. He has you brainwashed, but without him you'd see—"

"Enough!" I interrupted. "Enough, Alastair. I think you need to sit down and talk to someone. Have you spoken to your family about the way you feel?"

"You think I'm crazy because I care about you! Unbelievable! I don't need to sit down with anyone to see the truth. I'm not the one who needs help, Marie. You are." Stuffing his fisted hands into his pockets, he turned on his heel and disappeared back into the shadows.

Shivers turned to full-on trembling as the adrenaline rush of our confrontation faded. My knees threatened to go out from under me, so I leant against the building for support and took a deep breath. I had no idea how to deal with this. Telling Kieran would only send him off into a rage, determined to sort out Alastair. I didn't want him getting into trouble, but I had a horrible feeling this situation was going to get a lot worse before it got better. One thing I knew for sure though, I couldn't keep secrets from Kieran.

As though I'd summoned him with my thoughts, he rode around the corner and parked his bike up against the pavement. He pulled off his helmet, took one look at my face, and came running over.

"What's wrong?"

"Alastair was just here. He didn't listen to anything I had to say last time. He's convinced we should be together, and I seriously don't think he's going to take no for an answer. It's like he's become obsessed."

"I'm going to fucking kill him," he said, looking around.

"He's gone."

"But he won't stay gone. That's the fuckin' problem. You did your best not to hurt him, love. But you've tried your way, now give me a chance to try mine."

"What are you going to do?" I asked warily.

"I'm going to explain why stalking my girl is a real bad idea." He was scarily calm, and it reminded me of his expression when he knocked Con on his arse.

"Kier, it's not as simple as scaring him. I think he's sick. Threatening him won't work. He needs to get help."

He paced a little, opening and clenching his fists as though he was trying to reign in his temper. When he seemed to come to a decision, he walked back over to me and cupped my face softly.

"Then make a report to the police. There's got to be some law against stalking. If nothing else, at least they'll start keeping a record of all the crap he's pulling. And until I can be sure that he's out of our lives for good, I don't want you going anywhere alone. He comes into the shop, you call the police."

"I can do that," I agreed, giving him a small, tight smile.

He rested his forehead against mine, as though he could sense my fatigue.

"Let's get you home. You look exhausted." He gently stroking my cheek. I closed my eyes and leaned into his touch as I inhaled the subtle hints of his aftershave. He threw his leg over his bike, then helped me with my helmet so that I could climb on behind him. Turning his head around to face me, he flipped my visor open to talk to me.

"By the way, I forgot to tell you. I have a surprise for you when we get back, but try not to freak out, okay?"

CHAPTER TWENTY-THREE

KIERAN

"You know we live in a one-bedroom flat on the second floor, don't you?" Irish said with amusement.

"We live here for now. We've got three houses lined up to see this weekend, and we're bound to like one of them. This will be for a couple of weeks at most," I reassured her.

"And what happens when we're at work?"

"I'll take him to the gym with me. I'm sure Danny won't mind. I'll run to and from the gym as well, so he'll get plenty of exercise."

She was trying to be practical, but I called her bluff to see how she really felt.

"If you hate the idea, I can take him to Ma's house. She's been toying with the idea of getting a dog for years. I'm sure she'd take him," I said. Okay, so that was a flat-out lie. Ma would never in a million years have a dog chewing up the place and shedding hair all over her furniture.

"I can't just give him to anybody though. It has to be someone who'd take good care of him. He's a rescue dog that had been abandoned." I threw that last part in for good measure, in case she was wavering about the idea.

"I wouldn't get rid of you, would I, baby? You're part of the family now, and you are so gorgeous. Yes, you are! You're absolutely beautiful," Irish said to the bullmastiff puppy that was scrabbling about in her arms and covering her face with drool. I laughed watching them play together.

I'd always wanted a dog, ever since I was a kid, but Ma wouldn't have it. I knew Irish was far too practical to have one. When I'd seen an advert on the rescue centre's social media page, I didn't give it two minutes thought. It was love at first sight, and I hoped she would feel the same. Besides, it was easier to ask for forgiveness than permission. Sometimes the impractical decisions that felt right in your heart were the best ones you ever made.

"Why would anyone ever abandon such a beautiful puppy?" she asked me angrily.

"They told me it looked like the owners moved house. For whatever reason fucked-up people who mistreat animals do it, they didn't want him and couldn't be bothered taking him to the rescue centre, so they just tied him up in the garage and left him to starve."

Just talking about what those evil fuckers had done made my blood boil. If I ever found out who they were, there was nowhere they could go that would be far enough to get away from me.

"What are we going to call him?" she asked.

"Baby, that's up to you. I got him, so you get to name him. Just remember that he's a guy and he's going to be part of our family for a very long time, so no girlie names like twinkle or sparkles or any shit like that."

"How about Driscoll? I reckon Danny's more likely to let you bring him to the gym if you name it after him."

I looked over at the dopy fucker, who was laid out on his back, legs in the air, as Irish rubbed his belly. "I like it," I said. "We can call him Dris for short."

"You do know how big they get, don't you? And they slobber all over everything."

"You love big dogs that slobber, admit it!" I said, crawling over to nuzzle her neck and nip her like a dog would. She burst out laughing as my kisses tickled, and Dris went nuts, trying to climb on top of me to get in on the action. Looking at Irish, who'd settled down to cuddle on my lap with Dris, I couldn't believe I'd ever fought the idea of us. I had everything I never knew I wanted, and I couldn't imagine life ever being more perfect than this.

* * *

"What the feckin' hell is that? And what the feck is it doing in my gym?" Danny said, cigarette hanging out of his mouth in disbelief.

"I adopted a rescue pet and called him Driscoll. I'm gonna train it to eat Irish's ex," I explained.

"I repeat. What the feck is it doing in my gym?"

"I can't leave him at home. He's too little. I figured it would be okay to bring him with me when I'm training. He wouldn't be any trouble. He'll sit in the corner, good as gold, I promise," I said in kind of a whiny, pleading voice. I was fucked if Danny wouldn't let me keep him here. There's no way the little guy was old enough to be left home alone, and I didn't know anyone who could watch him all day.

"I do not want a rodent in my gym, pissing all over the floor." His face completely deadpan.

"I'm training him, and me and the boys will take turns taking him out on runs. You won't even know he's here. And he never pees on the floor, I promise."

Dris made kind of a whining noise, and we both looked down at him. The little fucker stared at Danny longingly, tilted his head to one side, then pissed all over the floor. I closed my eyes in disbelief. There was no way I'd be allowed to keep him here now.

When Danny didn't bark at me to get rid of him, I looked to see the old man and the puppy still staring at one another.

"Clean that mess up and keep him out of my sight," he said, finally. Taking a puff of his cigarette, he shuffled back to his office.

"You jammy bastard," Con said in amusement. I turned around to see the guys all loitering and eavesdropping on my conversation, waiting for me to get a bollocking as well no doubt.

"I reckon the old man's getting soft in his old age," Tommy threw in. "No way would you have gotten off that lucky a couple of years ago."

"I'm sorry to interrupt, boys. I forgot my pipe and slippers," Danny said, scaring the shit out of us, but Tommy especially, who gave a little whelp and jumped a mile.

"Sorry, did I disturb you?" Danny asked sarcastically. "I was under the impression this is where fighters came to train, but correct me if I'm wrong." We turned to look at the office door and I wondered how he slipped back out without anyone noticing. That man sure did have some ninja skills when he wanted to.

"Well, then, what're ya waiting for! Get back to work, ya lazy fuckers," he barked when nobody moved or answered. We all jumped to it, Tommy included. I started towards the cleaning cupboard for a mop and supplies, but realised Dris wasn't with me. I turned back just in time to see him toddle through the office door at Danny's heels. I opened my mouth to say something, but the door slammed shut before any sound came out.

"Danny's gonna eat that thing for feckin' breakfast if you don't rescue it before he realises it's in there," Tommy warned.

"I'm more likely to piss him off by knocking on the door than Dris is," I replied.

"Pretty fuckin' genius naming the dog after him," Con said.

"It was Irish's idea, but she's going to fucking kill me if Danny eats her new puppy," I said, making him chuckle.

I cleaned up the pee, something I had a feeling would become a pretty regular part of my day from now on. A couple of times, Danny opened the door and Dris came out, so I used the opportunity to take him outside to do his business before he scampered back the way he came again. When Heath called us into the office at four for a meeting, I finally got to see how he was doing. Danny had dredged up an old blanket from somewhere. Folded on the floor, it served as a makeshift bed. In front of Danny's desk and near the warmth of the heater, Dris was fast asleep on it.

"Cheeky little fecker," Tommy mumbled. Con and I looked at each other and chuckled. Maybe the old man was getting soft after all.

"Right then, boys, it may have escaped your notice with all the feckin' slackin' that's been going on lately, but we've got fights to organise and titles to defend. Kieran first," Danny barked.

My face was still black and blue from my last fight, and my ribs were still giving me trouble, so I knew there was no way he would be scheduling me another fight yet. The fact that he was bringing it up though made me wonder if he knew what was coming.

"I'm not fighting again," I blurted out. "I mean, I'll always be thankful for the time and effort you all put in to training me and the faith you showed me, putting me forward in the first place. But I knew the minute I held up that belt that this life isn't for me. I belong behind the ropes. And in case any of you are thinkin' it, it ain't anything to do with Marie. I fought for me, so that I'd never be an old man lying in my bed and wondering what if. But now I'm finishing it for me too."

My answer was met with silence. Looking around the small room, I could see everyone's gaze focused on me. Some had understanding in their eyes; others held disbelief that I would win a world title, then throw it away again without going back for more. If being a great fighter was Con's calling, training a great fighter was mine.

Time and experience had given me some perspective, and I realised how different my life could have been after Da died without these guys and this place. I knew that I had it in me to be a world-class fighter, but when I looked back at my life and what I'd done with it, I wanted to know I'd made a difference. Whether he knew it or not, Danny hadn't just changed my career; he changed my life. He'd looked at me and seen not what I was, but what I could be. I wanted to know one day that I'd made the same difference in someone else's life. My heart was in training Con and the next generation of lads who came behind us. Maybe it wasn't the most sensible decision. Shit, I'd never make the money that Con was making, but I knew in my heart that it was the right decision for me, and that was enough.

"Fair enough, kid. Fair enough. You gave everything you had in that fight. I saw it, and so did the rest of the world, and no one's ever gonna take that away from you. If you've learned that behind the ropes is where you chose to be, rather than where you just happened to find yourself, then that's good enough for me. That being said, you and that mangy mutt of yours best not get too comfy. Heath's set Con up with another fight. I want you to help train him," Danny said.

"Who's it against and when?" Con asked, always cutting through the bullshit and straight to the point.

"Roman Malachi Reid in ten weeks. It's in America again though. More money, more TV coverage, more showboatin'.' I'd prefer a fight this side of the pond, but the yanks are insistin', so there it is," Danny explained.

Con looked over to Em to gauge her reaction. Speaking to her after Irish's freak out had been a revelation. How she'd learned to school her reaction to this sort of news, I'd never know. She would never tell him no, Con knew that, but if he had an inkling of the way she felt when he climbed into the ring, he'd give it up in a heartbeat, and he wasn't ready for that.

"What do you think?" he asked her.

"Can you beat him?" she asked back. He didn't scoff or roll his eyes or any of that shit. He simply looked her straight in the eye and nodded his head.

"Then the question isn't what I think, it's what do you think?" she replied. She would never judge him or pressure him. She just made sure he thought it through so he could come to his own decision.

"We'll take the fight," he answered.

We'll take the fight, not *I'll*. As soon as he said the words, a tingle of excitement ran down my spine. Reid was the newest heavyweight to come out of the US. Two years younger than Con, he was sharp, hungry, and dangerous. It would be a hell of a fight.

Em nodded and wandered over to Con. She slid an arm around his waist, and his eyes glazed over.

"Training starts tomorrow," Con demanded, before Danny could say any different. Danny rolled his eyes, while the rest of us chuckled. When training started, sex stopped, so Con would be making the most of his last night. I'd be surprised if Em could walk in the morning.

"Obviously, Con's indisposed for the rest of the afternoon, but if the rest of you feckers ain't busy, I've got a favour to ask," I said.

* * *

After our weekend at the beach, I insisted on getting a house with a fire. Finding a rental property with an open gas fire was no mean feat, but we eventually settled on a two-bedroom place with a wood burning stove. Signing the papers and getting credit checks done took a week. Of course fifty quid on the side to the agent probably helped to speed it up.

"Jesus Christ. How much stuff do you have?" Tommy said, humping another couple of bags over his shoulder to take in the house. With the guys' help, I'd nearly finished moving our stuff in. Irish's old rental place was furnished, so we had to buy most things new. We'd already picked out a bunch of stuff from Ikea, so we picked it all up that afternoon and Liam put it all together. Both of us had a background in construction, so you'd think I'd be doing it with him, but I couldn't do flat pack for shit. I'd nearly finished arranging everything when my phone rang.

"Where's all my stuff, Kier?" Irish asked when I answered.

"In our new home," I replied. "I wanted to surprise you, Irish. I figured we could spend our first night here tonight, with a bottle of vintage wine in front of an open fire. What do you say?" I asked seductively.

"Sounds very romantic," she agreed. "I'll see what wine's on offer at the supermarket, and you get the log burner going."

"Deal. I've got a couple of things to finish up here, so I'm going to send Tommy over to come and pick you up."

"Okay, Kier. I want to say goodbye to a few of my neighbours anyway. I'll see you soon. I love you."

"I love you too. Bye, love." I replied and hung up.

"Tommy! Can you pick Marie up at her place so I can finish up here?" I called up the stairs.

"Great! So on top of doing all your grunt work, I get to be a fuckin' taxi driver now," he grumbled as he ambled down the stairs.

"I'll do it if I can take your bike," he bartered. Tommy loved riding my bike, though I was pretty precious about it, so I didn't let him on it very often. He was desperate to get one of his own, but we both knew his ma would throw a fuckin' head fit if he did, and Tommy's ma wasn't someone you wanted to mess with. I hated the idea of Irish pressed so close up against him on the back of the bike, but I really wanted this place ready for her to come home.

"Fine!" I agreed, reluctantly. He grinned, happy now that he had an incentive.

"Man, I hope your girl's wearing a skirt. If she is, I'm coping a feel all the way home," he taunted.

"You even think about Marie like that, let alone cop a feel, and you'll be pissing blood for a week by the time I'm finished with you. She comes out in a skirt, you send her back in to change. First chance I get, I'm getting her some proper bike leathers."

It was funny to watch Tommy mindfuck Con by flirting with Em. I sympathised a little more now that it was being directed at me. Suddenly, his picking up Irish didn't seem like a good idea, but I really wanted to surprise her when she got back.

Tommy grabbed my leather jacket off the hook and, grinning, gave me the finger on his way out the door. I didn't stop him. He only wore a hoodie and he needed some sort of protection on the bike.

Thirty minutes later, Liam went to meet Albie for dinner, but I was pretty much done anyway. An hour later, they still weren't back and both of their phones were ringing through to voicemail Frustrated and worried, I grabbed Tommy's keys and was about to drive round there when my phone rang.

"Hi Ma," I said. "I'm just on my way out. Can I call you back?"

"Oh, thank God," she said and burst into tears. "Kieran, I don't know who was riding your bike, but the police just arrived. There's been an accident."

And just like that, my world fell apart.

CHAPTER TWENTY-FOUR

MARIE

You know that feeling where you're in a really deep sleep and you have to struggle to wake up? And when you do, for that split second of disorientation, you can't quite remember where you are or what day of the week it is? That was what it felt like when I opened my eyes on the side of the road. I had no recollection of where I was or what happened, but the second that realisation hit, so did the pain. Unimaginable agony was just everywhere. After that, I didn't care what my name was or anything else. I just wanted the hurt to go away.

I turned my head to the side, and fresh pain exploded inside my skull. A mangled torso lay unmoving a few feet away.

"Tommy," I whispered as the pool of blood beneath his head slowly crept towards me.

I was filled with sorrow, but also a sick sort of relief that it hadn't been Kieran.

Kieran.

I pictured him in my mind as I last saw him, his cheeky grin as he kissed me goodbye. It was the very last thought I had before everything went black.

CHAPTER TWENTY-FIVE

KIERAN

"Look! For the millionth fuckin' time, I'm her boyfriend. We live together. Why won't someone tell me what the fuck is going on?" I shouted.

She was just a receptionist. I knew that. Rationally, I knew that shouting at her was a dick move. But that's the thing, I wasn't rational. I was so fuckin' far from rational that I was gonna need restraining soon if someone didn't come and explain what the fuck was happening.

"Sir!" the receptionist said authoritatively. "I understand that you're upset and worried, I really do, but I cannot find out what is happening with you screaming in my face. Now please, take a seat, and I will find someone to come and speak to you. But if you don't sit down, I'm going to have to ask security to come down."

"Five minutes!" I told her and stormed away to sit down on one of the plastic chairs. I rested my elbows on my knees and ran my hand backwards and forwards through my buzz cut. They were the longest, loneliest minutes of my life. There were so many people I needed to call, but until I spoke to a doctor or someone, I didn't know what to say. Over and over I kept telling myself it was my fault. I moved us out of the apartment I asked Tommy to pick Irish up, I let Irish ride around on the bike without proper leathers. Anything that happened to them both could be laid directly at my feet, and it didn't matter whether they'd ever forgive me. If either of them were hurt, I'd never forgive myself.

"Mr Doherty. My name is Alice. I'm a nurse in the ER. Would you come with me please?" a lady said to me. Her brown hair up in a ponytail and wearing plain blue scrubs, she didn't look much older than me.

"Can you tell me what's going on? How are they?" I asked.

"Through here, Mr Doherty," she said and led me to sit down in a small anteroom.

Miss Kelly and an unknown male were brought into the ER when the motorbike they were riding collided with another car. Miss Kelly was thrown some distance during the accident, but the unknown male was knocked off his bike and thrown under the wheels of another vehicle. At this time, we are only able to release specific details regarding the patients' medical condition to their next of kin or immediate family, but I can tell you that Miss Kelly is in a serious but stable condition. At the moment, the unknown male is critical. That's all I can tell you at this time, but if you can get their families here, I'll be able to release as much as I know," she explained.

I was shell-shocked. I'd locked onto the word stable, until she'd thrown critical in there, and then I was fucked. I couldn't lose either of them. I just couldn't.

"My girlfriend. She has a serious heart condition. She needs medical attention for it," I told her.

"Don't worry, we know," she replied. "We found a medical warning card in her purse, and her medical records are in the system."

"The guy, the one the police thought was me," I explained, "his name is Tommy Riordon," I told her as she wrote it down on her clipboard, together with his ma's number.

"We'll call Tommy's parents now, but if you could direct any family members to come here, I'll be back as soon as I have more news," she said, and with a tight smile that offered little reassurance, she left me on my own again.

As soon as she left, I pulled out my phone and rang Con on speed dial.

"Hey, what's up?" he asked when he answered. As quickly as I could, I explained what had happened.

"Em," he hollered to his wife before coming back to me. "How are they both doing?"

"They won't tell me shit till their families get here. Marie is serious but stable, but Tommy is critical. I've given over everyone's numbers and the hospital is calling everyone now. Look, I know you want to get here for Tommy, but could you pick Marie's ma up? I'll text you the address now. I don't have her number, but I want to make sure she gets here as quickly as possible. Just tell her you're a friend of mine."

"Don't worry, brother. Em's met her ma before, so I'll bring her with me. We'll be there as soon as we can. What about your Ma?" he asked.

"She's gone to pick Dris up for me. I don't know when I'll be home and I don't want him alone, so she's going to take him back to her place and I'll keep her posted when I here anything," I explained.

"Okay Kier, we're on our way. You just hold tight," he ordered and hung up. As quickly as I could, I tapped out the address and texted it to him. Then I pulled up another number, keeping a promise I'd made, but never thought I'd have to keep.

"Hello?" Luca answered with surprise.

"It's Kieran. I know you're on the rigs, but I thought you should know—"

"What's happened?" he said, all business, and I told him. "Fuck!" he cursed down the phone.

"I've sent a mate to pick up your ma, but I don't know her number. Can you call her and let her know someone's on their way to get her? I don't want her panicking about how to get to the hospital."

"I'll call her now. We're scheduled on tomorrow's chopper for the shift change, so it's the earliest we'll be able to get out, but we'll be there by tomorrow night. Keep me posted the *minute* you hear anything though, okay?"

"Of course," I said, kind of wondering why he wasn't screaming at me for destroying his sister's life. If she hadn't met me, she'd never have been on the back of that bike. All her life she'd battled with a weak heart. Who'd have thought I'd be the one to nearly kill her?

"And thanks, Kieran. I appreciate you calling and keeping us in the loop," he said.

"No problem. I'll see you tomorrow."

"Bye," he replied and hung up. Two seconds later, I was vomiting in the bin next to me.

* * *

I thought the worst thing was getting the phone call. It wasn't. It was having to look into the face of Irish's ma while I explained what happened. Con had phoned John and Mary, Tommy's parents, who'd already spoken to the police and were on their way when he called. I didn't think I could handle calling another person.

Despite having stopped for Stella, Con walked through the door first. I stood as he hugged me. I struggled to keep it together. I didn't need to talk about shit with him. He knew how I felt. It had been his girl in here not so long back, fighting for her life, and Tommy meant as much to him as he did to me. He was our brother. There weren't words to describe what the thought of losing him meant. Em followed straight after, her eyes red from crying.

"Where's Stella?" I asked, finally.

"She's with the doctors, seeing if they'll give her any news." Con looked me in the eyes. "He's gonna pull through this. You know that, right? You could throw the fucker under a bus and he'd still come back fighting. He's just that tough. So stop borrowin' worry till we know what's what."

I nodded, getting myself together. Just then, in burst Mary and John, looking devastated.

"I'm so sorry," I whispered to Mary. Tears threatened to fall as another wave of guilt rolled over me. Tommy was their only child and the absolute centre of their universe. It would tear them both apart if he didn't make it.

"I'll let the nurse know you're here," Con said, after giving them both a hug. Minutes later, he walked back into the room followed by a serious looking doctor.

"Mr and Mrs Riordon. My name is Dr Owens. I'm a senior consult in the ER. Would you like to step outside a moment so that we can talk about your son's condition," he said gently.

"It's okay, Doctor. We're all family here. We don't need to step outside," Mary said. John, Mary's quiet and stoic husband, who was the complete polar opposite of his wife and son, wrapped his arm around Mary's shoulders and squeezed, as though he was bracing himself for bad news.

"The police informed us that your son was riding a motorcycle that collided with a car at a junction. They suspect it may have been a drunk driver or a stolen car, because the vehicle didn't stop. While Tommy's passenger was thrown from the vehicle, the collision knocked your son under the wheels of another vehicle. As far as we can tell, he's broken several bones and there's internal bleeding that we are going to need to operate on quickly. His heart has stopped twice, and we've had to defibrillate to bring him back. As soon as he's stable enough, we'll get him in to surgery. His helmet was pretty banged up and cracked in several places. At this point, we believe he has some swelling on the brain, but we won't know how serious that is for a few days, until the swelling subsides. We're going to do everything we can for him, but the next twenty-four hours will be critical," the doctor informed us gravely.

"Can we see him?" Mary asked.

"Not until after the surgery, I'm afraid. It really is absolutely critical that we get him into the operating room as soon as possible. If you'd like to wait here, one of the nurses will let you know as soon as he's been moved down to theatre," Dr Owns said.

He left the room and Mary collapsed on John, gut-wrenching sobs racking her body. I couldn't stand to see her like this, so I threw my big arms around them both. The day I lost my da, Mary had been the one to comfort me. She'd thrown her arms around me and the scent of flowers made everything just a tiny bit more bearable.

"It's my fault," I admitted to her painfully. "He was riding my bike because I asked him to pick her up. I wanted to finish getting everything moved into our new place. It should have been me."

Her sobs turned to sniffles as my words reached her. John released me and pulled a clean white handkerchief from his pocket and handed it to his wife. Wiping away her tears, she sniffed loudly, then looked up at me, her face a picture of determination.

"Now you listen here, Kieran Patrick Doherty. I'm going to explain this once, and it better penetrate that thick bloody skull of yours, 'cause I ain't up to explainin' it again," she said pointedly. "What happened to my boy had absolutely nothing to do with you. Misplaced guilt is a wasted emotion that makes a mockery of life. If it had been you in Tommy's place, what then? Your mother has already lost your father. Do you think she could survive losing you? Live the life you were meant to live, do the things that you were born to do, and take care of the people who need you. My Tommy needs your strength more than he needs your guilt, you hear me?"

"You are the strongest woman I know, Mary Riordon," I told her truthfully and wrapped my arms around her. She burst into a fresh round of tears, and I held her tightly as John rubbed her back. She let go as Stella walked through the door, and the two women comforted each other.

"Did they tell you what's happening?" I asked Stella earnestly. I didn't know anything more than that she was stable.

"She's doing okay, love," Stella reassured me. "She was out cold for a while, and she's pretty banged up, but as far as the doctors can tell, she hasn't broken anything. They are a little worried about the fact that she was unconscious for so long and the strain on her heart, so they're going to run some tests in a little while to make sure everything is okay. Her heart rate is high and she's having a little trouble breathing, but all in all she's very lucky. It could have been much worse." She pulled herself up short then as she realised what she'd said. It was worse. Much worse for Tommy.

"Have you seen her?" I asked her. I desperately needed to see her with my own eyes, to listen to her heart beating and know that she was still with me.

"I did, but only for a moment," she said. "She's in intensive care now, but I'm pretty sure they'll transfer her to a ward once her cardiologist has seen her. You'll be able to see her then."

"I'm so sorry, Stella," I said. I felt Mary staring after me, given her speech about misplaced guilt, but I owed it to Stella to apologise.

"Were you in the car that hit them and drove off?" she asked, but didn't wait for my answer. "Of course you weren't! So you have nothing to be sorry for. I've been in and out of hospitals many times in my life, Kieran, far too many times than any mother should ever have to. What I've learned in all of that time is that faith will carry you through anything. Faith in God, faith in life, faith in the power of good. Sometimes, faith is the only thing that makes sense when nothing else does. It is more powerful than anything else, even guilt. So use it."

She rubbed my cheek gently, like my own ma would to comfort me, and went back to talking with Mary. Marie knew Mary through their respective business, floristry and wedding dresses kind went hand in hand, so I guessed that Stella and Mary were acquainted the same way. It was Mary Riordon who'd sent Em, Tommy, and me to Marie's shop to help Em find a wedding gown, where I met my girl for the first time. It was just another thing I had Mary to thank for.

Without anything to do other than wait, Con, Em, and I walked miles to and from the vending machine, keeping everyone supplied with crap tea and coffee. Over the next couple of hours, the small room filled up quickly. Liam, Albie, Danny, Heath, Ma, and even Father Pat turned up. We were a family, and it didn't matter that we weren't all blood. Family held you together when you didn't even realise you were falling apart.

The door opened a little while later, and we all held our breath, hoping it was a doctor with some good news. We were more than a little disappointed to see the police.

"I'm PC Harding. Which one of you is Kieran Doherty?" one of the coppers asked.

"I am," I replied. "You here about the accident?"

"Yes. I'd like to ask you a few questions. Would you prefer to step outside?" he asked.

"No, we're all family. I think everyone would like to know what happened anyway," I told him, and he nodded.

"Take a seat," I offered, standing up to vacate mine. He had pulled out his notebook, and I could see he was struggling to write standing up. If he was intimidated sitting between Liam and the heavyweight champion of the world, he didn't show it. I answered all of his questions as best I could. We were all insured to drive each other's vehicles because we swapped rides so much, the bike was in perfect working order as far as I was aware, and yes, Tommy was a careful driver. With Marie on the back of the bike, he'd have been a choir boy. Tommy didn't take many things seriously, but the safety of our girls was one of them.

"I think I have everything I need for now. The more we know about the condition of the bike and the drivers, the better we can understand what happened. I will add this though. The road was wet, and Miss Kelly and Mr Riordon slid when they came off the bike. Witnesses have reported that Miss Kelly was wearing a heavy leather bike jacket and gloves, and that Mr Riordon grabbed her when they slid and managed to pull her into the side of the road away from the traffic. He let her go and continued sliding under the wheels of another vehicle. He probably saved her life."

He left the room in a stunned silence as we contemplated what he'd said. I pinched the bridge of my nose to hide the tears that were sliding down my face. My brother, who gave me more shit than anyone else I ever met, may have just given his life to save my girl's. It was a debt I could never hope to repay, and if he didn't make it, I might never even have the chance to say thank you.

Con folded Em into his chest as her soft tears penetrated the silence. Nobody said a word, until Mary Riordon spoke.

"That's my boy," she whispered.

CHAPTER TWENTY-SIX

MARIE

As soon as I woke up, I knew I was in a hospital. The smell, the ever constant sound of the place, even the beds, were all so familiar that I didn't panic. It felt just as normal as waking up in my own bed at home. What I couldn't remember was how I'd got there.

Then there was the pain.

I wriggled around experimentally, but every tiny movement was agony. Eventually, I rested back against the pillows and the pain settled into a dull ache. I wanted to see Kieran so badly, but I didn't have the energy to even reach for a buzzer to call the nurse. As soon as I thought about Kieran, and how his friends were helping us move, everything came flooding back. I knew we'd been in an accident, but the details were more than a little fuzzy. It had all happened so fast, and I was pretty sure I blacked out as soon as the bike went down. I worried about Tommy. He'd insisted when he got to my place that I put on jeans and that I wear Kieran's leather bike jacket and gloves. I hadn't wanted to. They were heavy and cumbersome, but Tommy refused to take me anywhere without them on. I'd only ever seen the comic, happy-go-lucky side of Tommy before. It was kind of sweet to see that he had a stubborn, protective streak.

A little while later, a nurse came in to check my blood pressure and smiled when she saw my eyes open.

"Well, I have a waiting room packed full of hot guys who are going to be very happy to see that you're awake," she said, making me smile.

"Can you tell me how Tommy's going? He was in the accident with me," I told her croakily, realising how parched my throat was as I spoke. She walked over and poured a glass of water from a jug by my bed and gave me a small sip.

"Now, you just relax and I'll see what I can find out. First things first, the doctor will want to take a look at you, and I have to let your family know what's happening. That hot boyfriend of yours is going to pace a hole in the waiting room floor if I don't give him some news soon."

I smiled as I imagined how much shit Kieran was probably giving the hospital staff.

The nurse came back a few minutes later with a doctor. He looked me over, checked my heart rate and blood pressure, then asked me a few questions.

"Your temperature is a little high, and your heart rate is too accelerated for my liking, so I'm going to recommend keeping you in for a few days for observation. You took a nasty crack to the head, but it's really how the trauma from the accident has affected your heart that we're concerned about at the moment. I should have the results of your blood tests by the end of the afternoon, and if everything looks good over the next few days, we'll think about letting you go home," he told me. It was a huge relief. I knew from experience how doctors would talk between the lines when they suspected a problem. The fact that we were talking about my going home meant they were just being cautious at this point.

"Hello, baby girl," Mum said from the doorway. By this stage, Mum had perfected the art of not crying by my bedside, no matter what condition I was in. I honestly didn't know how much courage it took to pull that off, because I was welling up as soon as she popped her head around the corner.

"Mum," I said in my scared little girl voice. She sat on the side of my bed and pulled me into her arms. Sometimes, when you have no idea what to say, a hug says it all for you. The nurse had given me a couple of pain killers, but I didn't even care about the discomfort. Holding me was Mum's way of checking I was okay, so I was content to let her.

"You certainly have a way of making your guardian angel work for her money," she said with a chuckle as she tucked my hair behind my ear.

"It's been a while since my last visit, so I figured the hospital staff might be missing me," I joked.

"Yes, well, do your mum a favour and see if you can leave it a little longer before you visit again. You're going to give me heart problems at the rate you're going," she retorted.

"How's Kieran doing?"

"Ah, that boy has it bad for you. Of course, he's been beating himself up that the accident is all his fault. I'm hoping that seeing you will calm him down a little bit," she replied.

I was pissed off, but unsurprised that he was trying to shoulder blame where there was none. I knew how protective he was of me, but bad stuff happened to good people all the time. A person could go mad looking for the whys or the wherefores of it.

"I love him, Mum," I admitted. "He's it for me."

"Your father would have loved him too."

"You think so?" I asked, tears threatening again.

"Good Irish boy like that? Of course he would. Besides, Kieran worships the ground you walk on. What man wouldn't want that for his daughter?" she replied, giving a little sniff of her own.

"Now, let's get him in here before starts harassing anyone else for an update," she said, refusing to let her sniffles turn to tears. She leaned over to kiss my cheek before leaving the room. A few minutes later, my unusually pale and shaken boyfriend walked through the door.

He stood nervously at the foot of my bed as he catalogued each scrape and bruise.

"I'm all right," I reassured him. "A little banged up, but I'm okay."

He still didn't say anything, and I could see he was struggling to keep it together. I opened my arms, and he dashed round the bed, falling into me.

"Oof, you weigh a ton," I groaned as he jostled everything that still hurt. Pulling back immediately, he touched my face gently, as though I was made of porcelain.

"I thought I'd lost you," he whispered.

"I might be little, but I'm made of tough stuff. It will take more than that to keep me down." I studied his face carefully. He looked far too pained for this to just be about me.

"How's Tommy doing?"

He shook his head briefly as a tear slid down his cheek. My heart grew heavy at his expression and my own tears began to fall.

"He's crashed twice, but they stabilised him long enough to get him into surgery. They're trying to stop the internal bleeding, but his chances aren't looking good," he replied, croakily.

I pulled his hand down so that I could hold him, and we both cried together. I knew Kieran would never let anyone else see him like this. But in this private moment, we shared our fear and pain and grieved over the carefree life that had been our friend's only hours ago.

When my tears dried, he explained what Tommy had done and how, quite possibly, he'd saved my life.

Mum stepped in an hour later, and Kieran left to give us some time together. Quite possibly the sweetest man I'd ever met, he returned with a cup of tea for Mum and a takeaway carton from a lovely Italian bistro about a mile away.

"They wouldn't let me get anything for Marie, but hospital food is rubbish, so I got you some hot lasagne with garlic bread. There should be a little pot of grated parmesan in their too," he said, handing Mum the brown paper deli bag.

"Kieran, you shouldn't have walked all that way for me. A

sandwich would have been fine. But thank you. I won't say that I won't enjoy this. Hospital food is rubbish," she agreed.

"Marie, love, I won't tease you with the smell of this when the doctor has said you can't have any, so I'm going to tease everyone in the waiting room instead and let you have some time together," she said, standing up.

"I did a food run for everyone, so you'll have plenty of company. I couldn't find Mary and John to ask them if they wanted anything, but I can always go back out for them," Kier said sadly.

"I don't suppose either of them will be hungry for anything until Tommy is out of surgery. We're better off taking care of ourselves now, so that we can take care of them when they need us," Mum replied pragmatically. Kieran nodded, and she patted him gently on the back before she left.

"What have you got there?" I asked, nodding towards the other bag he'd been carrying.

"Hospital stuff," he replied and carefully unpacked the bag. Holding each item up as he unpacked them, he explained. "Every fashion magazine I could find. A notebook and some fineliner pens, because you always carry them in your bag in case inspiration strikes. Fresh donuts, your favourite kind with the apple inside, in case you get hungry later and the doctor says it's okay. A packaged sandwich, soft drink, and some chocolate bars for the same reason. Toothbrush, toothpaste, soap, deodorant, slippers, and some clean pyjamas. I'll get your stuff from home later, but at least you can freshen up now if you want to," he said, putting the last of the items down.

"Kier," I sighed softly. "You didn't have to do all of this. Thank you so much. This is so thoughtful." I picked up the soft, cute pyjamas, made of white brushed cotton with pink polka dots, and imagined him going from store to store and searching out all of these things and food my mum would like just to make us both happy.

"I love you, you know that?" I asked him.

"Say that again," he pleaded, resting his forehead against mine.

"I love you."

"You know, the last eighteen hours have been the worst of my life. When I got that phone call, I didn't think I'd ever get to hear you say those words again. And, as long as Tommy is fighting for his life, I don't feel like I deserve them, but I needed to hear 'em so fuckin' bad. When I'm alone, it feels like the world is falling apart, but as long as I can smell you and touch you and feel that you're safe here with me, it's easier to convince myself that everything's going to be okay."

"Everything will be okay," I reassured him. "Have faith."

"I'm trying, Irish. I promise. I'm trying."

* * *

Although I was out of intensive care, the hospital had placed me in a small, private room on the ward. Around eight o'clock, when visiting ended, a scary nurse came and turfed Mum and Kieran out. Mum, well used to hospital practice, left quietly after giving me a gentle kiss on the forehead.

"I'll be in the waiting room if you need me," she whispered.

"Mum, no!" I protested. "I'm just going to sleep for the rest of the evening. You've been here since last night. Go home and get some rest. They'll have visiting again in the morning."

"She nearly died yesterday. I'm *not* fuckin' leaving!" Kier argued with the nurse.

"I've tried being nice...," the nurse spluttered frostily.

"When?" Kier asked.

"When, what?" the nurse replied, confused.

"When did you try being nice? 'Cause I must have missed it. I know you're just doin' your job, but you can't watch over her all the time, but I can. She's in a private room so I won't disturb anyone," he argued.

"You're disturbing me!" the nurse ranted. "And you're disturbing my other patients, and if you don't leave now, I will call security and you will be banned from returning to this hospital on the grounds of your abusive behaviour."

"Kieran," I said gently, calling over my angry boyfriend. He sat down next to me, and I whispered so that only he could hear me. "Take Mum home, please," I pleaded. "She's absolutely exhausted and she needs to rest. I don't want her travelling around London at night on her own. I'll be fine here, I promise, but I'd feel better if you made sure she got back safely. After that, I want you to get some rest. Everything will be better in the morning."

He grabbed my hand as I stroked his face, and he kissed my palm.

"All right, Irish. I can make sure she gets home safe," he agreed. "Try and get some rest." He kissed me gently on the forehead. Then, giving the nurse a nasty look, he gave Mum his arm to take. She held back a grin at his overly protective behaviour, but sent me a conspiratorial wink on the way out.

Soon after, lights on the ward flickered out and everything went quiet. I flipped through a magazine or two, but I was exhausted. Finally, a nurse helped me to the bathroom where I had a quick, painful wash and brushed my teeth. Putting on my new pyjamas depleted the last of my energy, but it was worth it. After the last round of observations for the day, I fell back against my pillows and was almost instantly asleep.

The ward was dark when I stirred. A delicious warmth pressed itself up against my cold body, and the subtle scent of soap and aftershave, which I knew so well, filled my nose with every breath.

"You are going to get in so much trouble," I whispered, burrowing in closer to his body, which rested on top of my blanket.

"The old trout has to catch me first," he replied. It was the last thing I heard before drifting back into a dreamless sleep.

* * *

The next morning, we were tucking into breakfast tea and toast when Con's text came through.

An altogether more cheerful nurse than we'd met last night rolled her eyes when she came to do morning obs to find Kieran sat in a chair by my bed, and I suspected that his stealthy midnight visit hadn't been quite as stealthy as he thought. I loved her all the more for not saying anything though. It was all too much to cope with, and having Kieran holding me all night had grounded me.

"Thank fuck for that," he mumbled to himself as he read a text.

"Tommy?" I asked hopefully.

"He made it through surgery. His heart stopped again in the operation room, but they brought him back and the surgery was successful. He has to go back into theatre to have the broken bones reset and pinned, but they've stopped all the internal bleeding, so he's stable."

Kieran was still worried, we both were, but I could sense a little of the weight falling from his shoulders. Hope, which last night was nothing but a tiny slither in the darkness, had become a full-blown crack this morning.

"He's one tough little bastard," Kieran remarked.

"I can't believe his heart stopped three times, and he's still here."

"He's got a strong heart," Kier replied. "He's been training at Driscoll's almost every day since we were kids. He doesn't smoke, he's never done drugs, and he's the most stubborn person I've ever met. If anyone stood a chance of pulling through this, it's him."

"I should tell Mum."

"I'll call her now, see if any of the guys can pick her up. I should probably check in with them anyway. Will you be okay by yourself for a while? I want to see if Mary and John need anything as well," he said. I could see he was torn about leaving me.

"Go. Honestly, I'm fine."

Less than an hour later, he was back. Con had finally convinced Mary and John to go home and get some rest, promising to watch over Tommy and call if there was any change. Liam had taken Mum's number in the waiting room yesterday and had already called to see if he could her bring her in. They were on their way.

"You need to get some rest today as well," I warned Kieran.

"I can get plenty of rest by your bed, Irish. I brought my laptop in last night so we can watch a movie or something after your Ma visits. I want to check in on Tommy again as well. They still won't let anyone in to see him, so the guys are taking turns in the waiting area in case there's any news. I wanted to take over so they could go home for a while, but they told me they've got it covered and sent me back to look after you."

"Your friends really are worth their weight in gold."

"*Our* friends, baby," he corrected.

"Hello, Miss Kelly. How are you feeling today?" the doctor said as he walked into the room. I recognised him as the cardiologist I'd spoken to yesterday, though I couldn't remember his name.

"I'm a little sore, but I'm feeling much better, thank you."

"That's good news. And Mr Doherty, isn't it?" the doctor asked, shaking Kieran's hand.

"Kieran," he corrected, before sitting back down, and the doctor nodded in acknowledgement.

"Would you mind if I had a few minutes alone with Miss Kelly?" he asked Kieran politely.

"Kieran's my boyfriend," I explained to the doctor. "If it's all the same, I'd prefer him to stay. I'm going to tell him everything you say anyway."

"Of course," the doctor replied.

Kieran thread his fingers through mine and squeezed. I could feel the tension in him as he waited to hear what the doctor had to say.

"So, what's the verdict, Doc?" Kier asked.

"As far as the accident was concerned, you were very lucky. You have a number of cuts and bruises from skidding, though having the heavy bike jacket and gloves on certainly helped to minimise any damage. The crack to your head caused a mild concussion, but your obs overnight have improved. Your heart rate and blood pressure have settled back down and everything looks good. The repair to your aorta seems to be holding well, and although the accident has certainly put undue strain on your body, I can't see that it will cause any lasting damage," he replied.

Kieran let out a huge breath and gave me a broad smile of relief. That was until he looked back at the doctor's face. "If everything's golden, why the long face, Doc?" Kieran asked.

"As I said, the accident itself did not appear to cause any lasting damage. However, your blood tests have revealed something that does give rise to concern regarding your long-term health," he answered. My stomach churned, as my mind raced through all of the things they could possibly have discovered. Never in a million years would I have guessed the answer. "Miss Kelly, the blood test revealed that you're pregnant."

CHAPTER TWENTY-SEVEN

KIERAN

"What the fuck?" were the first words out of my mouth. Probably not the best sentiment to express on finding out that your girlfriend was pregnant with your child, but *what the fuck?*

"How could this have happened?" Marie asked, looking as shell-shocked as I did.

"Are you on any kind of long-term birth control?" the doctor asked, rifling through Irish's medical notes.

"No," she answered. "I haven't found anything that hasn't caused side effects when taken with my other medication," she answered.

"And, have you ever had unprotected sex?" the doctor asked her.

"No," she replied quickly. "We use condoms."

"The bathtub after the fight," I corrected her. "And in front of the fire at the cottage." Her face reddened with embarrassment, and I realised I'd probably given the doctor more information than he needed to know.

"But that's only twice. Twice! In all the thousands of times we've done it," she protested.

"I'm pretty sure it still counts if it's in water," I said with a chuckle.

"Mr Doherty is right. No form of contraceptive is 100 percent effective, and unprotected sex, even once, can lead to pregnancy," the doctor explained.

Irish looked at me, probably trying to gauge my reaction as she figured this out in her own head. We were young and just starting out our lives together. Hell, we hadn't even moved in together yet properly, but I knew that Irish was it for me. Adding a little one to our family would be chaotic, but we'd cope. And secretly, the thought of her round and pregnant with my child did something funny to my heart.

"I think we both know the reason is that I have super sperm," I told Irish, wearing my most serious expression.

"You're not mad?" she asked me.

"I'm pretty sure it takes two people to make a baby, love. Besides, with half of your genes and half of mine, that's gonna be one pretty awesome kid," I reassured her. She squeezed my hand as she smiled. The relief on her face was palpable.

"I would estimate from your hCG levels that you are around eight weeks pregnant. So, if you choose to keep the embryo, then we would need to do an early ultrasound to check that everything is progressing as it should," the doctor said.

"*If?*" I asked disbelievingly.

"Mr Doherty, I'm sure it's been explained to Miss Kelly previously, but with the heart condition that she has, any pregnancy is extremely high risk. Whilst we continue to monitor her condition, there is always the possibility of going back into surgery if needed. Having a baby puts an abnormal strain on her body. But the pregnancy is highly unlikely to survive open heart surgery if further valve repairs become necessary. You need to consider very carefully whether continuing with the pregnancy is worth the risk to Miss Kelly's health," the doctor said gravely.

If it was possible to pinpoint the moment that the bottom fell out of my world, that would be it.

"This baby is a part of us, and I'm not terminating it. I'll rest as much as I possibly can throughout the pregnancy, and I'll be as careful as I can, but I'm keeping our baby," she said firmly, her hands resting protectively over her stomach.

"The fuck you are!" boomed Luca from the doorway.

"Excuse me," the doctor said indignantly. "This is a private discussion. Now, please wait outside until I've finished with my patient or I'm calling security."

Luca completely ignored him, and I stood myself between him and Irish as he stalked towards me angrily.

"I trusted you to take care of her. We all did. You know how fragile she is, and you know she could die if she tries to carry a baby full term. First you were fucking stupid enough to knock her up. Now you're going to go along with this ridiculous idea that she can keep it!" he screamed at me. Despite my profession, I wasn't a violent man by nature, but it took everything I had in me to stop myself from knocking him the fuck out.

"Back the fuck off," I warned him. "Marie's had enough shit to deal with the last couple of days without you getting in her face."

"And who's fault is that?" he asked. "She wouldn't have been on that fucking bike if it wasn't for you!"

I frowned. I was responsible for both her and Tommy being involved in the accident; the fact was still a painful twist to my gut.

"Yes, it's my fault she was on the back of my bike. Yes, it's my fault she's pregnant, and if you want to beat the shit out of me to make yourself feel better, then fine, but not in from of Marie. What happens to the baby is our decision, not yours or anyone else's. The only thing I care about right now is her. You yelling and telling her what to do isn't good for her or the baby, so either calm down or fuck off, because if her blood pressure goes up even fractionally, and I'm kicking your arse."

He seemed to calm down slightly at that. When he had his temper a little more under control, he looked around me at Marie. I followed his gaze to find her scowling at her brother.

"Would you like me to call security?" the doctor asked her.

"It's okay, thank you. I can take care of my little brother. Would it be all right if Kieran and I had some time to talk things over though?" she asked him.

"Of course," the doctor replied. "I'm keeping you in a few more days for observation, so we can talk again when I'm on rounds tomorrow. If all is well, I should be able to discharge you in the next couple of days, and I'll then refer you back to your regular cardiologist."

"I hear one more raised voice from inside the room, and you'll be removed from this hospital," the doctor warned Luca on his way out.

Matt and Tristan walked in behind the doctor, and I groaned. The shit going round in my head was more than I could handle, and the only thing I wanted to do was talk it through with Irish. The twins stopped as they sensed the tension between me and Luca.

"What's going on, little sis?" Tristan asked her cautiously.

"I'm pregnant, and I'm keeping the baby," she explained, crossing her arms over her chest indignantly.

"The fuck you are!" Matt replied. "Your heart can barely keep one of you alive, let alone two."

"Hey!" I said, ready to knock another person out. Family or not, no one took pot shots at my girl.

"Jesus, that was harsh," Marie said, looking really hurt.

"How about asking your sister how she is, how she's feeling, and whether she needs anything from you other than a shitty attitude?" I asked him.

"Like we need you to tell us what our fucking sister needs?" Luca argued angrily.

"What she needs is not to be in a room where everyone is yelling. Which, coincidentally, is exactly what I need!" Stella Kelly said, shutting the door behind her with a soft click.

"How are you, sweetheart?" she said, bending to kiss and hug her daughter.

"I've been better, Mum," she replied sadly.

"So, I gather from all the shouting that I'm to have a grandchild then?" Stella asked her.

"I have to have an ultrasound, but the doctor thinks I'm around eight weeks," she replied.

"And how do you feel about this Kieran?" Stella asked me.

"We haven't even had time to discuss it before the boys came barrelling it, shouting the odds," Marie commented.

"I'm absolutely fucking terrified," I admitted, and the room fell into a sort of stunned silence. "My parents had that kind of epic love you see in movies. But when Da died, it nearly broke me ma. So I avoided any kind of relationship, because I don't think there can be many things worse than losing your soul mate. Only today I found one. I love Marie more than I thought it was possible to love someone. To lose her would fucking break me. But to lose her, knowing she died because I allowed her to carry our baby? Do you think there is anything worse in the world a person can fucking experience? But to give her a better chance at life, you want me to ask her to kill our child. And maybe right now, it is a tiny little bean, and maybe I wasn't expecting to be a father when I woke up this morning. But from this moment on, a father is exactly what I am. And a father's job is to protect and love their child. And you know what? I may fuck things up most of the time, but I think I'd make a pretty good dad. I had the best da in the world, and he wasn't that much older than I am when he had me. So if I'm half as good a father as he was, then I think our kid will be okay.

"Now, if Marie wanted to terminate the pregnancy, I would understand her decision and support her through it. Inside, I think I would bleed slow forever, but I wouldn't love her any less for it. I'd bleed because I put her in a position where she has to make that choice. But I think she wants our little bean as much as I do. So you tell me what to do here. Tell me what decision doesn't turn our happily ever after into an absolutely heartbreaking, fucking travesty."

For the first time since the Kelly brothers walked into the hospital, I thought they imagined themselves in my shoes. Tears were streaming down my girl's face, but she looked strangely proud of me. Wiping away those tears and sniffing loudly, she squared her shoulders and looked ready to do battle.

"Kieran, you haven't left this hospital in days, and our poor dog is going to forget what you look like. Mum and my brothers will stay with me today. I want you to go to your Mum's house and get some rest. Then go and visit Tommy for a bit. We're seeing the doctor again tomorrow morning, and we can talk afterwards. Would that be okay?"

I looked at her brothers, trying to judge whether or not they'd give her a hard time if I left them alone. All three looked like they'd run out of steam at my speech though. When I caught Stella's eye, she winked at me.

"Go and get some rest. I'll be here," she reassured me. Finally nodding my head in agreement, I leaned down to kiss my girl.

"Give me a call if you need me, and I'll come straight back," I assured her.

"Would you do something for me?" she asked.

"Anything."

"Take a shower," she whispered.

"Shut up. You love my manly smell, woman," I answered,

smiling. I kissed her goodbye, then eyeballed Luca on my way out. He'd pissed me off, but truth be told, he was right. I was the one who'd put us in this position, and now I had to find a way to live with it.

I made it all the way down to the hospital car park before I lost my shit again. Since my bike was totalled, I'd been using Tommy's truck. Waiting by the side of it was Marie's dick of a stalker.

"My name is Alastair—"

"I know who you are," I interrupted. "What do you want?"

"I want you to walk away from Marie and never look back."

"I'm seriously not in the mood for this shit," I replied tiredly.

"Everything was great before you showed up. Our relationship was just getting off the ground when you came along and stole her away from me. I'm not naïve enough to think that you don't have feelings for her, but whatever you have isn't enough. All you've done since you've come along is fuck everything up. I'm done with asking Marie to leave you. Now I'm telling you to get out of her life for good."

"You have no relationship, you fucking psycho. I get why you would fall for her, I really do, but this shit stops now. Marie is my girl. The mother of my child, and I ain't going anywhere. So I'm giving you one last warning. Stay away from my family, or I will fuck you up."

"She's pregnant?" he said in absolute shock. I didn't get the chance to answer before he was pacing backwards and forwards and rubbing his hands through his hair like a crazy person. "No, no, no, no, no, no, no... you're fucking everything up. It was all going to be so perfect. She was going to have my children. She was going to marry me, and you're ruining everything," he ranted, but it was almost like he was talking to himself.

"The fuck you say?" I replied, getting seriously worried that this guy wasn't so much a creep as a sandwich short of a picnic.

"It doesn't matter. She's still mine. The baby will still be mine. You're nothing more than a petty thug. Marie could do so much better, and she will, as soon as she sees what bottom-feeding pond scum you really are. I'm going to give her everything she ever dreamed of."

My patience with this fucker had just about come to an end. But despite that, I had the feeling that Marie was right. This guy needed professional help. He looked half crazed, and what he was saying was completely nuts.

"Look," I said tiredly, "why don't you come inside with me. We can speak to one of the doctors together. Maybe figure out what to do." Who was I kidding? I had no fucking clue what to do. But the idea of going inside and trying to find anyone who could diagnose his problem was a hell of a lot more appealing than walking away and imaging him sat at home making obsessive stalker scrap books of all his fantasies featuring my girl.

"Why couldn't you just die like you were supposed to?" he screamed at me. "That's all you had to do! Nobody would miss you. In fact, I would be doing the world a favour, so why couldn't you just do what you were supposed to? Marie might mourn you for a little while, but she'd have me there to support her. With a baby, she'd have to give up that stupid shop, and we could raise it together," he said, painting his own rosy fucking picture of his world without me in it.

"What did you say?" I asked him, wondering if I could possibly have misheard. "You caused the accident?"

"Nobody else should have gotten hurt. You ride that bike everywhere. All I had to do was clip the back wheel with the car. You should have been taken care of. Instead, you sent your friend out on a wet day to pick her up on that death trap," he screamed at me.

"How could you fucking do that? Marie was on the back. You must have seen her!"

"I thought it was one of your friends. She was wearing jeans, boots and a man's jacket. I didn't know it was her until it was too late. It wouldn't have been her if you hadn't let her ride around on that bike! The only one responsible for her injuries, is you," he argued.

I lost it. I'd been drowning in guilt over this accident and he'd been the hit and run driver all along. All the pain and suffering I'd experienced over the past few days was behind every punch as I laid into him. One good hit to the face got him to the ground, but I kept going.

"You stupid fucker! Do you know what you've done? Tommy could be fuckin' brain damaged and Marie could have been killed! You put her in hospital all because you couldn't take no for an answer," I shouted.

"No, you put her there! The minute you put your grubby little hands on what's mine. What's always been mine," he wheezed.

There was no more talking after that. He curled into a ball as I hit him over and over. By the time a strong pair of arms lifted me off the ground, Alastair's face was a bloody mess.

"Get off me," I screamed, knowing it was Con who held me back.

"Enough, Kier, he's done," Con replied.

"You don't know what he did!" I protested.

"I heard enough. Now let's get out of here," he told me. He dragged me to his car and shoved me into the passenger side. The tyres squealed as we peeled out of the car park, leaving that piece of shit where I left him. I took no notice of where we were going until he pulled up outside Driscoll's. The few fighters that were training or sparring turned to stare as we barged through the doors.

"Everybody out," Con ordered.

It was a testament to the respect he had that nobody questioned his orders. The gym was opened to all members, even when he trained for a title fight. If he wanted the place cleared, the guys knew it was serious. He sent a quick text from his phone then chucked it into his training bag as he pulled out a pair of wraps and chucked them at me.

"Put 'em on," he ordered. I said nothing as I pulled my hoodie and T-shirt over my head and dumped them on his bag. For one glittering, shining moment I had everything I ever wanted, and now I was watching it all turn to dust. There wasn't anything left to say. Wrapping my hands seemed pointless, given that my knuckles were split and covered in Alastair's blood, but I did as he'd told me, lacking the will to argue with him.

"In the ring," he ordered. Looking around, I could see that the place was already empty. I climbed through the ropes and squared off against Con. Bare chested and wearing low slung jeans like me, he'd taken the time to put on wraps as well.

"Let's go," he said.

I'd told him everything on the way over, and the journey had allowed me to force everything back into the bottle. Now Con was trying to push me, not only into opening the bottle and letting those feelings out, but into smashing the whole fucking thing.

"Don't be a fucking pussy. Either hit me or start walking," he goaded.

"Fuck off. Don't you think I've had a tough enough day without getting shit from you?" I asked, feeling more and more pissed off with each passing minute.

"So, are ya gonna stand there whining like a little bitch all night, or are ya gonna do something about it?" he asked, jabbing me in the face. I blocked and blocked over and over until he finally scoffed and muttered, "You don't deserve her."

Like someone releasing pressure from a safety valve, I let the pure, unadulterated rage pour out of me. There was no skill in the way that I pounded on him. What every punch lacked in technique, it made up for in power. He took a few hits, but Con was never one to lie there and take a beating, not even for me. It just wasn't in his nature to allow himself to be subjugated. Instead, he blocked and jabbed. He didn't look for openings to beat on me, and Lord knows I'd left him many. But he didn't make it easy on me either. With every hit, I thought about how it would feel if Marie or the baby died, or if Alastair lured her away from me. The tipping point was imagining the agony of watching another man marrying my girl and raising my child. When I had nothing left to give, I threw my head back in pain and dropped to my knees, sobbing like a little fucking girl. Kneeing down beside me, Con grabbed my neck and pressed his forehead against my own.

"What the fuck am I going to do? I had everything, the whole fucking world in my hands. How did it all turn to shit so quickly? I can't lose either of them. And if Tommy doesn't wake up, how can I live with that for the rest of my life?"

"Then fucking do something about it!" he ordered.

"Do what?"

"You get your shit together and you fight for what you want, Kier. It's what we do."

CHAPTER TWENTY-EIGHT

MARIE

It was a universal truth that hospital beds were the loneliest places on earth. The second loneliest place was the chair beside the bed. With nowhere to go to escape from my worries, I stared at the walls, my hands covering my tiny belly, and I prayed for the life of my unborn child. I suspected that those very same walls had heard more prayers than the walls of a church.

It saddened me that more people seemed to want my little bean terminated than want it alive. Rationally, I knew it was because the people who cared about me truly believed my body couldn't handle carrying a baby. Matt's gibe that I could barely keep one person alive, let alone two, had hurt. But none of them had any idea. Not really. Because there was no force on earth more powerful than a mother's love. I didn't need to hold our baby in my arms to understand that. I felt the truth of it in every part of my body. And I would be anything, do anything I needed to do, to keep my baby safe. If it took every last beat of my heart and every last breath in my body, then so be it. But the thing of it was that I didn't feel weak or tearful. Maybe that would eventually come when the hormones kicked it. But the more I prayed, the more empowered I felt. With every fibre of my being, I knew.

I could do this.

"Hello, love. You know, you should try and get some rest," Mum said as she slipped quietly into my room.

"You know I never sleep well in hospitals. Five minutes in my own bed, and I'll be out like a light," I replied with a chuckle.

"You'll be back home in a couple of days."

"My new home," I reminded her. "Kieran moved all our stuff to the new house before I ended up in here."

"Have you both decided what you're going to do?" she asked me. Her tone was completely partisan, and I loved her for it.

"I wanted to give Kieran some space to really think things through. But, Mum, I really want this baby. I know it isn't logical or rational to want to put my body through this. I would never have planned a pregnancy, but now that it's happened, I'm all in, and I think Kieran is too. It's my body. My risk to take. And I know that my brothers won't support my decision, but if they take it out on Kieran again, we're going to have a serious falling out."

"Your brothers are scared. You may be their big sister, but they've been watching over you their whole life. They have no control over this, and it scares them. You just need to do what you always do."

"What's that?"

"Defy the odds," she explained. "Even if that means staying in bed for the rest of your pregnancy. You do what it takes to give this baby the best start and your own body the best chance."

"You're not going to fight me about keeping it?"

She sighed heavily in response. "I've watched over you every day since you were born, and not a day goes by that I don't worry about you. It's the nature of being a mother. But you've become a strong, independent woman, and you do things that most people in your situation wouldn't have dreamed possible. You're also the most stubborn of all my children. There never was any talking you out of something when you put your mind to it. So no. I'm not going to try and talk you out of it. You're a grown woman and it's your body. However, I reserve the right to nag you about taking care of yourself if I think you're overdoing it."

"Thanks, Mum. I knew you'd understand."

"I know a lot's happened in the last few days, but have you thought about what you're going to do with the shop if you keep the baby?"

"I guess I'm going to have to look for someone to run it full-time. I don't want to sell it, but if they put me on permanent bed rest, I don't want to worry about missing or rearranging appointments all the time."

"Well, I had an idea that I'd like to run by you. You see, I've loved working at the shop these last few years, and even though I might be tooting my own horn, I think I'm pretty good at sales."

"You sell more dresses than I do."

"Exactly. There were times I thought I'd like to experiment with different window displays or showcasing open catwalk evenings, but it was your business, and I never wanted to step on your toes. We use

Moira for alterations during the busy period, but now that her children are in school, I know she'd like to look for a full-time position. If you like the idea, I'd like to take over the running of the shop, with Moira doing the alterations full-time in your place. Now, your designs outsell everything in the shop and have done for a while. I'd like you to think about designing full-time, so that we can eventually faze everything else out and the shop can stock your work exclusively. It's what you've always wanted to do anyway, and this way you could do it from home without the pressure of running your own business. What do you think?"

"Are you kidding? I think it's a brilliant idea! But, Mum, that puts a huge responsibility on you. Are you sure you want to take so much on?" I asked her, worried that she was going to overdo things just to try and help me out.

"Honestly, I've spend most of my life taking care of our home and raising a family. With the shop, I feel like I've found something I'm really good at and that I have a flair for. I enjoy spending all my time there. But I promise, if there comes a time when I'm finding it too much for me, I'll tell you, and we can look for a new manager."

"Hey, sis," a sheepish Tristan said from the doorway.

"Hello," I replied stiffly.

"Ah, don't be mad," Tom added as he and Luca followed in behind Tristan.

"What do you mean don't be mad? You tore strips off my boyfriend and embarrassed me in front of my doctor. You're lucky I didn't let security toss you out on your arse."

"Do you blame us?" Luca replied. "I mean, we left for the rig and everything's hunky dory. A few weeks with Kieran and you're pregnant and laid up in hospital."

"None of that is his fault. I'm as much to blame about getting careless with contraception as he is. And it's not as if he's abandoning me to bring up this baby alone. None of you are being fair to him or acting the least bit like adults. I love you all, I really do, but if you want to be a part of ours and the baby's life, you need to grow up and stop treating me like a little girl. We need help and support, not snide remarks and the back end of your shitty tempers. Now, either you're with us on this, or you can fuck off back to the rig, because there's no compromise," I told them firmly. Then, when I thought about what I said, I turned to Mum. "Sorry for swearing, Mum."

She waved me away and looked like she was trying not to crack a smile.

"She gets it from, Ma," Tristan said to the boys.

"Yeah, I don't remember Dad ever being that mean," Tom added.

"Well?" I asked, looking at Luca.

"I'm not happy about it. Having a baby with your medical problems is a really bad idea. But now that I've had some time to calm down and think about it, I know you wouldn't get rid of it. We'll give you all the help and support that we can," he said.

I crossed my arms, raised an eyebrow, and waited. Luca rolled his eyes at me.

"Fine. We promise not to beat the shit out of your boyfriend as well," he added.

"You could try," I scoffed.

"Hey now, you don't think the three of us could take him?" Tristan asked.

"I have my doubts," I replied with a wry smile.

The boys launched into a huge debate as to why and how they could take Kieran, and any of the Driscoll's boys, and I laid back against my pillows, relieved that my family seemed to be at peace again.

* * *

Kieran texted me throughout the day to check in, but I was rarely alone. My brothers rotated their visits between my room, the nurses' station and the cafeteria, and I wondered if the hospital was supposed to stick to allocated visiting hours. If they were, my brothers ignored them. Whether it was because I was in a private room, or because they'd been using their considerable charm on the nursing staff at any available given opportunity, I didn't know. Still, I wasn't complaining. Now that they'd seemed to come around a bit, they were actually a lot of fun to spend time with. After all, they were well practiced at keeping me entertained in hospital.

Em popped by quickly to say hello and to bring me some chocolates and a get-well-soon card, but she didn't want to leave Tommy for long. Nat came in as she was leaving.

"So I saw Tristan earlier in the lobby, and he tells me you've got a bun in the oven!" she said, throwing her arms around me and giving me a huge squeeze. She lugged a huge carrier bag with her and began to unpack my body weight in fruit onto my bed.

"He's got such a lovely way with words," I told her.

"I can't believe you're having a baby!" she said excitedly.

I knew Nat wouldn't really understand the implications of being pregnant with my heart condition, but I wasn't about to disabuse her of her happiness. It was kind of refreshing to be around someone so unreservedly enthusiastic.

"I know! I'm not sure what kind of a mother I'll make, but I'm looking forward to trying."

"You'll make a brilliant mother. I can't believe you're having a baby before me though!"

"Yeah, well, it wasn't exactly planned. Kieran blames his super sperm," I told her jokingly.

"I know it came as a bit of a surprise," she said, "but do you have any regrets?"

"Not about us or the baby. I regret not taking a taxi to our new place. I'd give anything for Tommy not to have been hurt. It's killing Kieran knowing that one of his best friends is fighting for his life and that there's nothing he can do about it, especially as it was Kieran's bike he came off. No matter what anyone says, I think he blames himself for the accident."

"That's crazy," she replied. "Bad things happen to good people all the time. It's not his fault."

"Try telling him that. I don't think he'll be completely himself until Tommy recovers."

"Is he excited about the baby?" she asked, smiling.

"I think so, but it's still early days yet. So don't go out buying anything, okay? I don't want to jinx it," I warned her, knowing that mentally she probably already had little bean's first wardrobe already picked out.

"Fine!" she huffed, good-naturedly. "I can't really buy anything anyway until I know how big the baby will be. And I don't envy you there."

"Why?" I asked curiously.

"Well, your guy is a heavyweight fighter and your brothers are huge. With genes like that, this baby is bound to be massive!"

I froze as I contemplated with alarm the idea of my tiny frame trying to deliver a twelve-pound baby.

"Ah, don't worry about it," she said, seeing the look of abject horror across my face. "From what you told me about the size of his 'you know what,' and the number of times you guys have been at it, this baby will probably walk out."

My jaw dropped in shock, and as she burst out laughing at my expression, I threw a grape at her to shut her up.

* * *

By the time Nat left, I was exhausted. I wasn't lying when I said I couldn't sleep in hospital though. Maybe it was something about sleeping in such a public place that made me feel vulnerable. But whatever it was, the rest I so desperately needed was elusive. Hearing the creak of my door and seeing the slither of light shine across my bed, I smiled, knowing that he wouldn't wait until morning to see me.

"Hey, Irish. How's my girl?"

We'd only been apart for a matter of hours, but that deep,

delicious accent that was so familiar still made me tingle. I heard him kick off his boots and shrug off his hoodie before he lifted the sheet and slid into bed behind me.

"Now are you talking to me or the baby?" I replied.

"It's a girl?" he asked, his body completely frozen.

"I was joking, you lunatic. I have no idea. I don't think you can even tell until around four months. Why? Would having a girl be a bad thing?"

"Depends."

"On what?"

"On whether any of the other lads end up having boys. I don't fancy the idea of having to chase any of their randy offspring away from my daughter," he replied, making me laugh.

"And if your boy becomes one of the randy offspring?" I asked, still chuckling.

"No problem. I'll just teach him to use contraception better than his da."

His arm wrapped around my waist and he pulled me back into the warmth of his body. His thigh settled in between mine, and all of the vulnerability and anxiety that I felt earlier about lying there alone just slipped away.

"Sleep now, love. I've gotcha," he whispered in my ear.

"I love you," I told him as I drifted off to sleep.

"Not as much as I love you," he whispered back.

* * *

The next morning, I woke to find Kieran sitting in the chair next to my bed, watching me intently.

"How is it you look so perfect first thing in the morning, and I probably look and smell like roadkill?" I asked him, making him chuckle.

"You look adorable, and you smell like home," he told me, and I melted.

"I love it when you go mushy on me."

He gave me a pained smile.

"What is it?" I asked him seriously.

"I didn't want to tell you last night, because I knew you wouldn't sleep, but Alastair stopped me in the hospital car park yesterday. He pissed me off by telling me to stay away from you, but he started acting all crazy when I told him you were pregnant. Irish, he admitted that he was the driver of the car that hit you. He assumed it was me with one of the boys on the back, and that with me out of the picture, you'd fall into his arms and live happily ever after,"

"Oh my God. You're kidding me? I figured that he wasn't well, but I never imagined that he could be capable of something like this. How could he?"

"Look, it gets worse. After everything that went down with your brothers, and after finding out that he put you and Tommy in hospital, I lost it. I beat the crap out of him. I would have kept going as well, but Con pulled me off."

"Are you okay?" I asked, only just noticing his split and bruised knuckles.

"Yeah, I'm better for lying in your arms all night. You anchor me when I'm feeling lost, you know?"

I nodded in reply. I did know, because he did the same for me.

"I don't know what sort of shape he's in, but quite frankly, I couldn't give a fuck. I'd be dead right now if he had his way. And if Tommy dies, he'd better fucking hide, because if I find him, I'll finish what I started."

"What are we going to do?" I asked. It terrified me that I'd never realised that Alastair was capable of something like this.

"*We* are not going to do anything, love. Your job is to rest and take care of yourself. I'm going down to the police station with Con later today, and I'm going to give a statement about what went down. Hopefully, they'll find something at the accident that ties it to Alastair. If not, the police will at least interview him and maybe they'll work out how fucking crazy he actually is."

"Shouldn't I come with you? They'll want to interview me as well, won't they?"

"If they do, they'll come here and I'll be with you. In the meantime, I think I gave him enough of a beating to scare him off, but I want to let your brothers know what went down so they can make sure you aren't left alone until I get back."

"He wouldn't try anything here though, would he? I mean, we're in a hospital. There are cameras everywhere."

"No, I don't think he would either, but I'd rather be safe than sorry. When it comes to you and the baby, I'm not taking any chances with your safety. Plus, I know you'll worry the whole time I'm gone. At least now you'll have your brothers to distract you," he said, smiling.

He leaned over to grabbed my hand and laid a kiss in my palm before wrapping his big hand around mine. The way he stared deep into my eyes was so intense. Neither of us looked away until the doctor came in on his rounds.

"Good morning, Miss Kelly, how are you feeling today?" he asked.

"Ready to go home," I told him truthfully.

"Looking at your observations, I think we'll be able to grant that wish today. Have you thought any more about what we discussed yesterday?"

I looked towards Kieran for confirmation, and he nodded with a smile.

"We understand the risks, and plans are underway for me to give up work so that I can relax and take it easy during the pregnancy. We've decided to keep the baby," I told him. When he asked for my decision, there was no hesitation. With Kieran's hand in mine, I'd never felt so loved, so protected, and so sure of the future.

CHAPTER TWENTY-NINE

KIERAN

"I understand. I'm still going to refer you to your own cardiologist who will be in touch shortly. I imagine that he will want to see you for a further consultation and to set up regularly scheduled appointments throughout your pregnancy. In the meantime, I'd like to do an ultrasound before I discharge you, if that's okay with you," the doctor said.

"That would be great, thank you," Irish replied.

She looked so fucking pretty. Sure, she was scratched and bruised, but without even a stitch of makeup, she was still the most beautiful woman I'd ever seen.

A few hours later, we were waiting patiently outside the ultrasound department when Irish caught me staring.

"What?" she questioned.

"You've been rocking this 'Sarah Connor' vibe since you woke up this morning, like you're ready to point a gun at the next person who threatens our kid. It's pretty fuckin' sexy.".

"Sarah Connor really does it for you, huh?"

"Nah, but I'm picturing you in full tactical gear right now, and that's really doing it for me."

"You always know how to make me smile."

"No matter how difficult things get, I promise I'll always be there to make you smile," I vowed.

Leaning forward, she kissed me gently on the lips and, slipping her arm through mine, laid her head on my shoulder. All around me the world stopped, and the subtle scent of apples filled my lungs. Through the pain and noise, the heartache and chaos, she was my peace. Her strength and optimism gave me hope that somehow, despite all the shite the world was throwing my way, everything was going to be all right.

"Marie Kelly?" a nurse called out, breaking the spell. Hand in hand, we followed her to a small room where another technician was waiting.

"Hi. My name is Miranda, and I'll be doing your ultrasound today. Can you lay down on the bed for me and lift your top up until it rests just beneath your bra?" she asked Irish. Felling like a bit of a useless prick, I sat down in the "Dad" chair next to the bed and reached for Irish's hand.

Earlier this morning, I'd downloaded a pregnancy app to my phone that would show me day by day how the baby was growing and what Irish would be feeling. Tommy would have loved giving me shit about it. Fuck, I missed him. It was funny how you didn't realise how deeply a part of your life someone was until they were gone. He might still be alive, but I felt like he was lost.

A bit of research told me that bean really was about the size of a bean. That being said, I wasn't expecting much from the scan.

I was so wrong.

When that sound, so quick and strong, echoed around the room, I fell in love all over again. I pictured myself holding my father for the very last time, and I felt like he was right there with me in the beat of my baby's heart. It was the most beautiful music I'd ever heard. Irish looked up, eyes filled with tears, and for the first time since I'd lost my father, I knew.

I'd found the miracle that made my life complete.

"Well, congratulations, Mum and Dad. The baby has a good, strong heartbeat, and from the measurements I've taken, I'd estimate you to be about nine weeks along. So, all being well, you're looking at a spring baby," the technician said. She handed me pictures that she'd printed out for us to keep. Staring at the fuzzy image, I wondered how someone so tiny had the power to bring a man like me to my knees. Because from this moment on, my life would never be the same.

* * *

"Are you and the boys good to stay with her today? I don't want to leave her alone with Alastair still running around," I said to Luca.

"You do know that we were looking after her long before you came along, don't you?" he replied sarcastically.

"Yeah, well, she's mine to look after now, and I don't want her alone."

"I get that you worry about her, but I think that we can handle Alastair," he scoffed.

"He deliberately drove a car into the back of my bike and put Tommy and your sister in the hospital. Are you seriously willing to take the risk that he won't try something else now that he knows she's pregnant? Because I'm fuckin' not," I said angrily.

I liked Irish's brothers, but I was getting seriously fucked off with this shit. If Tommy or any of the boys were here and I asked them to look after my girl, they'd have guarded her with their lives.

"He did what? I knew he was doing some creepy stalker shit, but nothing like this" Luca replied, his expression becoming stormy.

"It's a long story and I'll explain later. Just don't leave her," I told him.

"We're not going anywhere. One of us will be with her all day," he reassured me.

I nodded, hoping I was doing the right thing. I hated leaving, but Irish had enough to worry about without the constant threat of Alastair hanging over our heads. What I wanted to do was find him and beat the shit out of him again. But my child's father needed to be a better man than that. It was time I started thinking with my head, instead of my fist.

We walked into Irish's room and saw her dressed and sat on the bed.

"Have you been discharged?" I asked.

"The nurse is doing the paperwork now," she replied. Her packed bag waited at the foot of the bed, and I could tell she was eager to leave.

"Won't you let me come with you?" she pleaded.

"No, love, you need to be resting. I don't want you or the baby in that dirty fuckin' building full of criminals."

She rolled her eyes at me. "It's full of police as well you know."

"Yeah, forgive me if I don't want my hot, pregnant girlfriend around a bunch of guys in uniform either," I replied, moving to stand between her legs.

She grabbed the collar of my jacket and pulled me forward until our noses were touching.

Luca coughed loudly, letting us know he was still there.

"Yeah, I'm just gonna take Marie's bag down to the car. Try and remember when I'm gone that she's my sister. There's some shit brothers really don't need to see," Luca mumbled the last bit to himself as he grabbed Marie's bag.

She looked anxious as she slipped a hand inside my jacket, running it down my chest until it rested over my heart.

"It's so strong," she whispered.

"That's because it beats for you."

Her smile was a punch to the gut every time. I traced my calloused thumb gently across her bottom lip, mesmerised by its softness.

"I feel like I should go with you, like it's the right thing to do," she said.

"Do you know what I've been dreaming about these last few days?" I brushed her hair over her shoulder, so I could lean in to kiss and nuzzle the underside of her jaw.

"What?" she asked breathlessly.

"You and me. In our own bed. In our own house. I wanna strip you bare so we're skin to skin and smell you as I sleep. Even if the doctor says we can't have sex for a while, I still want you that way. I want to kiss every inch of your body, so when you close your eyes, it's me you dream of," I said in between kisses.

"It's always you."

A feeling of fierce possessiveness, like nothing I'd ever felt before, rolled over me. I wanted to wrap her up in cotton wool and keep her safe from the rest of the world until the baby came. I knew she'd never agreed to it. She was far too independent to let me closet her. But this aggressive need to protect and defend what was more sacred to me than anything else in the world was consuming me. Death laid his hand upon her once, upon the one person to epitomise life itself. If I had to sell my soul to keep her, it wouldn't touch her again. I vowed, that when she closed her eyes for the last time, it would be as an old lady, warm in her bed.

"One more day," I promised her, "and I'll make it happen."

"One more day," she agreed, rolling her head to the side to make room for me. I slid my hand into her hair as I resumed my path of kisses. It was pure, blissful torture to be so close to her, knowing that I had to leave. Her touches were feather light, fingertips stroking along skin, lips brushing across lips. Each touch branded her even more deeply into my soul.

One more day.

That was all, but I felt a terrible sense of foreboding in our parting, and suddenly, one more day seemed like an eternity away.

"Jesus Christ, are you two still at it?" Luca said from the

doorway.

"I'll see you tonight, but I'll call you later, okay?" I said. "Con texted to say that Tommy is allowed visitors, so I want to see him before I come home."

"Do you think his family would mind if I visit?" she asked.

"Of course they wouldn't. If you feel up to it, I'll take you tomorrow," I told her.

"I'd like that. I'll see you tonight." She kissed me goodbye, and Luca coughed again, making her giggle. It was that beautiful sound that followed me. The sound I wanted to listen to for the rest of my life.

* * *

My morning at the police station felt like a complete waste of fucking time. The officers I spoke to seemed like decent guys, but they weren't exactly optimistic about my chances of getting Tommy and Irish the justice they deserved. Irish hadn't made a single complaint to the police about Alastair's stalking, so it would really be her word against his. After a lengthy argument, they agreed to investigate, but unless they could find the car, there was nothing to tie the manipulative little shit to the accident. Even then they warned that a decent barrister might be able to argue that someone else had been driving.

It was only last night, when I was wondering what Danny would make of all this, that it occurred to me that there might be another party with a vested interest in sorting out this mess. Needing to cover up the tattoos and make myself halfway presentable, I rushed home to change into my universal suit. The one and only suit I owned that only made an appearance for hatches, matches, and dispatches. Liam had taken Dris to Ma's, and I realised something. Our house that I'd loved so much was just a shell. It took Irish and Dris to make it a home.

I looked up at the imposing red, brick building. It smelt of old money, if that were possible. I smoothed my hand nervously down my black, silk tie. Taking a deep breath, I reached for the chrome handle of the monstrous glass door as I steeled myself to look like a man holding all the cards.

Four hours later, I walked down the sterile hospital corridor lined with rows of mundane artwork designed to make each of the halls completely indistinguishable from any other.

At the end of the long walk sat John, Tommy's da. With his head tipped back against the wall and his eyes closed, he looked like he was praying. The last few days had aged him immeasurably. His hands rested on his knees. Those hands, that had looked so strong and capable when I was boy, were now so weathered and frail. He opened his eyes as he heard my footsteps walking towards him, and he gave me a sad smile.

"Kieran, my boy. How are you doing?"

His wife was so vibrant and full of life, but John couldn't be more different. His calm, steadfast nature meant that they were the perfect balance for one another. He was her rock and the centre of her world. You only needed to be in the same room as them to see the love they had for one another was a palpable thing.

"Shouldn't I be asking you that question?" I asked, taking a seat next to him.

"I'm as good as can be expected, son."

"Where's Mary?"

"She wanted to go to mass, so your Ma's taken her down to see Father Pat."

"You didn't want to go too?"

"The nurse is in with him at the moment, and I like to be the last one to say goodnight to my boy. Besides, I don't need church to know that God's right here with me."

I swallowed hard against the painful lump in my throat. Leaning my elbows on my knees, I pressed the heels of my hands against my eyes, willing away the tears that didn't deserve to fall. Tommy was John's only son, a son that was completely devoted to his parents. They had raised a great man, a strong, powerful man with a heart of gold. To sit here now, night after night, never knowing when he would wake, was a travesty that no parent should have to endure. But they had endured it. They were enduring it with a strength of character that took my breath away.

"I'm so sorry, John. I'm so sorry for everything. Sorry that it was my bike he came off. Sorry that I asked him to ride it. Sorry that I haven't been here more since the accident. That I've let the boys be here for you and Mary when it should have been me," I apologised.

"Do you remember after your da died, you came to stay with us for a couple of weeks?" he asked me. I shook my head to answer no, not trusting my voice not to break.

"Well, ya did. And every night you used to cry in your sleep.

You didn't really wake up, so Mary and I were at a loss for what to do. Eventually, Tommy heard you. He never came to get us, or asked us what to do. He just climbed into your bed and gave you a hug till you stopped crying. There aren't many boys at the age you were then who'd have done that. But my Tommy, he didn't even think about it. Now, I don't suppose he ever told you about that, did he?"

I shook my head again, stunned that I'd never heard this story before.

"Well, that's Tommy for you. Always takin' care of the people he loves, whether they know it or not. And if he were awake, that's what he'd be expecting you to do. Not moping around worrying about him. He'd be telling you to take care of that girl of yours. 'Course then he'd be warning you about how he's gonna be stealin' her away as soon as he was back on his feet, but that's Tommy," he said with a wry chuckle. "Now, I think I'm going to stretch my legs a little and get a cup of coffee. Maybe even have a sneaky cigarette, seeing as Mary isn't here to give me grief about it. You want anything while I'm gone?"

"No thanks, John. I'm just going to visit with him a bit, if that's okay?"

"You go right ahead," he replied. "Tell him his old man will be in soon."

I walked into the dimly lit room to see a nurse writing in his notes.

"How's he doing?" I asked her.

"He's holding in there," she replied with a genuine smile.

"When will he wake up?"

"Honestly? We don't know. He's been in a medically induced

coma since his surgery to allow time for the swelling on his brain to go down. We took him off the medication that keeps him in a coma this afternoon, but there's no hard and fast rule about how long it will take him to wake up."

"But he'll be okay though when he wakes up, won't he?" I asked, my voice breaking a little.

"I'm afraid we don't know that either. He sustained significant head injuries. Only time will tell whether any of those injuries resulted in permanent brain damage," she explained sympathetically.

I swallowed hard and nodded, like I understood exactly what she was talking about. But I didn't understand. Not at all.

"I'll leave you two to catch up." She replaced his notes and left us together.

Alone, but for the quiet beeping of his heart machine, I sat in the worn, padded chair, and just cried. Tommy's body was a fuckin' mess. His face, his arms, even his hands were completely battered. Everywhere I looked, tubes and wires were sticking out of him, but the worst thing of all was the quiet. Tommy had never been quiet in all the time I'd known him. I spent most of our lives trying to shut him up. Now, I'd give anything to hear him speak. When I was done, I wiped my eyes and chuckled.

"I know, I know, I'm a fuckin' pussy. It's what you're thinking, isn't it?" I said to him. "Well, you can spend the rest of our lives taking the piss out of me for cryin' over you, but you've got to wake up first, buddy. This fucked-up dysfunctional family only works with you in it.

"You know, since you've been lying here, I've been going over and over all the things I should have told you, like how you're the heart of us all. The one who makes us laugh, the one who protects and cares for the people we care about. The one who's always been there for us. Then I realised that you don't need me to tell you that, because deep down, I think you already know. What you probably haven't realised is how much we need you to come back. No matter what, the four of us were never alone, because we always had each other. Without you, we're all just drifting. Without you, we're anchorless.

"So, you don't get to choose to stay asleep. You don't get to decided that you're too tired to open your eyes, and wake the fuck up. Whatever it takes, whatever you need to do, you come home. Because otherwise, what's the fuckin' point? Where's the happily ever after for all the shit we've endured if we lose you? I don't accept that can happen. We need you back. I need you back. And I've seen enough of hospitals to last me a lifetime. So stop fuckin' around with this coma shit. It's time to come home now." Closing my eyes, I folded my arms on the bed, rested my weary head, and waited.

CHAPTER THIRTY

ALASTAIR

I never liked Marie's brothers. It wasn't as though we'd ever properly been introduced, but I didn't like how they acted around one another and how they were all so "familiar." Not having any siblings, I had no benchmark for their behaviour of course, but I thought that it was appropriate to have a little more decorum in familial relationships. Of course, her family would always be part of her life, but I'd insist on that distance once we were married. After all, it was the appropriate thing to do. And we would be married. Of that I had no doubt. Once she saw what that animal she was besotted with had done to me, the veil would fall from her eyes and she would see me for what I really was—a man worthy of being her husband.

The first time that I saw her, she was sat at a bus stop. I shuddered at the thought of her on public transport, but she'd get used to being chauffer driven soon enough. Her pink cheeks had been flushed from the cold, and she'd smiled as she'd given up her seat for some old lady. Something in her eyes spoke to me, and then and there I'd picked up the phone and cancelled every meeting I had that day and followed her. To work, to the supermarket, even to her home, and by the end of that day, I knew she was the one for me. The one who'd make me the perfect wife. The one who'd never leave me, not like my bitch of a mother and every single nanny who followed thereafter.

She'd told me that she didn't want to see me again, but I knew she didn't mean it. I was wrong about the other girls, but I was right about her. I was sure of it. I just needed to make her see what I could see. Maybe I was getting a little desperate and was doing things I wasn't proud of, but she'd forgive me in the end; I knew she would.

I waited for a long time to make my move. She was so rarely alone, but I knew this was a conversation that needed to be private. The eldest brother left her room, and it sounded like he was talking through a situation with his employer. He held his hand up in the doorway to indicate that he'd be five minutes, then walked into the waiting room to finish the call.

Five minutes was all I needed anyway. I slipped into her room before the door clicked shut and just starred. She looked tired, but still so exquisite.

"Get out," she ordered, pointing at the door.

"Now, just hear me out. You owe me that," I told her.

"I don't owe you anything. I know what you did to me and to Tommy. You could have killed us!" she said accusingly.

"You must know I didn't mean for that to happen. I was desperate. You couldn't see the real me with him around. You wouldn't even give us a chance."

"I don't have anything left to say to you, Alastair. Please leave." She sounded sad.

"Not until you promise that you'll leave him."

"You've got to be kidding."

"He's no good for you. You have to see that. Just look at what he did to me." I gestured towards my face. "Is this the kind of animal you'd rather be with, someone so ugly and common and violent. I would worship you if you'd only give us a chance."

"And putting two people in hospital, nearly killing one of them, isn't violent?" she scoffed. "Despite what you believe, Kieran is the gentlest man I've ever met. You nearly killed his girlfriend and his best friend with this obsession. I'm surprised he didn't hit you harder."

"No matter what, you'll never see him for what he really is, will you?" Why couldn't she see how perfect everything could be? How could he have such a poisonous hold over her? "Well, I'm not asking any more. For your own good, I'm telling you. Stay away from him."

"Or what?" she asked quietly.

Slipping a hand into the inside pocket of my bespoke Saville Row suit, I pulled out a USB stick and threw it on her bed.

"What is it?" she asked.

"It's the cctv footage of Kieran beating me in the hospital car park. An edited version of that violent thug nearly beating to death a well-respected member of the legal community."

"Any jury in the world would understand his reaction after what you'd done," she replied, still starring at the memory stick.

"What have I done? There's not a shred of evidence tying me

to the accident. I was an old friend coming to visit you in hospital when I was jumped by your jealous, violent boyfriend," I replied, perhaps a tad smugly.

"You can't do this," she whispered.

"Well, that rather depends on you, doesn't it? I can tell you from experience that he'll be convicted and will mostly likely face a prison sentence. He'll lose his boxing license, his title, and his livelihood. It will destroy his life. But if you leave him, then he can keep his career. All I want is you."

"I'm pregnant," she protested. "You can't make me do this. Not when we're having a child together."

"I won't lie. I was devastated when I found out. That baby was supposed to be mine. But I will raise it as my own. It will never take over the family business, but I won't make you get rid of it. In time, we'll have our own children and all of this unpleasantness will be a distant memory," I said magnanimously.

"Please don't make me do this," she pleaded, one last time.

"It's done, Marie. You have tonight to end things with him. Tomorrow, I want you in my office at twelve o'clock sharp. Bring a bag, because you'll be living with me from now on until our engagement is formerly announced and we can be married. You should say goodbye to your family for a while as well. After their involvement in this meaningless relationship of yours, I think that a little detachment is called for."

"You're a monster."

"No, sweetheart, I'm your guardian angel. You just can't see me for the devil who blinds you," I replied before letting myself out.

THE STORM

Sinking my hands into the pockets of my tailored trousers, I took the elevator to the basement and whistled a little tune as I strolled back towards my Aston Martin. Now that everything was coming up roses, I felt lighter than air.

CHAPTER THIRTY-ONE

MARIE

Light was streaming through the partially closed curtains, but I struggled to open my eyes. I couldn't ever remember crying as much as I had last night, and my eyes were puffy and swollen. I held it together as long as I possibly could with Luca there, but as soon as I could plead tiredness and escape to bed, I sobbed into my pillow until sleep finally claimed me.

Kieran's body spooned me from behind. His huge, tanned hand spread protectively across my belly. There would never be a child who was more loved that this one. If protecting it was the last thing I ever did, Alastair would never lay a finger on our baby. I just needed to find a way to protect the man I loved while I was at it. Last night had been my moment of weakness. With the dawn came strength and resolve. This giant of a man, with a heart bigger than anyone I'd ever met, had chosen me. He would defend and guard the baby and me with his life. I would offer him no less.

"What you thinkin' on so hard there, Irish?" he asked me sleepily.

"Alastair came to see me yesterday," I admitted softly.

"The fuck he did!" Kieran replied, now fully awake. "I fuckin' told Luca I wanted him by your side from the minute I was gone to the minute I got back."

"It isn't his fault. He went next door to take a call from work, and Alastair slipped in. Kier, he has footage of you beating him up. Unless I leave you and agree to move in with him and bring the baby up as his, he's going to press charges for assault and release it to the police."

Kieran reacted in the last way I ever expected. He threw his head back and laughed.

"That man is fucking delusional if he thinks that's ever happening," he said.

"Kieran, this is serious! He could end your career. You could go to prison for this!" I was horrified that he wasn't taking this seriously.

"Do you trust me?" he asked, rubbing slow circles across my abdomen.

"Of course I trust you."

"Then stop worrying and leave this to me."

"Kieran, whatever you're planning, I don't want you going to prison. It's not worth it. Maybe if I just took off for a bit and showed him that we were apart from each other, without actually going to him, that would be enough."

"Yeah, that's not happening, baby. Not ever. A couple of years in prison to know that my family is protected is a sacrifice I'd make, but trust me when I say it won't come to that." He looked so resolved and powerful that it was hard not to trust that he knew what he was doing. A scratching at the door caught my attention.

"What's that?" I asked, pulling the sheet higher up my body.

"A neglected member of our family wanting some attention I'd guess." He jumped out of bed to open the door. The minute he did, Dris came bounding in and made a pathetic attempt to jump on the bed. Kieran scooped him up with his big hands and dumped him in my lap.

"I've only been gone a few days. How'd you get so big? Huh, baby, how'd you get so big?" I cooed, tickling my gorgeous puppy as he covered my face in sloppy wet kisses.

"Ma's probably been feeding him like she used to feed me," he said, rubbing Driscoll's belly.

"Well, I'm afraid I burn water, so you might be running back to your mum for a few meals yet," I warned him.

"If my boy is half the size I am, he's going to need good nutrition and a shit ton of food," he replied. "Lucky for you, Ma raised me right and I'm a god in the kitchen, so expect to be nice and fat by the time the baby comes." He bent down to kiss where his hands had been.

"I'm sure you'll still find me attractive if I completely ballooned up. A guy isn't even supposed to see his girl without makeup for at least a year," I replied.

"Believe me, Irish, when I tell you that there is nothing sexier in the world than watching you eat food I cooked and knowing that I'm not only taking care of you, but in my own small way, I'm feeding our son," he said gruffly, and I melted into him just a little more.

"God, I hope she has your accent," I said with a sigh. I could listen to that deep, delicious Irish brogue of his for hours.

"*He*, baby," he corrected.

"Why are you so certain we're having a boy?" I twisted around to see his face.

"Have you seen the size of me?" he asked. "There's no way I could father something feminine and delicate. I'm telling you, it's a boy."

"It's pointless to argue with you about how your size has absolutely nothing to do with the sex of the baby, isn't it?" I closed my eyes as he slowly kissed a path from my collarbone to my jaw.

"Trust me, Irish," he replied. "I've got this."

* * *

At five minutes to midday, I stood at the imposing doors of Alastair's legal practice.

"I think I'm going to be sick," I admitted. "What if he calls the police? If they arrest you for causing trouble at the office, on top of the assault charges, they're going to send you to prison for sure."

"I'm not going to cause any trouble. And if he calls the police, we'll deal with it. Now let's get this over with so we can go home. The sooner I get you back to bed, the better," Kieran told me.

He seemed like he didn't have a care in the world. Either he knew something I didn't, or he gave a convincing act. I let him usher me into reception, already regretting that I hadn't listened to my gut and come alone.

"Hi. My name is Marie Kelly. I'm here to see Alastair Baxter-Hall," I said to the receptionist with as much calm as I could muster.

"Of course, Miss Kelly. Mr Baxter-Hall is expecting you. Please let me show you to his office," she replied politely.

Everything about this place screamed power and prestige, and I felt like I was suffocating with every step closer to him. If the receptionist was surprised that I was not unaccompanied, she didn't show it. She knocked on a mahogany door at the end of a long hallway and waited.

"Come in," boomed Alastair's voice.

"Miss Kelly to see you, sir," she said.

"Send her in," he replied, and she held the door open for us to pass before shutting it gently behind her.

"What in the hell is he doing here? And where is your bag?" Alastair barked the second the door closed.

"I see my warning to keep away from my girl didn't hold much faith," Kieran said to him, but Alastair didn't take his eyes off me. He shook his head, like he was bitterly disappointed.

"I should have known better than to give you a chance to come of your own free will. I knew what a hold he had over you," he said to me.

"You should have done it properly the first time," Kieran told him. "Because over my dead body is the only way of getting to my girl."

"I hoped it wouldn't come to this, but I'm pressing charges. You're going to need a father for that baby when he's in prison, and I intend to be it," Alastair said.

I stared at him with my mouth open in shock. How could he be this delusional? If he had Kieran arrested, I would hate him until the day he died.

"I can see why you fell in love with her," Kieran said to him. "She's so easy to love. Her choosing me wasn't just a leap of faith. It was a fuckin' miracle. Her love is a gift, but it don't mean anything if she doesn't give it freely. No matter how much you want to, you can't force her to fall in love with you. I count my blessings every day I wake up knowing that she picked me. And I know, I've always known, that I'm nowhere near good enough for her. I can't give her the fancy shit you'd be able to, and I'm never gonna have a big law firm or some fancy degree from some fancy law school. But I love her. I will love her until the day I die, and I will always put her happiness before my own and never, ever, put her in harm's way. Can you say the same?"

"You talk a good talk, Mr Doherty, but the truth is that if you were putting her happiness before your own, you'd have walked away long ago and let her have a life you couldn't dream of giving her," Alastair rebutted.

"Can you say the same?" Kieran persisted.

"Of course I can," Alastair fired back angrily.

"Then, explain how you could drive a car into the back of my bike, knowing there was a chance she'd ride on it with me," Kieran asked, and we all fell silent.

"You left me no other choice," Alastair said to me. "No matter what I did, you were never going to be mine as long as he was around. I had no choice...," he said, trailing off as he contemplated how far he'd gone.

"You have to let me go now, Alastair. I've made my choice. It's over," I said, willing him to put an end to this craziness so we could get on with our lives.

"It's not over, Marie. You'll see. Once this goes public," he said, pulling out another USB drive and waving it around, "you and everyone else will understand what he's really like. When he's gone, we can start all over again. You never really got to know me the first time, but now with the baby coming, you could give up work and we could spend some time together. Maybe go on a holiday somewhere hot."

He was getting more and more frantic as he illustrated all of the ways life would be better, and my blood ran cold as reality set in. There was never going to be any getting away from this. He was never going to stop.

The door opened sharply and in walked an older gentleman, who was holding a mobile phone.

"I've heard enough, Mr Doherty. I agree to your terms," he said to Kieran.

"Dad, what are you doing here?" Alastair asked the older gentlemen. "You're just in time to meet Marie."

He moved towards me with his arm wide, like he was really going to introduce me to his father. I took a step back and wrapped my arm around my stomach protectively.

"Wait... what do you mean you agree to his terms?" Alastair said as his father's words sank in.

"Mr Doherty came to me yesterday with a rather outlandish

story. There were elements of it that rang true—your behaviour towards his girlfriend and the suggestion of stalking. On its own I would, perhaps have believed that history was repeating itself. But then he accused you orchestrating a bike accident, the result of which put two people in hospital. At that point, I suggested that he leave my office. But he insisted on laying out his proposition, that if he could get you to admit to the accident, that I would see to it that you were sectioned, so that you could get proper help," Alastair's dad explained.

"He's lying, Dad. Whatever he said, he's lying," Alastair protested. He was pulling manically on his hair as he paced backwards and forwards.

"I heard you, son. Mr Doherty telephoned me before he came in here. I heard everything," he replied sadly. "I blame myself for allowing it to get this far. When I think of all the families I paid off, the people I bribed to make your little indiscretions go away, I'm horrified. I always knew that you were highly strung, that you let your crushes become infatuations. But you're a bloody good lawyer. You're in line to take over the business when I'm gone. I... I never dreamt I was helping to cover up a mental illness. That you could become violent."

"I'm not ill, Dad. Why would you think I was ill? Things have never been more clear. Those other girls weren't real. Like you said, they were just infatuations. I'm in love with Marie. She's going to be the perfect wife for me. Just like Mum was for you," Alastair protested.

"Is that what you think?" his dad said. It was like he'd aged in the few minutes he'd been in the room. I guess shock did that to people, but I couldn't quite bring myself to feel sorry for him. Alastair was sick. From what I'd heard, the signs of his mental illness had been apparent for a while. And, instead of supporting his son and getting him the help he needed, he'd brushed everything under the carpet and covered it up to avoid any embarrassment.

"Alastair, my marriage to your mother was an arrangement. I was getting older and I needed an heir. She was a beautiful young woman who wanted to marry a man with money. She upheld her end of the bargain, and when she'd had enough of motherhood, we reached an amicable financial settlement, and I hired suitable nannies to raise you until you could join me here."

I looked at Alastair's broken face, and I felt a great swell of pity. His whole life, he'd never been loved, never been wanted, except as a pawn in the family dynasty.

"I thought she died," he whispered.

"Why would you think that?" his dad asked.

"I don't remember her and you never talked about her. I thought you loved her and she died, and that's why you never talk about her or why there aren't any pictures, because the memories are too painful," he replied.

"Oh, son, what have I done?" his dad said to himself. Walking over to Alastair, he hugged him, and Alastair sank into his embrace. His Dad looked stilted and awkward, and I cried inside for the messed-up kid who needed more hugs than his useless father could ever hope to make up for now.

After an uncomfortable few seconds, his dad patted him on the back, looking embarrassed and unsure of himself.

"It's time to go, son. I'll share out your cases with the other associates until you're well enough to come back."

Alastair just nodded. Everything he'd done was for his father's approval. To live the life he thought his father had. To realise that everything he thought he wanted was a lie, had devastated him. Alastair desperately needed help. If it was the only decent thing his dad would ever do, I prayed he got it for him.

As they walked out of the office, his dad turned to Kieran.

"I assume you'll drop this complaint with the police about my son's involvement with the accident now that I'm ensuring that he'll get the help he needs? If the media gets wind of this, the damage it will cause to the reputation of this firm will be immeasurable."

"You assume wrong," Kieran replied. "I won't go to the press with this, like we agreed, but I'll do everything in my power to make the police press charges. I owe it to Tommy and his family. I owe it to my girl." The finality in his voice made it clear that there was no arguing with him. I rubbed my baby, this time for comfort. I had trusted him, and he hadn't let me down. He'd done the right thing, the honourable thing, this man that would be the father of my child.

Alastair's father nodded sadly, understanding Kieran's resolve, before leaving with his son.

Kieran held out his hand to me, his strong, capable hand. I took it, and everything was right with the world.

"Come on, Irish," he said, lifting our joined hands to kiss the back of mine. "Let's go home."

CHAPTER THIRTY-TWO

KIERAN

I will remember January tenth for the rest of my life. It was the day that Tommy woke up.

For ten days, every one of us guys took it in turns to stay by his side while he endured test after test, all of them designed to figure out what worked and what didn't. Considering that Tommy was still only a probationary firefighter, I was surprised to see so many firefighters stopping by to check in on him.

On the final day of assessments, we all found ourselves waiting outside for Mary and John to deliver the news, whatever it may be.

Despite her protests, I persuaded Irish to stay at home with Dris. Hours of waiting on a hard, plastic hospital chair wasn't good for her or the baby. Em didn't even get the opportunity to try one out. As soon as he sat down, Con hauled her into his lap, settled her body in close, and spread a huge hand possessively across her abdomen. In between kisses, he peppered her with dozens of questions. Was she hungry, was she thirsty, was she comfortable, was she warm enough? Em answered every question with different variations of "I'm fine" and a gentle smile.

"When's the baby due?" I asked.

"What? Err...? What do you mean? What was the question again?" Em said nervously.

"Three weeks after yours is due," Con replied, wearing a huge grin.

"Con!" Em protested, smacking him on the chest.

"Sorry, Sunshine, but he guessed!" Con replied, not looking the least bit sorry.

"Admit it, you couldn't wait to tell him," she accused playfully.

"Baby, I'd broadcast it on national television if I could," Con agreed.

"Knowing that you're on national television every time you fight, I wouldn't put it past you to do just that," Em replied, laughing.

Con gazed at her adoringly before pulling her in for a kiss.

"How'd you know anyway?" Con asked me when he finally pulled his lips away from his wife.

"Are you kidding me? In case you weren't aware, you're a tad overprotective lately," I pointed out.

Con frowned, looking confused, which I thought was pretty fucking comical.

"Con, my girl has a serious heart condition, so I got reason to worry, and if I acted half as crazy around Irish as you do around Em, she'd have punched me in the balls by now," I told him truthfully, making him frown even harder.

"Honestly, it's fine, love," Em told him with a smile. "I like that you want to take care of us."

As soon as she said the word "us" it was like he got a hit of testosterone. He nuzzled her neck, making a giggle, and rubbed her belly gently. I rolled my eyes at their antics and began to regret not bringing Irish with me. There wasn't a morning that I didn't wake up and wonder what a lucky son of a bitch I was that she chose me.

She was already sporting a tiny little bump. Ma told me that plants grow strong when you feed and talk to 'em. I figured the same was probably true for babies, so I talked to little bean every morning before we got out of bed, and I fed my girl every chance I got. I was already planning what to cook her that night, now I knew Em was expecting. No way was Con's boy gonna be bigger than mine.

"I wish you could see your face right now," Em said to me, smiling. "You laugh at Con, but your face gets all dreamy when you're thinking about Marie."

Con laughed, and I gave him the finger. I was about to give him shit when Tommy's door opened and three doctors came out. Taking that as our cue, we all rushed into the room. When I saw Mary sobbing into John's shoulder, my heart sank.

"What's up, ladies?" came a croaky, fragile voice from across the room.

"About time you woke up, ya lazy bastard," I said, grinning. I walked over to hug him as best I could, considering all the machines and crap around his bed. Moving out of the way so each of the lads could get their turn, I made my way over to Mary. John let her go to pass her a handkerchief from his pocket. She blew her nose loudly, then threw her arms around me. It was only then that I could see from her smile that they'd been happy tears.

"Oh, Kieran, the doctors say he's going to be fine. He's going to need intensive physiotherapy for his leg and plenty of rest, but now that the swelling has gone down, they said it doesn't look as though there's any lasting brain damage," she explained, the words pouring out of her with relief.

"At least, no more than there was before," Con said, smiling.

"I was so worried about you!" Em exclaimed, giving Tommy a big kiss.

"Hey now, let's not get carried away!" Con protested, frowning. I wrapped my big arms around Mary and smiled across at my friends. Everyone ribbing and taking the piss felt strangely normal, and we'd all missed normal so very much.

"The fire service been in touch yet?" Con asked.

"Yeah, the guys have been in, but I haven't seen any pen-pushers yet. Not much point yet until they know whether I'm ever going to be fit for active duty again," Tommy replied.

"You will be," I reassured him. "If it takes all of us in the gym with you every day for a month, we'll get you back in the truck."

"Well, there's something to look forward to," he joked. "I might take you up on the offer though. My leg's pretty fucked, so it's gonna take a fucking miracle to get it back where it was. Anyway, enough worrying about this shit. What's been happening while I've been gone?"

"Well, Marie's pregnant and due in the summer. And Con knocked Em up, and she's due three weeks after Irish," I told him.

"Lovely way you have of announcing that I'm expecting," Em chastised.

"Fuck me! How long was I out!" Tommy joked in surprise.

"Super sperm works fast," I informed him, making Em giggle.

"You're pregnant!" Mary squealed. Letting go of me, she threw herself at a terrified looking Con, then enveloped Em in a big hug.

"Well, I don't blame you both for taking advantage of my incapacitated state. Impregnating them before I have a chance to lure them away from you sure is probably the smartest thing you fuckers have ever done," Tommy commented, making everyone laugh.

"Love you, Tom," I said truthfully.

"Still not fucking gay," he said, giving me the finger. Then everything really was as it should be.

* * *

As I found myself sitting on the shitty, plastic hospital chairs, once again staring at crappy artwork, I realised that for everything good that happened in the universe, there was an equal and opposite shitty reaction. Tommy got better, while Irish got sick. Despite giving up working in the shop and being confined to bed rest, her little body just couldn't take the strain of handling my demanding offspring. By thirty-two weeks, the doctors insisted that they couldn't wait anymore. They were certain, that if they let Marie go full term, she would die, and if they couldn't deliver in time, the baby would too.

I knew without a shadow of a doubt that Irish would have given her last breath to give the baby as many days safely inside the protection of her body as she could. But if there was a good chance of saving both of them, I was taking it. When she argued with me, I explained that the greatest gift I could give my child was a mother. She cried for hours and agonised endlessly over the decision, but in the end, I didn't have to talk her around. She knew I was right.

This time, it was Em's turn to stay home. All of our family, Ma, Tommy, Albie, Heath, Danny, and Father Pat included, were all sat with me. Nobody offered stupid fucking platitudes about how everything was gonna be fine. No words could help when your girl and your child were lying on an operating table without you there, ready to go under the knife. This was no straightforward surgery either. They were delivering the baby by caesarean section and going straight in for a repair to her aortic valve.

"Do me a favour?" I asked the nurse as they wheeled her away. "Don't tell me what sex the baby is. Just tell me that they're safe. I want us to find out together."

"Of course," she replied.

The same nurse returned an hour later.

"You have a beautiful, healthy baby," she told me, and the waiting room buzzed with congratulations. "We need to keep baby Doherty in the NICU for three or four weeks to ensure that the lungs are developing as they should, but the steroid injections appear to have helped and the baby is breathing on its own."

"And Marie?" I asked earnestly.

"She'll be in theatre for a long while yet, but there were no complications with the caesarean," she reassured me.

"That's grand news, thank you," I told her. She smiled and

headed back towards the doors.

"Wait!" I called after her. "Why did you call the baby Doherty, and not Kelly?"

"Because those were Miss Kelly's instructions before she went into theatre," she replied and carried on walking.

It was the nearest I'd come to losing it since we got there.

* * *

Ten hours and eight coffees later, Marie's surgeon came to find us. Luca, Matt, and Tristan stood behind their mother, braced for bad news, but she reached for my and squeezed as I held my breath.

"Marie is out of surgery and looking good. As we discussed previously, there have been huge improvements in cardiac surgery since Marie's last operation, so we're confident that this repair will provide a long-term solution. There's no doubt that having another baby is out of the question, but there's no reason that Marie can't continue to live a normal and relatively healthy life," he said.

Ma burst into tears with relief, but Stella was as stoic as ever.

"Thank you, doctor," she said. "That is wonderful news."

"When can we see her?" I asked, not daring to believe his words until I could see her for myself.

"A nurse will come and get you in a couple of hours. When she wakes up and comes round a bit, we'll transfer her back to the ward and you can see her then," he replied.

Time dragged by ridiculously slowly, but it wasn't the purgatory I'd been chained to during the surgery. When the nurse finally arrived, I looked to Marie's mother. She was her next of kin and had more right to see her first than I did.

"It's all right, Kieran. Go and meet your child. I'll give you a twenty minute head start before I'm coming for a cuddle with my grandchild," she told me. I didn't need to be asked twice. I grabbed her shoulders, planted a huge kiss on her cheek, and went to find my future.

"Hey, love. Did you miss me?" she asked sleepily.

"Always," I replied. Taking a chair next to her, I picked up her tiny, beautiful hand and kissed the back of it.

"Is the baby all right?" she asked, her first concern always for our child.

"Of course," I replied. "Our baby has your heart."

The doors opened and a nurse rolled in a tiny incubator.

"Would you like to meet your son?" she asked with a huge grin.

"We have a son?" I asked in disbelief. Tears were streaming from Marie's eyes as the nurse carefully handed her our boy.

"You sure do, and premature or not, he still has a set of lungs on him," she replied.

"What are we going to call him?" I asked Irish.

"How do you feel about naming him after your dad and mine?" she suggested.

"You'd do that?" I asked, stunned that she would let me honour him like that.

"I think Jack Michael Doherty would be a fine name," she replied. "Are you ready to hold your boy?" She placed him in my arms, and after wrapping his blanket around him, I cuddled him into my chest.

There were no words to describe how I felt looking down at his beautiful face. He was only a few hours old, and still, I couldn't remember a time that I didn't love him. So often in life, I'd questioned myself, wondered if I could make it as a fighter, if I could hold it together in the face of someone already coping with so much. But there was no self-doubt in that moment. Because I knew with absolutely certainty that I was born to be a father.

For the longest time, I was positive that the pain of da's parting had frozen my heart forever.

I was wrong.

My thawed heart was overflowing. Because if there was one thing more precious to me than my last hug with my father, it was my first hug with my son.

EPILOGUE

KIERAN DOHERTY

"Come on, Pete, keep that guard up," I barked, bouncing a little from side to side as I called out instructions.

It amused me that music blared out from the speakers all day and the guys were anything but quiet as they trained, but never once did the noise wake my boy. But if I stood still for more than thirty seconds, all hell broke loose. I looked down at my little man. Strapped to my chest in a baby carrier, he would happily sleep for hours as long as I kept moving. I brought him down to the gym for a few hours almost every day. Marie hated to be parted from him, but I reminded her frequently that recovering from major heart surgery meant resting.

"Your dog's about to crap on the floor again," Pete pointed out.

"Bad dog!" I shouted to him. He turned his head to the side and gazed at me innocently. I wasn't fooled. It was the look he gave me every time he crapped on the floor.

"Outside!" I ordered, pointing towards the entrance. We'd

installed a flap in the downstairs door so he could come and go as he pleased, but the little fucker was lazy. Why walk all the way downstairs when you could crap where you're sitting? The dog completely ignored me as usual. I had the father thing down, but the art of canine training was beyond me.

"Driscoll, downstairs now!" Danny ordered. Immediately, the stupid dog got up and did as he was told.

"How'd you do that?" I asked.

"I use the same tone of voice I use with the rest of you," he explained, looking at me as though it was obvious.

Just then, a piercing cry erupted from my chest.

"Shit. I stopped moving," I said to myself.

"It ain't that. He's hungry. Look, pass him here," Danny told me. Taking him out of his carrier, he lifted him up over his shoulder and headed towards the office to put Jack's bottle on. Danny complained endlessly about everything. Everything except Jack. He fed him, changed nappies, and had him over his shoulder as he barked orders at the guys more than I had him in his baby carrier. He was the same old grumpy fucker, but he showed Jack a side he usually only reserved for Em.

We found out just how much Danny embraced having kids around when a brand new travel crib turned up in his office. There was no room to swing a cat in there as it was, but he'd made it fit. Jack loved it and Em cried. I'd learned that pregnant woman cry.

A lot.

If you leave your socks on the bedroom floor, they cry. If you buy them flowers on your way home from work, they cry. Danny dealt with her hugs and happy tears by groaning about what a pain in the arse hormonal women were. But the crib stayed.

Despite her pregnancy, Em spent almost every day that she wasn't working at the gym. It was the only way we could get Con to train. He had a world title defence in two weeks, and his baby was due in three, meaning his protective genes had gone into overdrive. Em had almost made it full term, but how she'd done it without killing Con, I'd never know.

Between taking care of Jack, training Con, and Irish's flourishing design business, my girl and I had little time to dwell on the past. And the past was exactly where Alastair had been relegated. The police informed us that a car reported stolen by Alastair had been found, burned out and dumped. Forensic testing matched paint left on the back of my bike after the impact, to the car He was currently in a psychiatric facility pending sentencing. Surprisingly, he had pleaded guilty to the charges, claiming diminished responsibility. I guess his father's firm thought that it was easier to deal with matters quickly than risk all the bad publicity that came with a trial. In the end, I felt sorry for the guy. It was hard not to when he had everything, except the one thing his money couldn't buy.

As for me? I knew as soon as I held Jack that my decision to end my professional boxing career, had been the right one. Nearly losing him and Irish had taught me to treasure each and every second I had with my family. Fighting had made my heart strong. They had made it full. I loved Irish more than I knew it was possible to love another person. Like da said, it was a freight train that hit me when I least expected it. And I wouldn't change it for the world. The only thing I planned on changing was Irish's surname.

I jumped up to the side of the ring and leaned on the ropes as I called out pointers to Pete, who was sparring with one of the older kids. Con was doing hanging sit ups, but when the office door opened and Em called out, "O'Connell, I think my water just broke," I thought he was going to fall off the bar. He caught my amused gaze and looked absolutely fucking terrified. I didn't know what the future held for any of us, but I did know that life in this crazy-arse family of ours was about to get a whole lot more interesting.

A NOTE FROM THE AUTHOR

Dear Readers,

I hope you enjoyed Kieran's story. From the moment Liam's character came to me, as I sat down to begin writing *The Hurricane*, I knew that his story wouldn't be an easy one. Told over the course of three books, you have followed his struggle to find his own happy-ever-after, and I love you for it. Always strong, steadfast and reliable, I wanted you to see a little more from one of my favourite characters as he meets the love of his life for the very first time. So for all of you who believe in the power of love, no matter how hard the struggle, here's a glimpse at Liam and Albie's first meeting...

R.J. Prescott

LIAM

Settling back into the worn leather sofa, I glanced lazily around the club. The atmosphere was thick with lust and hunger. A hunger I hadn't felt for a very long time. The place was full of people on the hunt. Some looking for a one-night stand, others looking for a relationship, but all of them looking for some sort of a connection. I stopped hoping for that a long time ago. The truth of the matter, was that I was gay. Shit, I'd never actually even said the word out loud when talking about myself. I wasn't a virgin. I'd slept with girls before. But it felt wrong. Shit, it made me feel so fucked up and empty inside that I hadn't touched a girl in years. No point. Not once I'd made peace with the reason that I felt that way. Realising that I was attracted to men, and doing anything about it, were two different things though. My family was strict Irish Catholic. To say that my parents would rather me dead than homosexual, would be a fucking understatement. So I would keep my sad secret and enjoy the company of friends on my birthday, while the void inside me remained empty.

"Liam, look after my girl for me, would you? Nobody fucks with her while I'm gone, understand?" Con said.

I grinned at the guy who'd been one of my best friends since childhood and gave him the two fingered salute. Fucker has the cheek to wink at me before walking over to the bar.

"Well, baby girl, you sure look pretty tonight. I guess you're around the gym so much it's hard to remember that you're an honest to God woman and not one of the boys," I told her.

She looked like a terrified deer, caught in the headlights. But she smiled at my comment, and dropped her shoulders as she relaxed a little.

"That's just the way I like it," she replied.

Seeing Em in this place was like watching a white dove, trapped in a building. All of us could see what she was, and protected her. But Con had claimed ownership the minute he saw her. He'd be the one to coax her down from the rafters and set her free.

"You know, you're a good influence on him," I told her, nodding towards Con.

"So I've been told. But I don't think that Danny is crazy about us being friends," she admitted.

"He's protective of you, that's all. He loves Con like a son, but he's unstable. If things go to shite for Con, he's worried about you getting hurt in the fallout," I explained.

"I appreciated his concern, but I think that being Con's friend is worth the risk," she replied, firmly.

"He's a lucky bastard, Em. I hope he knows how lucky he is," I said.

"He knows, shithead," Kieran said, plonking his arse down next to me on the sofa. I grunted in reply and tuned out the rest of their conversation. When Em turned pale, I paid attention, and followed her stare towards two girls. They were nothing special. The same sort of fake bitches you'd expect to see there on a Saturday night. When one of them straddled Kieran and he ran his hands up her thighs, Em bolted like she'd been given an electric shock. I let her go, but watched her like a hawk as she began talking to the friend of Kiera's fuck buddy. Nothing was happening to the dove on my watch. I was contemplating going over there, when a group moved through the crowd and took up flanking positions behind her. It was clear they were friends of Em's from the pissed off looks they were giving the other girl. None of them looked like a threat and I smiled at the knowledge that Em had more than just us watching her back.

Realising they were outnumbered, both girls stormed off and within minutes Kieran and Tommy headed towards Em's group, like hounds who'd caught the scent of fresh pussy. I didn't bother getting up. I was too busy to trying to control my hard on for the guy standing behind Em. From the minute I'd seen him, I was struck dumb. He was big, though nowhere near as big as me. Tall, with broad shoulders that tapered to a lean waist. I couldn't see his arse, but I had a feeling that it would be firm and round, and fucking perfect, just like the rest of him. One look was all it had taken to smack me upside the head. There was no point staring. For all I knew he wasn't gay. Even if he was, there was nothing I could do about it. Didn't mean I could bring myself to turn away though.

He glanced my way, and as our gazes met, I held my breath. My throat was dry and my palms were sweaty, but fuck if he didn't hold my stare. A slight blush spread across his cheeks, and he gave me a small smile before he looked away, like the intensity of our connection was too much for him to hold onto. Accepting a pint from one of his friends, he considered me nervously, then started to walk my way.

"Hi, I'm Albie. I'm a friend of Em's from University," he explained, holding his hand out to me.

"Liam," I responded gruffly. I placed my palm against his, and just like that my dick went from half-mast to hard as a fucking diamond. He let go of my hand and sat down next to me on the sofa. My skin still tangled from the contact.

"So I take it that you box with Cormac?" He asked, looking a little shy, but generally unfazed about striking up a conversation. I, on the other hand, who hardly spoke at the best of times, felt like a nervous teenage girl.

"We've been friends since were kids. Went to the same school and we spar at the gym together, but I ain't a serious fighter like he is. I work construction," I said. I was anxious. This guy and I were worlds apart. He was at University, which meant that he was smart. His hands were smooth and callous free, which likely meant he'd never done a hard day's labour in his life. I was a working class Irish builder, and this guy was so far out of my fucking league, it was laughable.

"You look like a fighter," he said, as his eyes skimmed over me appreciatively. I grabbed my drink, and knocked back about half a pint as I tried to regain my composure. I'd never flirted with a man before. Never really had the opportunity, even if I'd wanted to. Now, the hottest guy I'd ever seen was sat next to me, and I literally had no game. I wasn't a big drinker, but I needed the crutch.

"You look like you enjoy sports yourself," I replied finally. His pale blue shirt stretched tightly over his biceps and across an impressive chest, leaving me to imagine how it would feel to peel it off him and expose those firm pecks. When I dragged my eyes from his chest to his face, the intensity of his gaze surprised me. If I was mentally undressing him, it was clear as day that he was doing the same.

"I play rugby for the University. I would have like to have played professionally, but I wasn't good enough. So I looked for a University with a great rugby team. I figured I'd play a few more years while I got my degree. I'm hoping that, by the time I graduate, I'll have an idea about what I want to do after," he explained, shrugging.

"Don't they give you any kind of careers advice in college?" I asked, curiously. I admired his confidence that he could be so laid back about his future, but I wasn't at all jealous. I hated school with a fucking passion. Whilst going into construction like my father and brothers may have seemed like a foregone conclusion, I loved what a did. Whether it was building something from scratch or renovating, it gave me a buzz. I had plans one day to go it alone and set up my own construction company, but not yet.

"Sure, but it's tough to imagine myself in any of the careers they suggested. I was actually thinking about primary school teaching. I love kids, and their passion for rugby at that age is infectious. But I've never had any teaching experience, so I don't know if I'd be any good at it," he admitted.

Fuck, could this guy be any more perfect? If there was one thing,

I'd kept as much a secret as my sexuality, it was my desire to have a family. I loved kids too, and one day I wanted a bunch of em'. The idea seemed as unlikely as the notion of me coming out of the closet.

"Why don't you look into helping out with coaching a kid's rugby team. There's got to be dozens of schools around here that would kill for your kind of help. That way, you can see if it's a good fit for you before looking into it as a career," I suggested.

His face lit up like the morning sun at my crappy idea, and he grinned broadly.

"I can't believe I never thought of that before. Thanks," he said, and I relaxed. However nervous I was, talking with him like this felt right. For the first time in my entire life, I didn't feel wrong or dirty to be thinking this way about a guy. Just sitting here and talking, was as close to perfect as I'd ever felt.

The rest of the evening flew by. When Em puked over Con, he simply made sure that she was okay, whipped off his shirt and carried her out of the club. I lost track of when the other guys left, but security were ushering everyone out of the club to close, and Albie and I were still sitting there. Reluctantly, we made our way to the exit and I realised as the fresh air hit me, that this was it. We would both go our separate ways, and who knew if we'd ever see each other again.

"Do you have far to go?" he asked me.

"I live about six miles away, but I'll never get a taxi this late. I'll start walking and see if I can flag one down on the way," I told him. With hands shoved deep in his front pockets, he rocked back on his heels and regarded me apprehensively.

"Look I have a room in halls of residence about a mile or so from here. If you don't have to be up early tomorrow, do you fancy coming back to mine for a drink?" he asked.

"Sure," I answered quickly, like my throat wasn't dry at the thought of being alone in a room with him. He looked relieved at my reply, and smiled as I fell into step next to him. I didn't let myself dwell on what I was doing. All I knew was that I didn't want the night to end. It couldn't be over, not yet.

We said little as we walked, and all too soon we were outside a big heavy door. He let me in and I followed him up to his room. As he knocked on the light, I could see that the whole place was one large room with a double bed up against one wall, a desk against the other and a small sofa opposite a television taking up what little room was left.

"This is great," I answered truthfully.

"It's not bad for the money," he replied. "The kitchen is shared, but I get my own bathroom which is a big plus," he said.

"I like it," I replied. Books and papers were piled messily on the desk, and a few clothes were strewn haphazardly around the room, but the whole place smelled like him. I imagined him shaving shirtless, and splashing on aftershave and my thickening dick twitched.

"What can I get you?" he asked. Maybe it was my imagination, but his husky voice seemed to drop an octave. Was he offering me a drink, or more? He was there next to me, and we were alone. Suddenly, the moment seemed painfully intimate. All I could focus on was his pulse. That slither of skin in the opening of the collar of his shirt that throbbed furiously. I wondered if it would taste as amazing as it smelled. I shuddered as he moved closer. We weren't touching, but electricity arced between us.

I wanted to be brave. I wanted to be fearless. I wanted...him.

"Fuck it," he whispered. Wrapping a hand around the nape of my neck he crushed his lips against mine.

And I was lost.

Never had I experienced anything so visceral or powerful. My need for him was primeval. I have been starved of this feeling for a lifetime, and now that I'd had a taste, I wanted to gorge myself. He might have made the first move, but I took control. Spearing my hand in his messy blonde curls, I spun him around to press him against the wall. My tongue reached out to tangle with his, sending sparks of lightening straight to my cock. He moaned as he tilted his pelvis, and I pushed my hard cock against him, desperate to find some release in the friction. It wasn't nearly enough. He reached his hand around to grab my arse, pressing us even closer together, and it was my turn to groan. He angled his head to deepen our kiss. It was wild and uninhibited. It was more special than anything I'd ever experienced before. You could wait a lifetime, and never find as much peace as I did in that kiss.

I was seconds away from losing complete control, and shooting my load, when I reluctantly pulled away. Closing my eyes, I took a deep breath to calm myself, and rested my forehead gently against his.

"Don't leave," he whispered shakily. I rubbed my thumb gently across his swollen bottom lip.

"Never," I whispered back.

ABOUT THE AUTHOR

R.J. Prescott was born in Cardiff, South Wales, and studied law at the University of Bristol, England. Four weeks before graduation, she fell in love, and stayed. Ten years later, she convinced her crazy, wonderful, firefighter husband to move back to Cardiff where they now live with their two equally crazy sons. Juggling work, writing and family doesn't leave a lot of time, but curling up on the sofa with a cup of tea and a bar of chocolate for family movie night is definitely the best part of R.J. Prescott's week. She loves to hear from her readers so contact her at:

Website: http://rjprescott.com/

Facebook: https://www.facebook.com/rjprescottauthor/

Twitter: https://twitter.com/rjprescottauth

Instagram: https://www.instagram.com/r.j.prescott/

ACKNOWLEDGEMENTS

To my husband and my best friend, Lee. The reason I can write the stories I do, is because of you. No matter what, you never let me lose faith in myself. Even on my worst days, you carry me. There aren't enough words to describe how much I love you. To my beloved boys, Jack and Gabriel. You were both so little when I first started writing, and with every book you make me more and more proud. I love that I get to call myself an author. I love it even more that I get to call myself your Mum. Thank you Mum and Dad for all that you do for me. Everything I've ever achieved is because I had your love and support.

Lauren-Marie, you are a legend. I can't tell you how much your support and friendship means to me. You pick me up when I'm down, and keep me writing when I've run out of words. I look forward to many more books, signings and memories together for years to come. Also you are in charge of my passport forever seeing as I clearly am not to be trusted with remembering anything. Ever.

My beautiful friend Maria. You have mad ninja proof reading skills and could literally run the country with your mobile phone and calendar. My only regret about our friendship is that I didn't meet you sooner. You are one of the kindest, most generous and caring people I've ever met. Vin is a very lucky man, and I promise to regularly remind him of your awesomeness.

To the best family in the world, Gerry, Faye, Ben, Boo, Dave, Gareth, Laura, Dan, Sarah, David and Tiffany. You all make me feel that there is nothing I can't achieve, and no matter what you always love and support me. I feel so lucky to call you all my family.

Marie. Yours and Tony's friendship means so much to Lee and I. I always loved reading, but you opened me up to a whole world of romance and new authors, and then made me believe I could be one of them. We have been together since the start of this crazy journey, and I couldn't imagine it without you. Thank you for always making me believe in myself.

Rachel de Lune. Your books kick arse and I'm so lucky to have you in my life. You motivate me and keep me smiling, even in the seventh circle of editing hell. I hope you still remember me when you're an NYT best seller. It's only a matter of time.

Louisa Maggio. I can't even bring myself to call you my cover designer, because you are so much more than that. You are, and forever will be, my friend. Your talent blows me away, but more importantly you are kind, generous and have more integrity than anyone I have ever met. You bring my books to life and I will always feel so grateful to have you in my life.

To my editor Vernonica, thank you so much for everything. I loved your motivation and good humour and I look forward to more books together in the future.

Leigh Stone, thank you so much for bailing me out when I needed it. I look forward to working with you for many years to come.

To Lynsey and Nicola. Ladies, I don't know if a couple of sentences are enough for what I need to say. Meeting you guys has literally changed my life. Nicola, you have supported me from the very beginning and you always know when I need you, even before I do. Lynsey, I love your strength and your unwavering support. When I lost my literary voice, you guys made me believe that people would wait for me to find it. Some people have a way of finding you when you really need them, and I needed you so very badly when we first met. It is because of you that the Hurricanes exist, and I will never be able to thank you enough for everything that you have done for me.

Prescott's Hurricanes, you guys amaze me on a daily basis. You are kind, generous and supportive and thanks to this amazing group, I have forged so many friendships. When I lost my voice you helped me find it. I owe this book entirely to you. Without your posts, your messages and your support, this book would never have been written. You have made this last year so much fun, and from the bottom of heart I thank you.

To the lovely Mr Attree. Thank you for being my guide to all things Irish and for giving me the greatest band name!

Thank you so much to all of my friends in Bristol, Cardiff and around the world. Christine, Jodie, Kerrie, Kevin, Cynth, Amanda, Ruth, Ceri-Anne, Adele, Paul, Bronwen, and all my friends. Your support and encouragement means the world to me.

To the lovely Sue Roberts, thank you for your wonderful beta reading skills. You gave me a desperately needed perspective and your comments always help me to improve my writing.

To each and every blogger, author and reader who has offered me the hand of friendship and supported my books, thank you so very much. To be part of a community of kindred spirits, who understand completely what it is to lose yourself in a book, and emerge profoundly changed by the experience, is a privilege that I will never take for granted.

Finally, to you the reader. Thank you for taking a chance on me. I may have created the Driscoll's boys, but in every way that counts, they belong to you.

CPSIA information can be obtained
at www.ICGtesting.com
Printed in the USA
LVOW10s1918020817
543567LV00004B/683/P